Sometimes the answer is right in front of you.

As we sat in the hearse, a yellow school bus pulled up in front of the police station. On its side were the words *Camp Phoenix*. Seconds later a long line of teens paraded out the front door of the station and onto the bus.

"Eugene," Henry said, "how do *you* think Josh escaped?"

Eugene scratched his head. "He must have slipped out somehow. It's a mystery. Maybe he blended in with a group of people leaving the station. Normal folks go into police stations for any number of reasons—asking for directions, paying parking tickets, reporting a dog bite—you name it. It's the only think I can think of."

I found myself watching the kids filing onto the Camp Phoenix bus. They were all teenage boys. And suddenly it got me thinking.

"Wait a minute," I said, pointing to the bus. "I know exactly where he is."

OTHER BOOKS YOU MAY ENJOY

Charlie Collier, Snoop for Hire: The Copy Cat Caper	John Madormo
Charlie Collier, Snoop for Hire: The Homemade Stuffing Caper	John Madormo
Encyclopedia Brown, Boy Detective	Donald J. Sobol
Enola Holmes: The Case of the Missing Marquess	Nancy Springer
Gilda Joyce, Psychic Investigator	Jennifer Allison
The Puzzling World of Winston Breen	Eric Berlin
The Puzzling World of Winston Breen: The Potato Chip Puzzles	Eric Berlin
Theodore Boone: The Abduction	John Grisham
Theodore Boone: The Accused	John Grisham
Theodore Boone: Kid Lawyer	John Grisham
The Westing Game	Ellen Raskin
Wilma Tenderfoot: The Case of the Frozen Hearts	Emma Kennedy

CHARLIE COLLIER

SNOOP FOR HIRE

The Camp Phoenix Caper

CHARLIE COLLIER

SNOOP FOR HIRE

JOHN MADORMO

PUFFIN BOOKS
An Imprint of Penguin Group (USA) Inc.

PUFFIN BOOKS
An imprint of Penguin Young Readers Group
Published by the Penguin Group
Penguin Group (USA) Inc.
375 Hudson Street
New York, New York 10014, U.S.A.

USA / Canada / UK / Ireland / Australia / New Zealand / India / South Africa / China
Penguin Books Ltd, Registered Offices: 80 Strand, London WC2R 0RL, England

For more information about the Penguin Group visit www.penguin.com

First published in the United States of America by Philomel,
an imprint of Penguin Young Readers Group, 2013
Published by Puffin Books, an imprint of Penguin Young Readers Group, 2013

THE LIBRARY OF CONGRESS HAS CATALOGED THE PHILOMEL BOOKS EDITION AS FOLLOWS:
Madormo, John V.
The Camp Phoenix caper / John Madormo. p. cm.—(Charlie Collier, snoop for hire: #2)
Summary: The twelve-year-old private detective who sets up shop in his parents' garage solves more cases for fellow sixth-grade classmates. ISBN 978-0-399-25544-1
[1. Private investigators—Fiction. 2. Grandmothers—Fiction. 3. Family life—Illinois—Fiction. 4. Illinois—Fiction. 5. Mystery and detective stories.] I. Title.
PZ7.M26574Cam 2013 [Fic]—dc23 2012002315

Puffin Books ISBN 978-0-14-242762-0

Printed in the United States of America

1 3 5 7 9 10 8 6 4 2

To my daughters Caroline, Christine,
and Mary, for their encouragement,
their support, and for never allowing
me to take myself too seriously.

CONTENTS

CHAPTER 1

The Cereal Killer Caper

Henry impatiently tapped on his watch. "She's late. I can't believe it. The first day of our new three-man agency, and she's late."

"Correction," I said. "Two-man, one-woman agency."

"Whatever."

"Relax," I said. "There's probably a perfectly good reason for it."

"Like what?" Henry refused to let it go. "Charlie, I told you this was a bad idea. We don't need her."

It was no secret that Henry and Scarlett would never be considered BFFs, but they both had something to contribute to this agency, and I had to do my best to keep the peace between them, for all our sakes.

"I thought you were over all of this," I said. "Let me remind you that Scarlett comes highly recommended."

"What are you talking about?"

"Both my grandma and Eugene suggested that we

take her on. Don't you remember? They were impressed by the way she handled herself in the birdnapping case. They thought she just might make a nice addition to our little detective firm."

To be perfectly honest, I could understand how Henry felt. He was probably worried about getting squeezed out. The Charlie Collier, Snoop for Hire partnership had been a two-man operation from day one—Henry Cunningham and yours truly. With the addition of a new associate, namely one Scarlett Alexander, I'm sure Henry felt that he might slip a notch in the chain of command.

"Well, she better get here soon," he said. "We don't have much time."

He was right about that. With my dad at work and my mom at the beauty salon with Grandma, there was no telling how long we'd have the garage to ourselves.

Henry picked up a handful of darts and began tossing. "Let me know when she gets here," he said disgustedly.

I for one was excited about Scarlett joining up with us. Not only would she add another brain to the mix, but the thought of being this close to her each day was dizzying. I only hoped I could concentrate. Oh, don't worry, I'm a realist. I know that a kid like me—one who closes his eyes when he steps on the scale—could never end up with a girl like Scarlett. But stranger things have happened. When she sees me in action each day—when she's able to witness my amazing powers of deduction—when she watches me solve cases with little to no effort—then who knows? Sparks could fly. But I'm not holding my breath. If I were only as suave and debonair as Sam Solomon, then things would be different. That's Sam Solomon, Private Eye, if you're wondering. It's a series of detective novels set in Chicago in the 1930s. I've read every one in print. I consider myself not only a fan of the master detective, but a student as well. I credit Sam with helping me sharpen my reasoning skills. I only wish he could help me sharpen my social skills.

"Ooh," Henry cried. "I missed the bull's-eye by a quarter inch."

Before I could congratulate him, there was a knock at the door.

"Finally," he said as he tossed the remaining darts at the board.

"Come in," I said.

When the door opened, I tried to maintain my composure. I didn't want to look too eager.

"Hi, guys," Scarlett said as she entered. "Sorry I'm late."

"Oh, that's al—" I started to say.

Henry was somewhat less forgiving. "That's it? *'Sorry I'm late'*?"

"Something came up. Is that all right?" she snapped. "Something important."

Henry sighed. "And if you just happened to be on a stakeout, and you just happened to show up late, and you just happened to miss the perp in action, are you gonna say 'sorry I'm late'? It's unacceptable. Tell her, Charlie." He folded his arms and smiled confidently.

Scarlett placed her hands on her hips and glanced in my direction.

I was well aware that once Scarlett joined the agency, I'd be breaking up squabbles between these two on a daily basis. I was prepared for that. But in this particular instance, I was being asked to take sides. The wrong move here could haunt me for a lifetime. I paused to think it over. On the one hand, Henry was right—punctuality in our business was important. But he also needed to understand that trust was equally important. Sometimes you had to give someone—in this case, a business partner—the benefit of the doubt. I had to handle this in a delicate manner.

"Henry, I'm sure that Scarlett would have been here on time if she could have," I said. "Right, Scarlett?"

"Of course," she said.

"And I'm sure that she had a very good reason for being late," I said. "Right, Scarlett?"

Scarlett began tapping her foot. She didn't look happy. "Why don't you just ask me why I was late? I know you're dying to."

"I don't want to pry."

"Well, I do," Henry said. "What was so important?"

I pulled a lawn chair out from under the card table and motioned for Scarlett to sit down. We needed to deal with this in a civilized manner.

She reluctantly lowered herself into the chair. We joined her at the table.

"Well?" Henry said.

"Would you believe we had a flat tire?" she said.

Henry's eyes narrowed. He seemed skeptical. "You can do better than that."

"It's true," she insisted.

I needed to seem supportive, even though it did seem like a pretty lame excuse.

"Flat tires happen, and there's nothing you can do about them," I said. "Let's move on."

"Not so fast," Henry said. "I want to hear the details."

Scarlett sighed. "Not that's it's any of your business, but all right, I'll tell you. We were driving on Thiry-Third Street when we heard this thumping sound, and the car started to pull to one side."

Henry folded his arms and made a face. He wasn't going to make this easy.

"So my mom got out and noticed that the front passenger's-side tire was flat," she continued. "We didn't want to have to wait around for the motor club, so we decided to try to change it ourselves. I'd watched my dad it do it before."

"You should become a novelist," Henry said. "This is some of the best fiction I've ever heard."

"For your information," Scarlett said, "I happen to know what I'm doing. I opened the trunk and took out the jack and the lug nut wrench."

The expression on Henry's face suddenly changed. He knew as well as I did that people just didn't throw out a term like *lug nut wrench* if they didn't know what they were talking about.

"So we popped off the hubcap, loosened the lug nuts just slightly, jacked up the car, took the lug nuts completely off, and set them in the hubcap."

Henry was speechless. She *did* know what she was talking about.

"We got the spare tire from the trunk, put it on . . ." She sighed. "And that's when the trouble started."

"What do you mean?" I said. "It sounded like you were doing everything right."

"Everything was perfect until my little brother decided that he wanted to help. So I told him he could hand me the lug nuts. He was so excited that he ran over, but he accidently kicked the hubcap, which sent the lug nuts flying. They ended up in a ditch somewhere on the side of the road. We were never able to find them. So then we had to wait for the motor club." She glanced at Henry. "Are you happy now?"

"Whatever," he said. "Let's just get to work."

I would have been perfectly fine with doing just that and putting this squabble behind us, but I kept thinking about that flat tire. I figured that there had to be a way to solve the problem even with the missing lug nuts. I thought about it for another minute, and then I had it.

"You didn't have to call the motor club," I said. "You had everything you needed to put that tire back on."

"What are you talking about?" Scarlett said.

"All you had to do was take one lug nut from each of the three good tires, and use those. Then you could have replaced them later."

"Yeah," Henry said. "And you could have been here on time. Just see that it doesn't happen again."

Scarlett slid her chair out and stood. "It's not going to be like this every day, right? Because if it is, I want no part of it."

I needed to do something, and fast. I was not about to let Scarlett walk out that door. Partner or not—best friend or not—Henry was being unreasonable and someone had to tell him. It was just like what happened to Sam Solomon in Episode #15—*The Cereal Killer Caper.*

In this particular story, Sam was investigating the owner of a local diner who was suspected of trying to poison one of his customers with a tainted bowl of cornflakes. Sam immediately sought out the services of two old friends, a husband and wife team of chemists, to analyze the fatal feast. They were good—very good—but they were always at each other's throats. The mismatched lovers, whose expertise Sam desperately needed, were constantly trying to sabotage each other's findings. In time, Sam was able to convince them to put their petty jealousies aside and to work together for the good of the client.

And suddenly I knew precisely what I had to do.

"Scarlett," I said, "please sit down. Henry, I have to be perfectly honest—I can't take this either. If we spend all our time arguing, we'll never accomplish a thing. We might occasionally disagree on what strategy to employ on a particular case, but if we're constantly bickering, then we're doing our clients a disservice. Scarlett is an official associate of this agency, and we have to work together—no matter what." I stood up. "Now, I want the two of you to shake hands. It's the only way."

Scarlett extended her hand. She was willing to bury the hatchet. Henry, however, just sat there with his arms folded.

"Henry, we can't move forward until we put this behind us," I said.

Without making eye contact with Scarlett, Henry sighed and reluctantly shook her hand. It was a weak effort on his part, but at least we had made some peace. Neither of the combatants, however, looked too pleased about it.

I knew this was about as good as it was going to get

for now, so I decided to take advantage of the cease-fire and move on.

I rubbed my hands together. "Okay, what's on the docket for today?" I asked.

Henry reached over his shoulder and grabbed a legal pad off the workbench behind him. He glanced at it and then held it up for both of us to see. The page was blank.

"No clients?" I said.

"Nada," Henry replied.

"Then what are we doing here?" Scarlett said.

"Not everybody makes appointments," Henry said. "We do take walk-ins, you know."

Scarlett got up, walked over to the door, and opened it. She stuck her head out.

"You're right," she said. "There's a long line of people out here."

Henry jumped up and ran over to see. There was no one.

Scarlett flashed a devious smile.

"Real funny," Henry said as he slammed the door shut.

Here we go again, I thought. I needed to maintain some order. "Listen, I thought we had a truce. C'mon, both of you, sit down. Let's get to work."

"What work?" Scarlett said. She picked up the legal pad off the card table and held it up.

"We have other business to discuss," I said.

"Whatever happened with that thing that Eugene was talking about? I thought there was something going on. The other day when he was here, he said something about a big case that he needed our help on. What's up with that?" she asked.

"Yeah," Henry said. "What about that?"

I knew what they were talking about, but I didn't think they'd like the answer. Shortly after we had wrapped up the Rupert Olsen birdnapping caper, Eugene had shown up and had asked us to join him on a new case—one he described as *a matter of national security*. We were all excited about helping out, but we never heard anything more about it. So a couple of days ago, I rode my bike over to Eugene's office to ask him about it. It was now apparently on the back burner.

"I spoke to Eugene about that case just the other day. It's on hold for the time being."

"Why?" Henry asked. "What happened?"

"Something else came up. Something bigger. Eugene got called away on a special assignment," I said. When Uncle Sam called, Eugene—despite the fact that he was in his eighties—dropped whatever he was doing to report in.

"What kind of assignment?" Scarlett said. "To where?"

"All he said was that he'd have to get back to us on this other case and that he needed to brush up on his Portuguese."

"He's headed to Puerto Rico?" Henry said.

"No, not Puerto Rico. Portugal, probably," I said.

"Or Brazil," Scarlett added.

Before I could compliment Scarlett on her knowledge of world languages, I heard a car engine in the distance.

"That's my mom," I yelled. "How could they be back this soon?"

Henry looked at his watch. "It's only four fifteen. I thought your grandma had a four o'clock appointment."

I quickly folded up the lawn chairs and hung them on hooks on the garage wall.

"She did," I said. "Something must have happened."

Henry broke down the card table and slid it behind a ladder. "A little help over here, if you don't mind," he said to Scarlett.

"Well, I've never done this before. I don't know how you guys do it," she said.

"Scarlett, you'd better take off," I said. "I'll see you at school tomorrow." I didn't have to tell her twice.

She shot out the side door and disappeared.

Henry and I followed. Before exiting, I grabbed a football from one of the shelves.

"What's that for?" Henry asked.

"We need a cover. C'mon, let's make it look like we've been here for hours."

The instant we slammed the door behind us, we could hear the garage door opener.

"We're lucky," I said to Henry as I tossed the football in his direction. "If my mom had seen Scarlett, she would have asked all kinds of questions."

Seconds later, Gram and my mom walked out of the garage and into the backyard.

"Hi, boys," my mom said.

"Hi, Mrs. Collier," Henry said.

"Back so soon?" I said.

"You won't believe why we're early," my mom said. "No more than a minute after your grandmother sat down in the chair, there was a robbery."

"A robbery?" Henry said.

"What happened?" I asked. "Are you guys okay?"

"These two masked men came into the beauty salon and told Shirley to open the cash register."

I tossed the ball to the side and walked over to where they were standing. "They were masked? So you couldn't recognize them, huh?" I said.

"It was all so fast," my mom said. "To tell you the truth, I didn't know what happened until it was over."

"Did the police come?" Henry asked. "Did you give them a description? How old did they seem? Were they tall or short? Fat or skinny? What kind of clothes were they wearing?"

"Slow down, Henry," my mom said. "I'm not sure I can answer any of those questions. I just don't know."

I noticed that Grandma had been particularly quiet.

Considering her background as a cryptologist in World War II and with the time she spent working alongside Eugene at his detective agency, I was fairly certain that she had paid closer attention to specific details than my mom had.

"Gram, do you remember anything?"

"I remember everything. They were young—probably teenagers. I could tell from their voices. They seemed nervous—bouncing up and down a lot. One of them was wearing cowboy boots. The other had on gym shoes—orange ones with black laces. The one who did all the talking—the one in gym shoes—walked with a slight limp. The one with the boots kept scratching the top of his head. Probably dandruff."

"Wow, Gram, that was amazing. Did you tell the police all this?" I said.

"They didn't even bother to ask," Gram said. "When they see a senior citizen, they figure bad eyesight, poor memory, and too darn scared to be of any use. I could have helped them corral these bad boys. Too late now."

"Maybe you should call them, Mrs. Collier," Henry said to Gram.

"I've got an even better idea," she said. "Why don't you boys go find those young thugs? Think of it as your civic duty. Could be your next case."

"Please, Mom, don't encourage them," my mother said to Grandma. "That's way too dangerous. I'm sure that Henry's parents feel the same way we do—we'd prefer that these boys take up other hobbies—ones that'll keep them out of trouble. Am I right, Henry?"

"I'd rather not say," he said.

"I thought so," my mom said with a grin. "Charlie, dinner in an hour. Henry, you're welcome to stay."

"Thanks anyway, Mrs. Collier, but my mom's expecting me."

I watched my grandmother and my mom enter the back door of the house.

Before she closed the door all the way, Gram turned back and whispered, "Think about it, okay?"

I nodded.

"Hey, I'm gonna get going," Henry said. "Nothing more to do here. Looks like the agency's closed for the day."

"I'll see you tomorrow," I said.

As I watched Henry walk off, I thought about what my grandmother had said. I just couldn't see how we would ever become involved in a case like this. It was hard to imagine a client strolling into our office and asking for help in apprehending these robbers. This was a job for the police—not a private detective agency—and the boys in blue had a heck of a lot more resources at their disposal than we had. But Grandma's theory that teenagers might be the culprits was intriguing. And who better to understand what goes through their heads than someone like me? Granted, my thirteenth birthday—marking my official entry into the teen world—was still a few months away. But I was fairly certain that I had more in common with these perpetrators than a whole police force full of adults. I decided, however, after a bit of reflection, to drop any notion of getting involved in this robbery business and instead to concentrate on the problems of other sixth-grade classmates. They might not be as exciting, but after having nearly been turned into a stuffed human trophy in our last case, I was more than happy to settle for a few ho-hum adventures in the near future.

CHAPTER 2

The Reign in Spain Caper

After having finished up a particularly challenging homework assignment, I went downstairs to say good night. My parents were on the couch watching television. Grandma was sitting on the recliner with her feet up. She was decked out in a man's navy blue suit and was wearing a Richard Nixon mask as she read the paper.

"Those boneheads in Washington have done it again," she said. "In my time, we knew how to set a tough foreign policy agenda."

There was a time when I didn't quite understand my grandmother's habit of assuming other identities, but since my conversation with her a few weeks back, it now made perfect sense. When she and Eugene teamed up after the war to start up their own private detective agency, Grandma spent a lot of time undercover, and that meant new personalities whenever necessary. This was an unusual look, but I kind of liked it.

With remote in hand, a familiar sight, my dad changed the channel to the late news. A report on the robbery was just beginning.

"That's it," my mom said. "That's what I was telling you about."

"I wonder if they'll show you and Gram," I said.

My dad turned up the volume.

"Police are reporting that two masked men held up a beauty parlor in downtown Oak Grove earlier this afternoon," the news anchor said. "Many of the patrons at Trudy's Salon on Grainger Street were unaware of what had taken place. The robbers, whose faces were covered with ski masks, demanded all of the cash in the register."

A video clip accompanied the story. It showed the outside of Trudy's, confused bystanders on the sidewalk, customers milling around inside the shop, and police dusting for fingerprints and ended with a short sound bite from Shirley Watson, the clerk on duty at the time.

"It all happened so fast," Shirley said. "Before I knew it, they were in the shop and demanding money. I thought it best to give them what they wanted. I don't think they got more than about a hundred and fifty dollars. It was all so scary."

"Were you able to offer a description to the police?" a reporter asked.

"Like I said, it all went down in less than a minute," Shirley said. "I don't remember anything about them."

"She's an idiot," Gram shouted as she ripped off the Nixon mask. "Open your eyes, for Pete's sake."

"This is the third robbery of this nature in the past two weeks," the news anchor said. "Thieves, dressed in a similar manner, also hit Man's Best Friends, a pet shop on North Ellsworth Street, early last week. Eyewitness reports suggest that the suspects may be juveniles."

I immediately looked in Gram's direction.

She nodded and winked. She hadn't missed a thing while at the beauty shop.

"Police are making an attempt to connect these crimes but as of today have been unable to do so," the newsman concluded. "All of these robberies remain unsolved."

My dad clicked the mute button on the remote.

"What's going on here?" he said.

"I can't believe this," my mother said. "Who'd think that something like this could happen in little Oak Grove, Illinois? It makes me afraid to go out."

"Don't worry," Gram said. "The police'll solve it." She glanced at me and smiled. "Or somebody else will."

The next day at school was relatively uneventful. I found myself thinking a lot about the recent rash of robberies in the area and about how my grandmother was suggesting that the Charlie Collier, Snoop for Hire agency should take on the case. Without a paying client, however, I knew that Henry would never be interested. I, on the other hand, had no problem with pro bono work. Sometimes you just had to pitch in for the common good even if you didn't get paid.

I wasn't sure why I kept coming back to this case. I thought I had talked myself out of even considering it. I guess I just didn't want to disappoint Grandma. But I really wasn't sure if I wanted to commit my friends to such a high-profile case—one that was sure to involve some personal danger. I just didn't know what to do.

As we entered Mrs. Jansen's science class, the last period of the day, Scarlett tapped me on the shoulder.

"So are we on for today or not?" she asked.

I turned to Henry, who was listening in.

"The appointment calendar is empty," he said.

"Well, then I'll assume I have the rest of the afternoon to myself," she said.

"Don't forget about possible walk-ins," Henry said. "You don't want to miss out on a killer case just because you were wasting your time doing your nails or something equally lame."

I was just about to don my referee shirt when Mrs. Jansen conveniently intervened.

"Okay, kids, please take your seats," she said.

Scarlett glared in Henry's direction as she walked to her desk.

"I've got a little brainteaser for you today," Mrs. Jansen said. "And it has to do with the theory of gravity."

As was usually the case, whenever Mrs. Jansen uttered

the word *brainteaser*, half the class looked in my direction. Some smiled. These were the ones who enjoyed watching my powers of deduction in action. Then there were the others—the ones who scowled at me. These were the kids who would have loved nothing better than to see me fall flat on my face. To be honest, I had gotten pretty used to their reactions over the years. For the last couple of weeks, however, things seemed to have gotten better. After successfully cracking the birdnapping caper, the legions of jealous classmates had diminished. But it appeared that the honeymoon was over. They were back, and their forces seemed to have grown.

"Let's refresh our study of gravity for a moment," Mrs. Jansen said. "Who can give me a working definition?"

Stephanie Martin, one of those annoying kids who nods and smiles all the time when the teacher is speaking, raised her hand.

"Yes, Stephanie," Mrs. Jansen said.

Stephanie jumped to her feet. "Well, if I understand it correctly, gravity is the natural force of attraction between any two massive bodies, which is directly proportional to the product of their masses and inversely proportional to the square of the distance between them. Will that do?"

Mrs. Jansen smiled. "That was actually a little more than I was looking for, but I'll take it."

Stephanie sat back down and continued nodding. She just couldn't help herself.

"And who can tell me the name of the seventeenth-century mathematician and scientist we most associate with the theories of universal gravitation?" Mrs. Jansen asked.

Stephanie didn't wait for her name to be called. She shot up, nearly knocking her desk over in the process.

"That would be Sir Isaac Newton," she said.

"Very good, Stephanie. But remember to wait to be called on next time, okay?"

Stephanie nodded. What else would you expect?

"Okay, here we go," Mrs. Jansen began. "How many of you like to ski?"

A few hands went up.

"And how many of you would consider yourselves hikers?"

A few more hands were now raised.

"Well, imagine this. You're skiing or hiking down a snow-covered mountain when you look behind you and see a wall of snow coming right at you. You find yourself in the midst of an avalanche, and there's no escaping it. Before you know what's happened, you're buried alive."

Gasps filled the room.

I closed my eyes. I wanted to get the full effect. It always made it easier to figure out a brain buster when I imagined being right in the middle of it.

"And you know that you'll never survive unless you get out from under that drift," Mrs. Jansen continued. "You frantically start to dig your way out . . . but there's just one problem—you don't know which way is up. For all you know, you may be digging into the side of the mountain. But if you were really clever, you would know which way to dig." Mrs. Jansen smiled and leaned against the blackboard.

It didn't take me long to figure it out. I looked around the room for hands to go up. At first there were none.

"Oh, what the heck," Henry whispered from the seat behind me. He slowly raised his hand.

"Henry, what do you think?" Mrs. Jansen said.

Henry stood. "Well, if I didn't know where to begin, I'd start digging in equal directions all the way around me. Then I'd stop every couple of minutes and see if I could hear sounds from any particular direction. As soon as I did, then that's where I'd concentrate on my digging."

"But what if there were no sounds?" Mrs. Jansen said. "What if no one knew you were buried? And don't you think that before you could dig in all directions, you'd probably run out of air?"

Henry knew he had missed the mark, but he had no intention of surrendering the floor. "I can hold my breath a pretty long time," he said. "I might just be able to pull it off."

"And you might not," Mrs. Jansen replied. "We're actually looking for something else . . . but nice try."

Henry dropped down into his seat. I could tell he

was seething. It wasn't that he couldn't accept defeat, but he always hated it whenever someone said "nice try." To him that meant "you're wasting my time, loser." But I thought that whenever Mrs. Jansen used those words, it was as if she was saying "now, that was a well-constructed hypothesis, but it came up just a hair short." Henry, however, would never buy that.

"I can't believe no one knows this one," Mrs. Jansen said. "I'll give you a little hint—think about the topic that we were talking about right before I posed this scenario. Gravity?"

I was just about to raise my hand when I realized that I might not have to. If past performance was any indicator, I'd get a chance to speak up—Mrs. Jansen always eventually looked to me if she'd stumped the class. Then it wouldn't seem as though I was in a hurry to show up my classmates. It would be almost as if I had no choice. No one could blame me for that.

"Well, it looks like I'm going to have to give you the answer," she said.

What was she doing? What about me? She was supposed to ask me now. She just couldn't assume that no one in the room could solve her brain buster. Why wouldn't she just ask me? I wasn't sure what to do. It would just kill me to hear her rattle off the same answer that I would happily have supplied had she only asked. Whenever I was faced with a dilemma of this nature, I would always think about Sam Solomon. What would

Sam have done in a situation like this? I immediately thought of Episode #22—*The Reign in Spain Caper.*

This was the story of a deposed Spanish prince who narrowly escaped a murder plot and was now seeking asylum in the US. The prince had hired Sam to find out who had tried to kill him. When Sam determined the identity of the assailant, he didn't want to tell his client. It turned out to be his twin brother, born only minutes after the prince, who because of that was second in line for the throne as long as his brother was alive. Sam knew that if he told the prince who had actually hatched the plot, it would break his heart. The two boys had been inseparable their entire lives. But Sam also knew that as painful as it might be, he owed it to the client to share this information with him.

So there you go. Problem solved. Sometimes you have to speak up. You can't withhold the truth just because someone might not want to hear it. It was your obligation.

"Well, I'm a little disappointed no one could figure this one out," Mrs. Jansen said, "but here's what you would do."

"Wait!" I yelled as I jumped to my feet. At that moment, there was complete silence in the room. Everyone, and I mean everyone, looked right at me.

"Yes, Charlie?" Mrs. Jansen said.

"Can I take a shot at this one?" I asked.

"Why, of course. I didn't see your hand up, so I assumed I had stumped you too."

Not a chance, ma'am. I'm Charlie Collier, Snoop for Hire. This happens to be my business.

"So," Mrs. Jansen said, "you're buried alive in an avalanche. How do you know which direction to dig?"

I glanced back at Henry. Even he rolled his eyes. But that was okay. We'd been playing this game with each other for years. He could handle it.

"Well, first of all, I'd clear a little bit of the snow away from my face. And then I'd do something that I would never do at school." I noticed a few eyebrows rising when I said that. "I would spit—and then whichever direction it went, I would know that was *down*. Then I'd just dig in the opposite direction. And that would be *up*."

Mrs. Jansen smiled. "And there you have it—gravity. It might just save your life someday."

I dropped down into my seat. Mrs. Jansen continued her lecture on the theory of universal gravitation, and little attention was focused on me for the remainder of the period. What a relief. I had demonstrated my heightened powers of deduction once again and had lived to tell about it.

Henry and I met up at the bus stop after school. We saw Scarlett walking in the opposite direction. With no pending appointments, she must have felt that her services weren't needed. If someone did happen to walk into the garage and she wasn't there, it wouldn't be as if we were working with a handicap or anything. That was how it had been for a long time, and we had done just fine.

Since my mom had rescheduled Grandma's appointment at the beauty parlor for this afternoon, Henry and I were certain that we would be able to open the agency for at least a couple of hours before they returned. We didn't expect Mom and Gram to surprise us again. It was unlikely that anything like a robbery would ever happen again at the same location. It seemed safe enough to proceed.

During the bus ride home, I had to listen to Henry rehash the whole *why-does-Scarlett-have-to-join-the-agency* discussion. It seemed useless to argue with him, so I just tuned him out during the ride and at strategic points would offer an occasional "uh-huh" just to make him think I was still listening.

When the bus pulled up to my stop, about a half block from my house, we decided to race to the garage. This was a competition that I would always lose, but since I had bested Henry so often in the brainteaser arena, this seemed to help balance things out.

After about a half hour of waiting for a potential client to enter our establishment, we decided to play a friendly game of darts. *Friendly* was probably not the right choice of words. Henry was so competitive that whenever he fell behind, he would look for a chance to rebound and gain the upper hand.

As soon as I was up by a few points, Henry brought out the heavy artillery.

"Okay, genius, try this one on for size," he said. "You're standing in a one-room house. It has only four walls. And each wall faces south. There's a window on each wall. A bear walks by one of the windows. What color is the bear?"

I noticed that the sun was going down. I reached over and hit the light switch. I was actually just trying to buy myself a little extra time to solve this one if it became necessary. And since we always kept the doors closed in the garage to avoid being caught by my parents, we usually needed the overhead light to see what we were doing.

"Are you stalling, Charlie?" Henry said.

"No way."

Henry might think that he had stumped me, but that wasn't the case at all. I didn't like to rush things. I was never able to think straight when I did. I set my darts on the card table and thought about what he had just said. I knew that he was trying to throw me off with his reference to the bear. The most important part of this riddle had to do with the line "each wall faces south." That was the key. I stroked my chin and thought hard. How could *each* wall possibly face south? I tried to imagine a scenario where this might be possible.

"Why don't I just tell you?" Henry said.

"Never," I replied. "Give me another second." I could do this. I knew it. I tried to picture a map—then a globe. And within a few seconds, I had it.

"Time's up," Henry said.

"Here's your answer," I said. "There's only one place on earth where a one-room house with four walls facing south could exist—the North Pole. And the only bears you'd find up there are polar bears. The answer is *white.*"

Henry sighed and dropped his arms to his sides. He seemed defeated.

"Why do I even waste my time?" he said.

"Don't give up now. You're gonna stump me one of these days. You just gotta be patient."

But before Henry could continue to beat himself up, there was a knock at the door.

He immediately seemed to light up. "A walk-in," he said with a smile.

"Come in," I said.

When the door swung open, neither Henry nor I could believe who was standing there. It was the last person we would ever have expected to seek us out.

CHAPTER 3

The Missing Lynx Caper

Filling the doorway, with his hands in his pockets and staring at his shoes, was Sherman Doyle.

"Sherman," I said, "what brings you over here?"

"I was just taking a walk," he said. "And I saw the light on. So I thought I'd stop in."

A few weeks ago, I would have shuddered if Sherman had shown up here unannounced. But that was before. After working together on the birdnapping caper, I had learned a lot about this kid—and he didn't scare me now. He was still a little strange, but I didn't fear for my life anymore.

"Would you like to sit down?" I said.

Sherman pulled out a lawn chair and barely squeezed into it. This was one big kid.

I sat down opposite him.

"So, Sherm," Henry said, "is this a social or a business call?"

Sherman was staring at the concrete floor. It seemed as if he wanted to say something but couldn't get the words out. I waited until he raised his head and made eye contact.

"Is there anything we can help you with?" I asked.

Sherman cleared his throat. "I was hoping to talk to you about something."

Henry sat down and joined us. He seemed to be interested in what was about to happen.

"So what is it?" I said, leaning forward in my seat.

"It's about my brother," Sherman answered.

Henry's eyes widened. He kicked my leg. He knew this was going to be a whopper.

Most of the neighborhood kids knew about Sherman's older brother, Josh. He was unlike other sixteen-year-olds. Joshua Doyle had a love affair with nature. All he ever talked about was saving the rain forests, preserving the ozone layer, or protecting any number of endangered species. And Josh wasn't just a talker. A couple of years earlier, he took on a bulldozer that was attempting to clear a grove of maple trees and ended up in the hospital with a leg injury. From that day, he had favored his bad leg and walked unsteadily.

But Josh never complained. When asked about it, he would refer to it as his "badge of honor." He dropped out of high school to spend more time saving the planet and its creatures. As noble as his mission sounded, most residents in the area referred to Josh not as a dedicated environmentalist and animal lover, but rather as a crazy, misguided punk. He was sincere, but at times, he was reckless.

"Is your brother having some sort of problem?" I asked.

"No, not really. I don't think so. Well, maybe." Sherman spoke in disjointed sentences. He was having a hard time spitting it out.

"Why don't you tell me about it," I said. "Maybe we can help."

"Well . . ." Sherman struggled for the right words, then just blurted it out. "He's missing. Josh is missing. For about a month now. My mom and I are getting worried."

"Wait a minute," Henry said. "How many times in the last year did he leave home? No offense, but he runs away all the time, doesn't he?"

"But he always comes back. He's never been gone for more than a week or two. And he always tells me where he's going," Sherman said. "This time he didn't."

"What's the chance he's just off on another one of his *causes*?" I asked. "I seem to remember hearing that he hitchhiked to California one time to save the sequoias."

"And didn't he hop a freight train to Washington once for something?" Henry added.

"He took on the lumber companies to save the spotted

owl that time," Sherman answered. "But this is different, I know it."

"Has your mom gone to the police?" I asked.

Sherman sighed. "Yeah, but whenever they hear that it's Josh, they just go through the motions. They fill out some paperwork, question a couple of people, and then they call my mom and say, 'Sorry, Mrs. Doyle, with his history, your son probably ran away again.'"

"Is that what happened this time too?" I asked.

Sherman nodded.

"Let me get this straight," Henry said. "Are you saying that you want to hire *us* to find Josh? Is that why you're here?"

Sherman smiled weakly. "You see, we can't afford a real private eye—" He stopped short. Sherman suddenly realized that he might have offended me. "I didn't mean it like that."

"I know what you meant. No offense taken," I said.

Sherman dug into his jeans pocket. He pulled out a handful of change.

"I can cover a few days, I think." He began counting the coins.

"Don't worry about that," I said.

Henry threw his head back. Even though things were different now between Sherman and us, Henry was never a fan of giving away the product, no matter who the client was. "We might incur a few expenses on this one, Charlie," Henry said as he picked up the money jar and began shaking it. He glanced at Sherman sheepishly. "Nothing personal, big guy. It's just business."

"I'm not lookin' for a handout," Sherman said. "I can pay."

I was always a little squeamish about collections. Henry, on the other hand, had no problem making it very clear to clients that payment in full was expected at our intial meeting. Although this time I had to intervene. We had just been through a harrowing experience together, and Sherman had played a major part in our escape from Rupert Olsen's basement. Offering a little consideration was the least we could do. And on top of everything else, Sherman was sharing some pretty personal details about his family. I didn't think it would be asking too much to help out a friend in need. We certainly weren't vultures.

"Sherman, I would consider it an honor to help you find Josh. And just to show you how much we appreciated your help in solving the birdnapping case, I'm willing to take on the case for no charge." I held up my hand to discourage Henry from speaking.

He shook his head, turned, and walked away. He obviously didn't concur with my decision, but at least he wasn't about to make a scene.

"Thanks, Charlie," Sherman said. "I really appreciate it."

I grabbed a pencil and a pad of paper from the table. "Okay, when's the last time you saw Josh?"

"I think it was February twenty-second. No, it was the twenty-first. No, it *was* the twenty-second."

"And did he say anything before he left?"

"No, and that's why I'm worried. He always tells me where he's going. And then he makes me promise not to tell my mom. 'Just tell her I'm chasing windmills,' he'll say."

"Chasing windmills?" Henry said. "What's that supposed to mean?"

"Haven't you ever read *Don Quixote*?" I asked.

Henry returned a blank stare.

"Miguel de Cervantes?" I said. "Never mind." I turned to Sherman. "Is there anything else you can tell me that might help?"

"Not really." Sherman thought hard, then dug into his pocket. "Oh, here's a picture of Josh." He handed it to me.

I studied it. "I'm going to want to talk to some of his friends, maybe even your mom," I said.

"Let's leave my mom out of this right now. She's pretty upset. She doesn't even know I'm here."

"Well, I guess I'll start with his friends, then," I said.

"Josh doesn't have too many close friends," Sherman said. "He does have what you might call an on-and-off girlfriend. But I think my mom's already talked to her."

"I'd still like to talk to her myself," I said.

"Okay, I'll try to come up with some other names too," Sherman said as he stood up. "Well . . ." He seemed to fumble for the right words. "Thanks . . . thanks a lot . . . I'll see you at school." Sherman was halfway out the door when he stopped abruptly. "You guys won't tell anybody about this, right?"

"Clergymen, physicians, attorneys . . . and private investigators—we all respect client confidentiality," I announced.

"But you won't tell anybody, right?" he repeated.

"Not a soul," I said.

Sherman apparently hadn't gotten the gist of what I had said. It didn't matter.

"And one more thing," I said. "Not only will we locate Josh, we will personally deliver him to your front door. That's a promise."

"Okay," he said enthusiastically. "Thanks." And with that, he disappeared just as quickly as he had arrived.

I could barely keep from grinning. We had done it. We landed a real case. And we had gotten it all by ourselves. This wasn't one of Eugene's hand-me-downs. The brainteasers would have to wait. We were about to conduct a full-scale investigation. It was our first official missing persons case, and I for one was pumped. I found myself thinking about Sam Solomon and Episode #18—*The Missing Lynx Caper.*

This was the story of an eccentric owner of an exclusive Manhattan boutique that dealt in priceless furs. When the wealthy merchant disappeared into thin air, his daughter hired Sam to locate him. And let me tell you, when it came to tracking down a missing person, Sam had the instincts of a bloodhound. As you might guess, it didn't take long for the veteran detective to determine that the missing man wasn't being held for ransom as the police had thought. He had been kidnapped by an animal rights activist who had intended to do to the victim what the victim had done to countless minks, lynx, beavers, foxes, etc. And thanks to Sam, this enterprising businessman was able to escape a *close shave*—literally.

I could barely contain my enthusiasm. "So what do you think, Henry? This is what you call a legitimate case. This one could be legendary." I didn't get quite the reaction I was expecting.

"I really wish you would have taken his money when he offered it," Henry whined. "We may never see it again."

But compensation was the last thing on my mind at that moment. We were about to undertake a real caper. And once the investigation got under way, I knew that Henry would buy in and forget about the money issue. Well, actually, he'd probably never forget about the money issue.

• • •

The next day at school, we met up with Scarlett at lunch to update her on what had happened the previous afternoon. We told her about how Sherman had wandered into the garage and had presented us with a killer case. We explained all of the details we had up to that point. She unfortunately didn't handle things the way we had hoped.

"You mean to tell me that an actual client walked into your office and you guys didn't call me? I would have come over," she said.

"Even if your nails were still wet?" Henry said. It wasn't what you would call the most sincere response.

She waved him off. "I thought I was a partner now."

Henry jumped in. "Allow me to clear up this matter. Technically, you're an *associate,* not a partner. There's a difference. You see, Charlie and I are partners. You're a member of the agency now . . . and I can't believe I just said those words . . . but you haven't risen to the level of partner yet. Does that help?"

"I don't care what you call me," Scarlett snapped. "I just want to help. Would it have killed you to call?"

"Neither of us has a cell phone," Henry said.

She folded her arms and sneered at me. "And you don't have a phone in your house?"

Suddenly I had become the target. I wasn't even part of this conversation.

"Scarlett," I said, "it all happened so fast. I didn't even think about it."

"Charlie's mom and grandma were due back from the beauty parlor any minute," Henry said. "There was no time. But don't worry, we'll be sure to notify you if anything like that ever happens again." He smiled. He was definitely enjoying this moment.

She sighed. "Okay, then, what's next?"

"We're meeting up with Sherman after school," I said. "He promised to give us some contact info for a few of Josh's friends."

"I'm afraid to ask," Scarlett said, "but am *I* part of this meeting with Sherman? Or do you plan to exclude me again?"

Right at that moment, I was wondering if Scarlett was second-guessing her decision to join up with us. I knew how Henry felt about things, but there was no way I was going to let her get frustrated enough to bolt.

"Of course you're welcome at the meeting," I said. "What happened yesterday was a fluke. You're a full-fledged partn—" I caught myself. "You're an official associate of the agency, and we value your opinion." Out of the corner of my eye, I could see Henry with his finger in his mouth pretending to gag.

Scarlett smiled. "So, where do we meet?"

"At the bus stop," I said.

"I am sooo looking forward to it," Henry said sarcastically.

"Me too," Scarlett said with a phony smile. She waved to a girlfriend, flicked her hair at us just for effect, and was off.

We had managed to withstand a pair of brutal classes before meeting up with Sherman after school. He was waiting for us at the bus stop. When he caught a glimpse of Scarlett, he looked at us funny.

"It's all right. She's a member of the agency now," I said.

"But she's not a partner," Henry added.

Scarlett rolled her eyes. "Just let it go, will you?"

Sherman dropped the backpack that hung from his shoulders, slid his hand into a side pocket, fumbled for a piece of paper, and handed it to me.

"Here's the stuff you asked for," Sherman said, pointing to a name on the note. "That guy is probably Josh's best friend, although like I said, he doesn't have many friends." Sherman slid his finger down to the next entry. "And that's the *sometimes* girlfriend."

"Perfect," I said. "We'll get right on it."

Forcing a half smile, Sherman grabbed his backpack and was on his way.

"He's still a weird guy, you know," Henry said.

"He's just a little misunderstood, that's all," I said. "But strange or not, he's our client now and we owe him the best-possible effort." When I took a second look at the note Sherman had given us, I noticed that he had done a thorough job of supplying us with the necessary information. He had provided not only phone numbers but addresses.

"So now what?" Henry asked. "Back to the office to plot out our course of action?"

"We can't," I said, thinking out loud. "I know for a fact that my mom's home. But tomorrow could work. She's volunteering at a food pantry in the afternoon. That should buy us enough time to plan out our strategy. Okay, then, we reconvene tomorrow at sixteen hundred hours at the usual location. Got it?"

"Sixteen hundred hours?" Scarlett said.

"That's three o'clock tomorrow afternoon," Henry said smugly.

I didn't want to have to correct him, but I knew I had to do it. "Actually, it's four o'clock," I said.

"Oh, big deal. So I was one hour off. She didn't even know what it meant," Henry said, pointing to Scarlett.

I smiled. Henry frowned. Scarlett rolled her eyes. It was business as usual.

CHAPTER 4

The Weakened Warriors Caper

I was on my way to my bedroom after dinner to catch up on a little homework when I passed my dad, who was in the living room reading the newspaper while at the same time watching TV. My grandmother, dressed in an exterminator's uniform, was busy spraying something all around the room.

"Lift your feet," she told my dad. "Gotta get at some of those crawly things."

"Mom, what's in that thing?" my dad said, pointing to the canister strapped to her back.

"Just to be safe," she said, "you'd better hold your breath for a couple of minutes."

"What?!" he yelled.

Gram turned and winked at me. She always loved making my dad a little crazy, and he never failed to fall into one of her traps.

Gram turned and pointed at the TV. "Looks like they're at it again," she said.

"Police have released this closed-circuit video of the burglary at Jamison's Furriers on East Lansing Avenue last night," the newscaster announced.

"Another theft?" I said. Caught on tape was a pair of thieves wearing ski masks. One was stuffing furs into a large plastic garbage bag. The other one stood by the entrance and seemed to be watching for bystanders or police. When the suspect stationed at the door exited the store, he hobbled out.

"Can you believe this?" my dad said as he looked up from his paper. "What's this town coming to?"

"Did you see that guy who limped out?" Grandma said. "He looks like the same one I saw at the beauty parlor."

"Police say the thieves made off with an estimated fifteen thousand dollars in merchandise," the newscaster continued. "No arrests have been made in this case or in any of the other robberies in the area during the past week. Although the suspects have all worn masks, witnesses have indicated that the thieves had young-sounding voices. Police believe that a well-organized gang of teenagers may be responsible for many of these holdups."

"Told you," Gram said. "Told you it was a young punk." She waved me over to where she was standing.

"By the way," she whispered, "have you thought about what I said? Maybe you kids could lend the authorities a hand solving this one?" She glanced at my dad to make sure he hadn't overheard her.

I leaned in and lowered my voice. "Actually, Gram, we just took on a new case."

She smiled and raised her eyebrows. "Really? What's it about?"

"It's a missing persons case," I said.

She motioned for me to follow her.

"These fumes could kill a body," she said for my dad's benefit. "I need a little fresh air. Charlie, why don't you join me."

I followed her out onto the front porch.

"So, missing persons, huh? I always enjoyed those kinds of cases," she said. "They start out real slow—then before you know it, you're running for your lives."

"I'm not expecting anything dangerous, to tell you the truth."

"That's just it," she said. "It always seems to be the cases that look so easy that get you into trouble."

"I'll remember that," I said.

Grandma took the canister of pesticide—or whatever it was—off her back and set it down on the porch.

"Hey, did you know Eugene's back in town?" she said.

I shook my head.

"If I were you, I'd bounce this one off him," she said. "He just might be able to save you a little heartache in the long run."

Now, that was an outstanding suggestion. Eugene had to have a bunch of experience tracking down folks for clients.

"You know, I think we just may do that," I said. "Since this is our first missing persons case and all, I wouldn't mind hearing what Eugene has to say."

Gram put her arm around me. "Charlie, you and me—we're kindred spirits. We think alike. We enjoy the same things. We need to stick together." She hugged me.

I always enjoyed my time with Gram. She wasn't anything like your typical senior citizen. She really had her act together. She was more *with it* than my parents—although it didn't take much to accomplish that. Sometimes I would think about life without her, and I would immediately have to stop myself. It was just too painful. I hadn't realized it when I was younger, but since Grandpa died about five years ago, I had become more and more aware that she had this wealth of knowledge.

It was at Grandpa's funeral, actually, that I finally figured it out. My uncle Bill delivered the eulogy. He quoted an African proverb that went something like "When an old person dies, a library burns to the ground." It was a great analogy. It isn't until we lose someone—

someone with a lifetime of experience—that we realize how much we could have learned from that person if we had just taken the time to do so. It was at that moment that I made a vow to spend more time with my grandmother and to try to learn from her as much as she was willing to teach me.

She squirted some of her pesticide—or whatever it was—into the air. "C'mon back in with me," she said. "There's a big ugly bug on the couch whose days are numbered."

"I didn't see anything," I said.

"He's reading the newspaper," she said with a grin.

I laughed. That wasn't exactly what I meant about *learning from my grandmother*, but it sure was entertaining.

"Why do we have to tell him about it?" Henry said. "It's our case, right?"

While we ate lunch in the cafeteria at school the next day, I told Henry that it might be a good idea if we stopped by Eugene's office and asked for a little advice. I didn't expect his reaction.

"Don't get me wrong," Henry said, "Eugene's an awesome guy and everything, but he's pretty busy. I doubt if he'd even have time to see us. Listen, we'd be doing him a favor by leaving him alone. If we go over there, he'll feel obligated to help us. And for what? A missing persons case? C'mon, how tough can it be anyway? You ask a few questions, tail a few people, plan a few stakeouts, and before long, you find the guy. Piece o' cake."

"These are just the kinds of cases, the ones that look so easy, that end up being a lot more dangerous than you think. At least, that's what my grandmother told me."

"Again, Charlie, no disrespect to your grandma, but every case is different. There's no reason to believe that this one'll be any tougher than the others. I think we can handle it on our own."

I knew that Henry was not about to budge. But I also knew that the name on the door happened to be mine, and so I decided to pull rank. I simply informed him of my plans to ride my bike over to Eugene's office after school. And that was precisely what we did. Henry, Scarlett, and I rendezvoused at my house at sixteen hundred hours as planned and set out across town to Eugene's. Interestingly, Scarlett liked the idea of asking Eugene for a little advice. I'm not sure if she really felt that way or if she was looking forward to visiting her grandfather, the barber in Eugene's building. Or maybe she just wanted to get under Henry's skin.

We pedaled for about twenty minutes and decided to stop at a park to rest. We were in the middle of town, about a block from city hall. We immediately noticed dozens of vehicles and at least a hundred or so people on the front lawn of the municipal building.

"What's going on over there?" Scarlett asked.

"I don't know," I said. "What do you say we ride over there and find out?"

"Do we have time?" she said.

"We won't stay long," I said. "C'mon, it looks interesting."

When we reached the city hall grounds, we realized that we had stumbled onto a full-blown media event. Reporters and camera crews from various stations in town were in place for what appeared to be a press conference. We locked our bikes to a light pole and sat down on a curb, waiting for the show to begin.

Within seconds, a well-dressed group of city hall brass emerged from behind a curtain and moved briskly to the podium. Leading the group was the Oak Grove mayor, Andy Wilde, flanked by others I didn't recognize. Mayor Wilde approached the microphone.

"Thank you all for coming today," the mayor began. "I'd like to share some very exciting news. It involves our youth and their future. As you are well aware, there has been a series of robberies in our community in the past couple of weeks. Although no arrests have been made, witnesses have indicated that the suspects are all young people."

As the mayor spoke, I found myself staring at one of the men on the stage. He was big. I'd say 250 pounds. But not overweight. He resembled a bodybuilder. His head was shaved, and he was dressed in military fatigues.

His arms were folded as he listened to the mayor. The only way I could describe the expression on his face was intense.

Scarlett leaned over. "Who is that big guy up there?" She had obviously noticed him too.

"I don't know," I said. "But I have a feeling we're about to find out."

"Our system of dealing with juvenile lawbreakers is failing," the mayor continued. "But we think we've found a new, hopefully more successful alternative. And I'd like our distinguished guest, Colonel Harvard Culpepper, the director of Camp Phoenix, to share this with you."

The mayor stepped back and yielded the podium to the colonel. The large man in fatigues shook hands with the mayor and smiled at the reporters.

"Ladies and gentlemen," Colonel Culpepper said, "a few days ago, I walked into the office of your fine mayor with a plan, a mission, so to speak—a remedy to bring about the salvation of our youth." He nodded to the mayor, who returned a similar gesture. "As we have seen," the colonel continued, "the current system of dealing with juvenile lawbreakers simply sucks up these young people and regurgitates them back into a life of crime. There is no rehabilitation. They feel no remorse. But there is a better way," the colonel said, raising his arms into the air.

There was something riveting about this speaker. I couldn't take my eyes off him. As the colonel spoke, my attention was suddenly diverted to a pair of individuals off to the side of the stage, seated in folding chairs. They didn't appear to be very old—maybe teenagers. But it was hard to be sure because of their appearance. They were dressed in full army fatigues, with helmets and large yellow goggles that all but hid their faces. I was wondering if these were some of the kids from the camp that the speaker was referring to.

Colonel Culpepper pounded on the lectern. "Instead of incarcerating these lost souls," he said, "let them spend time under my tutelage at Camp Phoenix, and like the mythical bird that was consumed by fire, let them rise from their own ashes—just like these fine young men." The colonel pointed directly to the two boys seated on the stage. He turned to them, and then as if he were a drill sergeant, barked out orders. "Atten-hut." The pair jumped from their chairs and stood motionless at attention. "Forward . . . march." The two teens moved forward in perfect formation, although one of them had trouble keeping up with the other. His foot seemed to drag a little as he marched forward. The colonel looked out at the sea of reporters, his chest puffed up, and smiled. He then turned back to his recruits and simply waved them back to their seats.

I couldn't help but notice the reactions from some

of the reporters in the audience. With each gesture or refrain from the speaker, several members of the press reacted with raised eyebrows. They glanced at one another skeptically and rolled their eyes. I was sensing that they had little faith in the colonel's proposal or in his demonstration.

"Through an intensive rehabilitation program at our compound," Culpepper said, "I guarantee that the young hoodlums in your community will be awakened to a new dawn. They will finally understand that there are consequences for their actions."

Culpepper stopped abruptly. It was as if he had paused to admire his own words. At that moment the mayor jumped to his feet and began applauding. His cheerleading effort was met with mild enthusiasm from a handful of audience members.

The colonel leaned into the microphone. "Now, an undertaking of this nature would be impossible without the cooperation of our citizenry. Therefore, I am happy to announce that late last evening, in a closed-door session, the mayor and council accepted my proposal and have instructed the city treasurer to redirect the necessary funds to Camp Phoenix to help defray the costs of this program."

With that announcement, some of the reporters shook their heads as they wrote down the colonel's words on their legal pads. Others let out long, loud sighs. From a few feet away, I could hear one reporter say, "So there's the rub."

"Let me close by saying that we are confident and exhilarated." Culpepper turned and smiled at the mayor.

Oak Grove's chief executive jumped from his seat and encouraged the crowd to join him in applause. Like before, a lukewarm response followed.

"Colonel, we are excited to be embarking on this historic journey," Mayor Wilde said as he looked to the reporters. "Now, are there any questions for our distinguished guest?"

Henry leaned over. "Let's get out of here."

"I hate to agree with *him,*" Scarlett said. "But let's go. It's getting late."

"In one minute," I said. I'm not quite sure why I wanted to stay. Maybe it had something to do with Grandma suggesting that we take an active role in finding out who had committed the current string of robberies. Or maybe it was because of this dynamic speaker. Whatever it was, I was unable to move.

"Mayor, I have a question for Colonel Culpepper," one of the reporters shouted out.

"By all means," the mayor said. He stepped back and yielded the microphone to his guest.

"Colonel," the reporter said, "what do you have to say about reports linking you to a paramilitary group in the area?"

Culpepper's expression turned deadly serious. "I'd say you have your facts wrong, friend. I've never participated in such a group." He paused. "Next question."

A second reporter waved his hand. "Mr. Culpepper, this Camp Phoenix of yours has been called nothing more than a *boot camp for bad boys*. What do you have to say to that?"

"If that's what you want to call it, then fine," Culpepper said. "But I'd prefer if you would refer to it as a rehabilitation program for wayward teens. I'm fine with that."

"And you think your approach will be more successful than the social workers and counselors now working with those same young people?" the reporter said.

"Have you read the papers lately?" the colonel said. "Watched the news? Whatever our system of justice is doing for these young people, it isn't working. What these kids need is some tough love. They'll come out of my program in better shape physically and mentally. And they'll have respect for authority. I guarantee it. And if you don't believe me, all you have to do is ask Mayor Thompson over in Clifton City, just past the interstate. Our program has virtually cleaned up the juvenile crime in that community."

I was spellbound by this colonel fellow. I could have listened to him all day. He was so positive. I was beginning to think that he might be on the right track with this program of his. And if it were to cut down on crime in the area, then what would be the harm?

"Are you ready?" Henry snapped.

"I guess so," I said.

We snaked our way through the crowd and walked back to where we had left our bikes. Scarlett pulled her cell phone from her pocket and glanced at the screen.

"We shouldn't have stopped," she said. "We'll never make it to Eugene's and back before I have to be home. I have to go. I'm sorry."

"What are you talking about?" I said. "If we hurry, we'll make it."

"I better get going too," Henry said.

I threw up my hands. "What's going on here?"

"My folks have really been on my back about being late for stuff," Henry said. "This isn't worth getting in trouble for. We can just as easily go see Eugene tomorrow."

I couldn't believe what I was hearing. "Well, you two can go if you want, but I've got a job to do."

"So you're still going?" Scarlett said.

"Listen, we have a client," I said, "who's looking for some answers. We can't just stop when it's inconvenient."

"Yeah," Henry said, "a nonpaying client."

So that's what this was about. Henry's interest in this case had been diminished by the fact that we—or rather I—had offered to take it on for nothing.

"I should have known," I said. "Have you forgotten how Sherman helped us get out of Rupert Olsen's basement? Without him, we all might still be in there—permanently." I could feel my blood starting to boil.

"Have you forgotten," Henry said, "that we never would have had to go to that farmhouse if Sherman hadn't been kidnapping those birds for Olsen?"

"Stop it, both of you," Scarlett said. "This isn't getting us anywhere. Charlie, if you still want to go to Eugene's, then go. But all this arguing is just wasting more time."

She was absolutely correct. We had work to do. Or at least *I* had work to do.

"You're right," I said. "I'll see you guys tomorrow." I turned my handlebars and started off in the direction of Eugene's office.

I could hear Henry's voice trailing off. "You're gonna be late for dinner, and you're gonna get grounded. See if I care."

After I had pedaled for about a quarter of a mile, I looked back. Somehow I had expected to see them following me. But instead, there was no one. They really *had* gone back. And to make matters worse, Henry was probably right. There was no way I was going to be able to make it to Eugene's, share the details of this missing persons case with him, and get back home in time for dinner. For just a second I thought about turning back. But then as I always did in cases like these, I thought about Sam. What would Sam Solomon have done if he had found himself in a similar situation—alone and abandoned? And then it hit me—Episode #24—*The Weakened Warriors Caper.*

In this mystery, Sam had been hired to find out why several players on the Westport Warriors, a minor-league baseball team, had fallen ill. During his investigation, he learned that the team's owner had racked up some serious gambling debts and had begun betting *against* his own team. Sam soon discovered that the owner had supplied his players with tainted chewing tobacco that produced temporary flu-like symptoms. When Sam shared his findings with local authorities, they refused to take action for fear that the owner might move the team to another community and baseball in Westport would be no more. Sam was on his own with no support. But he didn't stop there. He took his evidence to the local newspaper, and following a series of scathing articles, the owner was brought to justice.

It seemed that Sam only knew one way of doing things. It didn't seem to matter that he was alone and abandoned. And you know what? It didn't matter to me either. My mind was made up.

CHAPTER 5

The Athens Grease Caper

By the time I made it to Eugene's office, the streetlights had just gone on. I was trying to collect my thoughts so that I could explain to Eugene, in a concise manner, the details of the missing persons case that Sherman had presented us with. But instead I found myself trying to come up with believable scenarios so I could explain to my parents why I had arrived home late for dinner. Being grounded, which I was no stranger to, was troublesome. I didn't really care how it might affect my social life. There wasn't much to it to begin with. But I was worried about losing precious time to devote to this case. I had always prided myself on my abilities to solve a case in a timely manner. I owed it to the client. And even though Sherman wasn't paying us by the day, it was a pattern that I wanted to maintain.

I parked my bike behind the building and climbed the stairs at the rear of the barbershop. The stairwell was dimly lit. There was one light, and it was flickering. But I had been to Eugene's office so often in the past few weeks that I could have navigated those stairs in my sleep. When I reached the office door, I knocked twice, scraped my fingernails on the face of the door, and knocked three more times. It was the official password.

From the other side of the door, there was a faint voice. "Come in."

I put my shoulder into the door to open it. This building was old, and most of its moving parts squeaked, rattled, or got stuck on a regular basis. When I stepped in, I found Eugene seated behind his desk.

"Charlie," he said. "Good to see you. How've you been?"

"Fine," I said. "When did you get back?"

"The day before yesterday," he said. He rose from his chair and came over to greet me. "Is this a business or a social call?"

"A little of both, I guess."

"Can I get you something to drink?" Eugene said.

I shook my head.

He pointed to a ratty, moth-eaten couch against the wall. "Sit down. Let's catch up a little."

I knew from experience that beneath the middle cushion on the couch was a nasty spring that had the ability to inflict bodily harm. I lowered myself onto a side cushion.

Eugene sat on the front edge of his desk. "So, what brings you here today?"

"Well, my grandmother suggested I stop by for a little advice."

"Advice?" he said. "Regarding what?"

"We've taken on a new case," I said.

Eugene smiled. "Really? Tell me about it."

Right at that moment, I realized that another spring was trying to make its escape from the cushion directly under me. I slowly lifted myself off the couch.

"Do you remember Sherman? He was the big kid who was with us on the birdnapping case."

"Oh, sure. He was the one that Olsen conned into stealing the birds, right?"

I nodded. "Well, believe it or not, Sherman is our new client." I moved toward Eugene and sat down on a chair opposite the desk.

"Does he have some sort of problem?" Eugene asked.

"Yeah. His older brother has disappeared. He wants us to help find him."

Eugene folded his arms. "Disappeared? Shouldn't he be going to the police?"

"He already did," I said. "You see, his brother is what you might call a *habitual runaway*. The cops have put in a lot of man-hours in the past trying to track him down."

"One of those," Eugene said. "I see. What have you uncovered so far?"

"Nothing really. We just started. But Gram wanted me to talk to you about missing persons cases in general. She says that they can seem pretty tame at first but after a while can get pretty wild."

Eugene slid off the front of the desk, walked around it, and plopped down on the chair behind it.

"Almost cashed in my chips on a missing persons case," he said.

"Really?"

"Yeah, they can be tough," he said. "You just don't know what you're getting yourself into. It's either a situation where somebody takes off and doesn't want to be found, or it turns out that the person has disappeared against his or her will. It's that second one that can get a little dicey."

"I don't know which one it is yet," I said.

Eugene's expression turned serious. "If it turns out to be the latter, I want you to stop what you're doing and contact me immediately. You see, Charlie, it's one thing to look for something you've lost—but it's quite another to go looking for something and then to discover there's someone out there trying to keep you from finding it. That's when it gets dangerous." Eugene leaned forward and rested his elbows on the desk. "You got it?"

"Got it," I said. I glanced at the clock on Eugene's wall. There was no way I'd be able to make it home before dinner.

"I gotta get going," I said. "I'm already gonna be late, and it's not gonna be pleasant."

Eugene turned to look out the window. "It's dark outside. Did you ride your bike over here?"

"Uh-huh."

"Come on. I'll give you a ride home. You can toss your bike in the back of the car."

"Are you sure?" I asked. "That would be great."

How do you like that? What a stroke of luck. I had made the tortured decision to continue on without my friends, knowing that I'd probably be late and face certain death when I got home. But it was all going to work out. I couldn't believe it.

Eugene's car was parked in the alley behind the building. It was one in a million. To my knowledge he was the only person in town, other than the funeral director, who drove a hearse. It was a black 1966 Cadillac in mint condition. I had only been in his car one other time, but I'd felt a little odd when I rode in it. People looked at you funny. It was almost as if they were expecting to see a dead guy in the back. I remember Eugene telling me one time that he had gotten a real deal on this particular vehicle. He explained that since the hearse is the lead car in a funeral procession, it has to drive slowly enough for everyone else to follow. And most of the time, the trips from the funeral home to the church and then to the cemetery were relatively short. He said it was like buying a car from a little old lady who only took it out on Sundays—short trips and low mileage.

We tossed my bike in the back and were off. We probably could have fit a dozen bikes back there. Unlike Grandma, Eugene was a really safe driver. He never went over the speed limit and seemed to obey all traffic signs and signals. But my guess is that since he has enjoyed a pretty colorful past, he has probably been in his share of high-speed chases. I was more than content to enjoy a nice, safe, uneventful ride home.

On the way back I found myself thinking about the news conference we had stopped at on our way over to Eugene's. I was interested to see if the rash of robberies by teenagers would decline. And I couldn't help but wonder what this boot camp, as one of the reporters had described it, was really like. Was it like being in the army or something? I couldn't imagine teenage offenders getting too excited about being sent there. But then again, anything was probably better than sitting in jail.

"Eugene, can I ask you something?" I said.

"Sure."

"Have you heard of Colonel Harvard Culpepper?"

He threw his head back and laughed. "Don't get me started."

"Really? You know about the guy?" I asked.

"What I know about him, I don't like. Does that answer your question?"

I wasn't expecting that kind of reaction. The colonel,

from what I could tell, seemed like a decent enough sort of fellow. After all, anybody who's willing to rehabilitate a bunch of teenage lawbreakers couldn't be all bad, right?

"What don't you like about him?" I asked.

"I don't trust him. First of all, he calls himself a *colonel.* The man never spent a day of his life in the military. To those of us who served, it's an outrage."

"Then why does he do that?" I asked.

"Because he belongs to some *play army.* They get all dressed up and pretend to be soldiers—just the way you probably did when you were a kid. Except *you knew* it was playing."

I hadn't seen Eugene quite this emotional before. I didn't want to set him off any further, but I wanted to know more about this guy.

"There was a press conference today and this colonel was there," I said. "Did you see it?"

"I listened to it on the radio."

"One of the reporters asked him if he was in . . . I think he called it a paramilitary organization . . . and he said *no.*"

Eugene immediately pulled the car over and turned off the engine.

I thought for a minute I was in trouble.

"Charlie, you know me. You know what I do. And you should have some idea of the kinds of sources I have and some of the information I'm privy to. And they tell me that Culpepper is indeed in a paramilitary group. A lot of folks in these outfits are anti-government. They play with real guns. They're dangerous. And I have no idea what our mayor is thinking by allowing this crackpot to take these young people to his compound."

"So, why do you think this is all happening?" I said.

"It's pretty simple," Eugene said. "There's an election in a couple of months. All this crime is the worst thing for an incumbent mayor. Makes it look like he can't run the city. So what does he do? He calls a press conference to tell the voters that he's come up with a new way to combat the problem. The only problem is that it's the wrong way."

Eugene sighed, started the car back up, and pulled the hearse into traffic.

"What do you think the mayor should have done?" I said.

"That's the million-dollar question. No one knows. Our justice system isn't perfect, but it's the best we've got. The important thing is—don't panic. Be patient. Just sit back and let the system work. But, of course, when you're running for office, there's no time for that."

I felt as though I had learned more about politics in the last five minutes than I had in a year of social studies classes. This was good stuff. And it made a lot of sense.

"Charlie, why are you so interested in this Culpepper character anyway?"

I asked myself the same question. If it hadn't been for Gram, I was doubtful that we'd even be having this discussion.

"Well, Gram seems to think that we—you know, me and Henry and Scarlett—should try to help solve this rash of robberies in the area. She thought it could be our next case. So when we stumbled upon that press conference today, it all seemed to be kind of connected."

Eugene put his finger to his lips. He was in deep thought.

"Wait a minute," he said. "I thought you told me you already have a case? The missing persons one."

Eugene made a sharp turn at the corner. I could see my house in the distance.

"We do," I said. "To be perfectly honest, I don't really think we'll get involved in this robbery business. But it is pretty interesting stuff."

"That it is," Eugene said. He pulled up in front of the house and looked at his watch. "Unless I'm mistaken, you're right on time for dinner."

"Thanks a lot, Eugene," I said. "You saved me from house arrest."

"Hey, I might need your help one of these days," he said. "I can't afford to have one of my best associates grounded by his parents." Eugene smiled.

This guy was the best. He helped me get my bike out of the back of the car and waved as he drove off.

I thought just how fortunate I was to have somebody like Eugene, and my grandmother for that matter, as mentors. Not everyone was lucky enough to have somebody as wise as these folks at his beck and call. I knew I could learn a ton from them. Heck, I already had. As I walked my bike into the garage, my thoughts drifted to Sam Solomon and Episode #20—*The Athens Grease Caper.* I wasn't the only one who had someone looking out for him—someone with the right advice at the right moment. So did Sam.

For years the ace detective would have dinner every night at the Olympiad, a Greek restaurant on Chicago's north side. He was especially fond of the owner, George Kostopoulos, a wise old sage. In this episode, Sam met up with an informant at the restaurant who was supplying him with details on a gun-smuggling ring. Sam was to pose as an interested buyer. Later that night, George told his friend that he had a bad feeling about Sam's informant and warned him that he might be falling into a trap. The next day Sam took George's advice and observed the gun smugglers from a distance before meeting up with them. And as you might guess, Sam spotted his informant in the company of the smugglers. George was right—and probably saved his friend's life. It was sure nice to be in similar company.

CHAPTER 6

The Unfriendly Fire Caper

At school the next day, Sherman spotted me on the playground at recess.

"Charlie," he called out. Sherman ran over and surveyed the area. He apparently didn't want our conversation to be overheard. "So how goes the hunt for my brother?"

It was always nice to be able to tell the client that you were making progress—even slight progress. But in this case, we had accomplished little to nothing. I didn't want to mislead him into thinking that we were hot on Josh's trail, but I didn't want him to get discouraged either.

"To tell you the truth, Sherman, it's a slow go. But don't worry, we're only in the initial stages of the investigation. Tomorrow's Saturday. We'll make some headway then."

"Did you talk to any of those people whose names I gave you?"

Right at that moment, I really wanted to lie to him, but it just wasn't the way I conducted business.

"Not yet," I said. "But we plan on talking to both of them first thing in the morning." I really didn't know if that was going to happen, but I needed to give Sherman something.

"Okay," he said. "Thanks. Be sure to let me know if I can help. My mom's getting real worried about Josh."

"Tell her not to worry. We should have something soon."

Sherman nodded and walked away.

I didn't want to have another conversation with him without having news of some kind. He was the client—granted, a nonpaying client—but a client nonetheless. And we had given him our word that we would do our best to not only track down his brother, but to bring him home.

I scanned the playground for Henry and Scarlett. I spotted Scarlett in her usual clique of popular girls. That group always intimidated me. As much as I wanted them to notice me, I was always afraid that one of them might crack a fat joke, and I didn't know if I had the courage to smile through it. I decided to take a chance.

"Hey, Scarlett, you got a minute?"

She appeared slightly annoyed but managed to break away from her friends to join me.

"Yes?" she said in a rather impatient tone.

"We need to do a little work after school on the Joshua Doyle case. I thought we could plan out our course of action for the weekend. Are you free?"

Scarlett sighed. She reached into her pocket and pulled out one of those elastic things and started putting her hair into a ponytail.

"Do we have to talk about this now?" she said.

I was beginning to think that Henry might have been right all along about taking on a new associate.

"Well . . . ," I said.

"I mean—am I on the clock twenty-four hours a day or what? I do have a social life, you know. Oh, that's right, you wouldn't know anything about that."

Scarlett of late was becoming a real Jekyll and Hyde. Whenever she was around her friends, she treated me like some annoyance in her life, but when she was working on a case with us, she was more than civil—even friendly—well, maybe not friendly. But she at least wasn't rude, unless she was talking to Henry, that is.

"I'll talk to you after school. Okay?" she said.

"I just wanted to give you a heads-up. That's all."

She flashed one of those phony beauty pageant smiles and left.

I didn't bump into her again until eighth period—Mrs. Jansen's science class. We made eye contact, but no words were spoken. Sometimes I just didn't get her. I knew I'd never run around with her circle of friends.

I didn't want to. I wasn't trying to crash the party. I just wanted to be able to have an occasional business conversation with her. That was it. Was that too much to ask?

I felt a tap on my shoulder. It was Henry.

"Hey, so what happened last night? Are you grounded or what?" he said.

I shook my head and smiled. "Grounded? For what?"

"For *what*? You had to have gotten home late," he said. "*I* barely made it."

"I went over to Eugene's. We had a nice conversation," I said. "And then I went home. No big deal."

Henry seemed to know there was more to the story. "And your parents didn't jump all over you?"

"They tried," I said. "But I set them straight. I told them that since I was the proprietor of my own private detective agency, I was old enough to make my own decisions. And old enough to set my own curfew." I grinned and sat down at my desk.

Henry plopped down in the seat behind me. "Get out. I don't believe you."

"I plan on conducting some interviews first thing in the morning," I said. "How could I do that if I had gotten grounded?"

Henry sat back in his chair. He seemed flabbergasted. I knew that he was trying to picture me standing up to my parents, but he was obviously having a difficult time imagining it. Good sense told him it was impossible.

"Okay, gang, let's get started," Mrs. Jansen said. "Quiet, everyone."

Henry slapped me on the shoulder. "Tell me the truth," he whispered.

I turned halfway. "Eugene drove me home. What did you think happened?"

"I knew it," he said—loud enough for the entire class to hear.

Mrs. Jansen stood at the front of the room with her arms folded. "Mr. Cunningham, would you like to share your comments with the rest of us?"

"No, not really," Henry said.

"Stand up," she said. Mrs. Jansen had one rule in class—there could only be one person speaking at any one time—either her or one of us.

Henry slowly got to his feet. "I'm sorry. It won't happen again, I promise."

"I'm disappointed in you, Henry," she said. "I want you to know that."

Mrs. Jansen was our favorite teacher by a long shot. No one else even came close. And we all hated it when she told us she was disappointed in us. Personally, I would have much preferred if she had yelled at us, or punished us, or publicly humiliated us. But to say that she was *disappointed* in us? Now, that was the worst thing imaginable.

Henry dejectedly slid back down into his seat.

"Okay," Mrs. Jansen said. "Let's get to work." She walked over to her desk and picked up a glass of water about three-quarters full. She held it up for everyone to see. "Here we have an ordinary glass of water." Then she reached into her pocket and pulled out something. Likewise, she held it up. "And this, if you can see it, is a cork. I'm going to put the cork into the water to see what happens."

Stephanie Martin, the nodder, raised her hand.

"Yes, Stephanie?" Mrs. Jansen said.

Stephanie jumped to her feet. "The cork will float," she said.

Mrs. Jansen smiled. "Well, I think we all know that the cork will float. At least, I hope so. I actually wanted to see if it does something else."

Stephanie, still nodding like one of those bobblehead dolls, returned to her seat. She was too clueless to realize that she had just been shut down . . . even in a polite way.

"Now, watch the cork carefully," Mrs. Jansen said.

We all watched it ever so slowly drift from the center of the glass to the side. So that was it? That was the big show? I didn't get it.

"Did you see that?" Mrs. Jansen said. "Who can tell me what just happened?"

Scarlett raised her hand.

"Yes, Scarlett."

"It just kind of floated over to the side," she said.

"Exactly. But who can tell me why?"

It suddenly got very quiet.

I had an idea *why,* but I decided to play dumb. I fought the urge to raise my hand.

Mrs. Jansen looked around. No takers. "The cork will always float to the highest point," she said. "And since the water level is highest on the sides, that's where it drifts to."

A few classmates glanced in my direction. They were smiling. I knew exactly what they were thinking. They were delighted that Mrs. Jansen had stumped me. It didn't even seem to matter that they hadn't figured it out themselves. How do you like that? I was now kicking myself for not raising my hand. Of course, I knew that the cork would drift to the highest point. Duh. Well, I'd show them. Next time they wouldn't know what hit them.

Mrs. Jansen continued to hold up the glass. "We're not done," she said. "Who can tell me how we can make the cork float in the *center* of the glass? Or is that even possible?"

Sherman cleared his throat.

"Sherman, do you have a guess?" Mrs. Jansen asked.

"It's a trick question. It can't be done," he said.

"Oh, but it *can* be done," she said. "Who can tell me?"

For the next five minutes we were forced to endure

a litany of lame attempts. No one was even close. Mrs. Jansen seemed disappointed that she had apparently stumped everyone. *Not everyone,* I thought.

"Looks like I'm going to have to tell you," she said.

I started to raise my hand. Then, just as quickly, I pulled it back down. A few minutes ago, I was certain that I would jump at the next chance to show up my fellow classmates. Now, for some reason, I was getting cold feet.

"Charlie, did I see your hand up?" Mrs. Jansen said.

"No," I said. "I mean . . . yes."

"So tell me, how we can make the cork float in the *center* of the glass?"

I stood up slowly. I could feel every eye in the room on me at that very moment. *Well, here goes,* I thought.

"Here's what I'd do," I said. "I'd fill the glass to the very top. Fill it with as much water as it can possibly hold. Then drop the cork in. If you did it right, a meniscus will form at the top of the glass. That's where the water seems to form sort of a convex shape above the glass. Since the highest point is now in the middle, the cork will float right there and won't drift over to the sides."

All heads turned to Mrs. Jansen.

"Let's find out if he's right," she said. She lifted out the cork and set the glass down on the front desk. Then she picked up a small pitcher of water and poured enough to fill the glass to its brim. She dropped the cork back in. This time it didn't move. It stayed right there in the middle. "Looks like Charlie's done it again," she said.

I stared straight down at the top of my desk. I wasn't certain what the reaction would be from other students. I didn't really want to know. I would have thought that after we had successfully saved all those exotic birds from certain death, these kids would see just how important reasoning skills could be. It wasn't just about solving riddles, it was about using your brain for bigger things. I wished I could make these kids see that. If they really wanted to, they could have learned something from these experiences so that the next time Mrs. Jansen tossed out a brainteaser, they might actually be able to solve it.

I knew one thing for sure—no matter how good it felt to solve these problems, the reaction from my classmates seemed to take some of the fun out of it. It was nothing like the rush I would get when a satisfied customer shook my hand after another successful case. Finding the solution to a brainteaser in class was different. At times, I didn't know why I put myself through this. Maybe I should just back off and let Mrs. Jansen answer all of her own brain busters. But in my heart I knew that I couldn't do that. I *had* to solve these problems—even if I didn't want to. I just couldn't help myself.

My only consolation was knowing that I wasn't alone.

There was someone else out there with the same problem—Sam Solomon. Even when he thought that sharing a piece of information might make his life miserable, he just had to do it. When Sam accepted an assignment, he would see it through no matter what. And there were plenty of times when he knew that presenting his findings to his clients would make his life very unpleasant. But, like me, it was out of his control. Sam was a man of his word, and no matter the consequences, his clients always got their money's worth. It was just like what happened in Episode #26—*The Unfriendly Fire Caper.* It was probably Sam's lowest point.

Sam had been hired by an insurance company to investigate the death of a firefighter who had died a hero while battling a blaze. The firefighter's widow and six children were in line for a $50,000 life insurance payout. Sam discovered that the firefighter had been at a bar when the blaze broke out. He had been drinking heavily and was in no condition to drive, let alone fight a fire. Sam knew that if he shared these details with the insurance company, it would void the policy. But what was he to do? Sam ultimately made the tortured decision to report his findings to his client. And as you might guess, for some time, Sam became a rather unpopular figure in his own community. Following the case, he began sending a few dollars each week to the widow to help her offset expenses.

As I thought long and hard about the decision Sam had made, I realized what my mission in life was. I had been given a gift, and it would be wrong—no, make that unthinkable—not to use it. I made a pledge there and then that if I were able to use my reasoning skills to solve a riddle or a problem or a brain buster or that million-dollar question that would blow the lid right off a case, then it was my obligation to do so. I took a deep breath, lifted my head, and looked around. This was a new Charlie Collier—one who was confident enough to deflect the jeers and the taunts and the criticisms of others. If these kids had been in my position, then they would have understood completely. And since they weren't, then there was nothing I could do to change it. This was my destiny. And I planned to live it to the fullest.

CHAPTER 7

The Thyme Bomb Caper

I got up early on Saturday morning. It wasn't my normal routine, but this was a new day for Charlie Collier, Snoop for Hire. My mission had begun. I was focused, confident, and unflappable. It was all about the client.

I called Henry and Scarlett and asked them to meet me at the intersection of Wellington and Ottawa at ten fifteen. It was midway between school and the address of our first person of interest—Zachary Kasper. According to Sherman, Zach was Josh's best friend. If we were going to locate our missing person, we would need to interrogate those people who knew him best.

When I arrived at the meeting point, Scarlett and Henry were waiting for me. Apparently our little squabble with Scarlett a few days ago regarding her punctuality had paid off. I was hopeful that I wouldn't have to immediately break up some silly altercation between the two of them, but when I rode up, things were relatively calm.

"*Now* who's the one late for an appointment?" Scarlett said.

I looked at my watch. "It's ten sixteen," I said. "Give me a break."

"Well, just see that it doesn't happen again," she said with a smirk.

Henry was smiling. He was enjoying the show.

"Okay," I said. "Let's get serious. Here's what's on tap for today." I pulled a piece of paper from my pocket. "We're headed to 414 North Kenmore Avenue, the residence of one Zachary Kasper—Josh Doyle's closest friend. If anyone knows where Josh is, he will."

"Don't you think that people have already talked to him?" Scarlett said.

"I guess so. What's your point?"

"My point is that he's probably already been questioned by Sherman's mom or the police, and if he hasn't told them where Josh is, what makes you think he'll tell us?"

Scarlett was probably right. Since Zach would have been a likely source of information, he already had to have been questioned by countless folks. And since Sherman came to us for help, then obviously Zach had been tight-lipped.

"But you forget about Charlie's amazing interrogation skills," Henry said tongue in cheek.

"Very funny," I said. "Listen, I realize that Zach has probably already been asked a lot of questions by a lot of people . . . and I also assume that he hasn't provided the kind of information that these same people were looking for . . . but my guess is that everyone he's talked to was an adult. If he's going to open up, he'd be much more likely to do so to a kid, don't you think?"

Scarlett looked skeptical. "I don't know."

"Charlie, if he knew us, then maybe your theory would be correct," Henry said. "But this guy doesn't know us from Adam. Why would he talk?"

We weren't getting anywhere debating whether or not a person of interest would talk or not. We wouldn't know until we found him and actually asked our questions.

"Let's just go find out for ourselves," I said. "We have nothing to lose. C'mon."

We made it to 414 North Kenmore Avenue in under twenty minutes. When we arrived, we found ourselves staring at a run-down two-flat. There was a broken picture window on the first floor. There were more weeds than grass in the front lawn. We had to steer our bikes around a broken bottle on the sidewalk. I noticed an uneasy look on Scarlett's face. We needed to make this a quick visit.

I climbed the stairs, managing to avoid a rotted-out step, and spotted the name Kasper written in an almost-illegible fashion on a piece of paper taped just below the top doorbell. I pressed it. The voice of an older woman came through a tiny, distorted speaker.

"What do you want?"

"I'm looking for Zachary."

"Zach," she yelled.

I waited for a few moments, wondering if they had forgotten about me.

"What?" a voice called out. It had to be Zach. He didn't sound particularly happy.

"My name is Charlie Collier. I've been hired to look into the disappearance of Joshua Doyle."

"You sound like a kid," Zach said.

I decided to ignore the comment. "I was told that you and Josh were friends. I was wondering if I could ask you a few questions."

"Listen, I don't know where he is."

"I promise not to take more than five minutes of your time," I said.

"You don't get it. I said I have no idea where he is," Zach insisted.

I wasn't going to give up. "The police apparently haven't been much help. And Josh's mom is really upset. Please," I pleaded.

In previous investigations, I had learned to adopt a relentless approach. I would never give in. I refused to accept *no* or *no comment.* I would continue to ask questions until I got the answers I wanted. If the interviewee was hoping that I would just go away, then he or she was mistaken. Zach Kasper would come to this realization sooner or later.

Zach sighed. "All right," he said disgustedly. "Five minutes. No more."

A second later, the buzzer sounded. I pulled open the door and was just about to climb the stairs to the second floor when I looked back at Henry and Scarlett. I reached back outside and hit the buzzer again.

A few seconds later, a rather irritated Zach replied. "Now what?" he said.

"Zach? I have two associates with me. Can they come up too?"

"No," he snapped. "Come alone or go away."

I whispered to Henry and Scarlett, "He'll only talk to me. I'll be down in a few minutes." I knew they wouldn't be happy about being squeezed out, but what could I do? Those were the rules.

The hallway was dimly lit, but the peeling paint was still visible. As I approached the Kasper apartment, something slithered by me and ran over my shoe. I chose not to look. I was relieved when a door up ahead opened and a skinny guy with wild hair, who looked to be about seventeen or so, poked his head out.

"You *are* a kid," Zach said.

I extended my hand. "Charlie Collier, Snoop for Hire."

Zach shook his head and smiled. "You're kidding me, right?" he said.

"Is there somewhere we can talk?" I was determined to get what I had come for.

"C'mon," he said.

As we passed through the living room, a woman who must have been his mother eyed me suspiciously.

"What's he want?" she asked Zach.

"He's trying to find Josh."

"Josh isn't here," she said sternly. "Why won't anyone believe us?"

"He knows that, Ma. Let me talk to him. It's all right."

Zach led me into his bedroom and motioned for me to sit down. I immediately noticed the posters that filled the walls. One of them featured a woman kneeling next to a lifeless body with the words *Kent State, Never Forget.*

On another, a teenage boy, dressed in 1920s garb, held a younger boy on his back. The words at the bottom read *He ain't heavy, he's my brother.*

On still another poster, a young Asian man stood in front of a wall of tanks in Tiananmen Square. I recognized that one. The words at the bottom read *Take A Stand—Preserve Human Rights.*

Knowing what I did about Josh, it was easy to see why he and Zach had become friends. Their causes were slightly different, but their values were similar. And they always seemed to be on the side of the underdog.

"Now, what makes you think I know where Josh is?" Zach said.

"His brother told me you might be able to help."

"Well, I can't help you," he said. "I haven't seen him in weeks."

"When did you talk to him last?" I asked.

"It's been over a month now."

"Did he say anything about where he might be headed?"

Zach sighed. He walked to the window and looked out.

"He told me he wanted to get the public's attention—that he had to stop a cruel and inhumane practice. And he would do so even if it meant breaking the law." He turned to face me. "People don't understand Josh. He loves the earth and all its creatures and just wants to save them." He picked up a baseball from the top of his desk and flung it at the wall, leaving a mark. "Our world is so screwed up. Step on the little guy. Destroy the earth. That's what we're doing. And then there's people like Josh who seem to get it. And what happens? They treat him like a criminal and throw him in jail."

"Is that what happened?" I said. "Is he back in jail?"

"Wouldn't be the first time."

I had a feeling that Zach was telling me the truth. He really didn't know where Josh was. He'd been pretty forthcoming. If he did know anything, I think I'd have been able to tell.

"So, if you had to track him down in an emergency, where would you start?" I said.

Zach sat on the edge of his bed. "Odds are he's trying to save something—or stop something. And knowing Josh, he probably broke some laws—if you want to call them laws. I'd check all the jails in the area."

"But his brother said that they checked the police department here in Oak Grove, and he wasn't there," I said.

Zach appeared to be losing patience. "Then call some of the others. I thought *you* were the private eye," he said.

"I will do that," I said. "But don't you think that *any* police department would have contacted his mom to let her know he was there?"

Zach laughed. "You don't know Josh. When he gets himself arrested, he clams up. He won't tell 'em anything. Not his name, address, nothing. To them, he's just another John Doe. They wouldn't know who to call." Zach lifted himself off the bed. "Oh, here in town, they know him. That's why he's not in the Oak Grove jail. If he were, the cops would've called his mom. Listen, if I were you, I'd check some of the other police stations in the area. You got a picture of Josh to show them?"

"Yeah," I said. I reached into my pocket and pulled out the picture that Sherman had given me.

"Okay, that's all I can tell you. You better go now," Zach said. "Your five minutes are up."

"Thanks a lot. I appreciate it."

Zach led me out of the apartment and walked me down the stairs. When I reached the front door, I smiled and waved, then turned to leave.

"Hey, kid," he said.

"Yeah?"

"I hope you do find him. I miss the guy. Good luck."

"Thanks," I said as I stepped out onto the front porch.

Henry and Scarlett were waiting patiently on the front sidewalk. By the looks on their faces, I could tell they were eager to know what I had learned.

"Well?" Henry said.

I jumped down the stairs, remembering to avoid the bad one.

"He doesn't know where Josh is," I said.

"Are you sure?" Henry asked. "Maybe he's lying."

I picked up my bike and hopped on. "He's telling the truth. I can tell."

"What are you—a human lie detector?" Scarlett said.

Henry folded his arms. He didn't appear happy with my results. "All I needed is two minutes with the guy and I'd have him talking. I'd show him who was boss." Henry considered himself the master interrogator. He wasn't afraid to get in someone's face. What he didn't seem to understand was that every source presented different challenges. Not everyone responded well to an aggressive line of questioning. He'd need to learn that.

"You gotta trust me on this one," I said. "C'mon."

"Now where?" Scarlett asked.

"Josh's old girlfriend. She lives about fifteen minutes from here in that direction," I said, pointing north.

"Aren't you gonna tell us what happened in there?" Henry said.

"I'll tell you on the way. Let's go."

As we traveled to our next destination, I shared the conversation that I had with Zach, word for word, with the others. I described the condition of the stairwell and the apartment, including the posters in Zach's bedroom. I told them about his mom, who didn't seem particularly friendly. They especially enjoyed the part where Zach hurled a baseball at the wall. And by the time I had finished, we were all on the same page again. Like me, they were now convinced that Zach was telling the truth—even Henry. Both he and Scarlett even thought that he had probably told me more than he had shared with the police if or when they had questioned him. His mom's tone seemed to indicate that the authorities might have paid them a visit at some point.

Following our upcoming chat with Josh's former girlfriend, we discussed the possibility of visiting police departments in the towns surrounding Oak Grove. The only downside to that plan was the distance we'd have to travel by bike to each location. If we decided to do so, we'd be putting in some pretty serious mileage. But, on the plus side, I'd be shedding some pretty serious calories. That would please my mom, although there was no way I could tell her about my new weight-loss plan.

It felt good to be making some progress. As we were pedaling through town, I thought back to my conversation with Zach. Trying to get information from him was like pulling teeth. It wasn't until he felt comfortable with me that he opened up. I had tried to remain calm and seem more like a friend than a snoop for hire. It had worked. And it reminded me of another Sam Solomon mystery—Episode #21—*The Thyme Bomb Caper.*

This was the story of a world-renowned chef at Chicago's Palmer House whose grandson had been kidnapped by a militia group. The chef had been warned that if he contacted the police, he would never see his grandson again. The chef had been planning a special main course—roast goose—for the president, who was in town to attend a campaign fund-raiser. But now the bird served at the president's table would have one additional ingredient—an explosive device. Sam had been hired by the president's staff to assist the Secret Service. Only minutes before dinner was served, Sam discovered the dirty bird following a lengthy interrogation of the chef. Rather than resorting to tough talk, he befriended the grief-stricken cook and eventually earned his trust.

Sam had taught me well. With some suspects, you had to get tough. But with others, like Zach, you had to seem more like an old friend. And oh, by the way, speaking of Sam—you'll be happy to learn that the chef's grandson was found unharmed. Thanks to Sam, there was one more cooked goose that night—the leader of the militia group.

CHAPTER 8

The Bartlett Pair Caper

Most of our ride across town was uphill. That kept conversation to a minimum. But it didn't stop Henry from taking another shot at trying to stump me.

"Hey, Charlie," he said as he slowed down to ride alongside me. "Before Mount Everest was discovered, what was the highest mountain in the world?"

Scarlett suddenly seemed interested. "Let me try too," she said.

"Is your name *Charlie*?" Henry shot back.

"I don't care," I said. "She can try if she wants to."

Henry didn't look pleased. "Okay, so what's the answer?"

"Well," Scarlett said, "there's Mount McKinley, Mount Rainier . . ."

I didn't want to correct Scarlett, but those peaks weren't even close. And even if she managed to name the really tall mountains in Tibet and Nepal and Pakistan, it wouldn't matter. I could tell by the smirk on Henry's face that this was not a social studies question. He was trying to trick me. It took me about thirty seconds to figure it out.

"The tallest mountain *before* Mount Everest was discovered?" I said.

"Yeah," Henry said confidently.

"The answer is . . . Mount Everest," I said. "Whether someone had discovered it or not, it was still the tallest." I glanced at Henry. The smirk was gone.

"Hey, that's not fair," Scarlett said.

"Scarlett, let me give you a little advice," I said. "Just about all of Henry's brainteasers are trick questions. First, you have to eliminate the obvious. Then think about each word in the question. In no time, you'll figure it out."

Henry squeezed his brakes and skidded to a stop. "Oh yeah? Let's see if she can answer this one."

We all stopped and moved over to the curb.

I pointed to Scarlett. "Okay, now remember what I said." Then I turned to Henry. "Let 'er rip."

"Let's say you're standing on a bridge over a river. You see a boat filled with people. But actually there's not a single person on the boat." Henry grinned. "Figure that one out."

Henry had asked me this one about a year ago. I still remembered the answer. If Scarlett faithfully followed the directions I had given her, I knew she could solve it.

"I'm standing on a bridge over a river," she began. "I see a boat filled with people. But there's not a single person on it?"

"That's what I said," Henry replied.

"You can do this," I told her.

Henry got off his bike and sat down on the curb. "We could be here for a while."

Scarlett's lips were moving, but she made no sounds. She seemed to be repeating the question over and over again. She was stressing different words each time she said it. At first she just appeared confused. But that soon morphed into a look of frustration. She sighed.

"Concentrate," I said.

"What do you think I'm doing?" she said disgustedly. She closed her eyes, gritted her teeth, and began breathing rapidly through her nose. A minute later, she sighed and shook her head. And then just as she was about to throw in the towel, she experienced that magical moment—the moment I've enjoyed countless times—when all of the planets align. She had it. She had solved Henry's riddle. Scarlett held her head up proudly. "There's not a *single* person on the boat . . . because they're all *married*," she announced confidently.

Henry threw his head back. He was now 0 for 2. He jumped onto his bike and took off. He didn't even wait for us.

I don't mind telling you I had a pretty tough time keeping up with him after that. In his present state of mind, Henry was quite capable of putting some real distance between us. I just put my head down and pedaled furiously. Unfortunately I didn't pay attention to where I was going. *HONK!* I had drifted too far into the middle of the street when a green minivan rudely reminded me of my navigation error.

Since I could see Henderson Park up ahead, I knew we were getting close. I pulled over to the curb. Scarlett joined me. Henry didn't even notice we had stopped. He was well ahead of us in his own little world. I took a look at the piece of paper that Sherman had given me with names and addresses. I was looking at the name—Deirdre Sweeney. Sherman had described her as Josh's on-and-off girlfriend. Hopefully she would have a better idea of Josh's whereabouts than Zach. If the address on the paper was correct, we were headed to 437 West Paradise Avenue. I was guessing it was about a half mile away now.

A couple of minutes later, when we turned onto Paradise, Henry was waiting for us. He had parked his bike on the driveway next to Deirdre's house, and he was leaning against an oak tree in the front lawn.

"What kept you?" he said in a nonchalant manner.

I thought it best to say nothing. When Henry got into one of those foul moods, there was no telling what he might do or say. I was just about to step off my bike when I was startled by a very unwelcoming voice.

"What do you want?"

I offered what must have looked like a weak smile. "My name is Charlie Collier."

The girl on the front porch crossed her arms. She must have been sixteen or seventeen, but by the way she spoke, she seemed older.

"And that's supposed to mean something to me?!" she shot back.

We hadn't been formally introduced, but I was fairly certain that we were talking to Deirdre Sweeney. There was a distrustful tone in her voice, similar to Zach's. What was up with these folks anyway? I wondered. Maybe they just assumed that everyone thought differently than they did. I guess they were conditioned to be on the defensive at all times. Regardless of the reason, her unfriendly greeting didn't make a body feel particularly welcome.

"We'd like to ask you some questions about Josh Doyle," I said.

"Never heard of him," she said.

Henry stepped in front of me and held up his hand. He was apparently going to demonstrate how to crack an uncooperative witness.

"Excuse me, miss. My name is Henry Cunningham. I have a few questions for you. You say you've never heard of Josh Doyle. Well, his brother tells us that you and Josh have dated in the past. Explain that."

"I don't know what you're talking about," she snapped.

A large, menacing figure in an undershirt and sweatpants appeared in the doorway.

"What's going on here?" the man said in a gruff voice.

"Nothing, Daddy," Deirdre answered. "Don't worry, I'll get rid of them."

"You selling something?" he shouted at us.

"No, sir," Henry replied.

"Just go back and watch TV," Deirdre said. "It's okay." Mr. Sweeney reluctantly exited. Deirdre bounced down the steps and approached us.

"Have you heard from Josh? Do you know where he is?" she whispered.

I liked to think that we were good at what we did, but never had a person of interest changed her tune so quickly.

"I was hoping you could tell *us,*" Henry said.

Deirdre sat down on the bottom step and stared forward.

"I haven't seen him for weeks. I'm worried about him," she said.

"So he didn't tell you where he was headed?" I said.

Deirdre shook her head. "He could be anywhere. But I have a feeling he's not too far from here."

"Why do you say that?" Scarlett asked.

"The last time I saw him, he said that there was something he had to do the next day. So he couldn't have gone very far. He didn't have any money for transportation."

"Did he say specifically what it was he had to do?" Henry said.

"He told me he needed to take a stand. He needed to get people's attention. He needed to keep them from harming those poor, defenseless creatures."

"What creatures?" I said.

Deirdre shrugged. "I don't know. I just don't know."

I could tell from the look on her face that she really cared for Josh. She seemed genuinely worried about his disappearance. I could sense the passion in her voice.

"And so that was it?" I said.

"Josh said that if everything went as planned, he'd see me in a couple of days. That was about three weeks ago." She stood up and climbed to the top of the porch. "If you guys hear anything, you gotta tell me. I'm worried. His knee was pretty swollen that day. He's got a bad leg, you know. He was having a hard time moving around when he left here." Deirdre paused for a moment, let out a long sigh, and disappeared behind her front door.

Henry lifted his bike from the driveway and smiled. "And that, my friends, is how you handle an interrogation," he said.

"But we didn't really learn anything new," Scarlett said.

"I don't know about that," I said. "I just have a feeling that at some point in the very near future, we'll think back to this conversation and realize that Deirdre gave us a valuable piece of information."

"Sounds like you're trying to justify the fact that we biked all the way over here for nothing," Scarlett said.

"You may be right. We'll see," I said. "But right now, let's head back to my house. I don't think my mom would mind making lunch for us. Then we can plot out our next move. C'mon."

I tried to sound confident, but I had no idea what our next move would be. And I wondered if Scarlett was right. Had we just wasted an entire morning? We were no closer to finding Josh than we had been when Sherman wandered into the garage days ago. We had put in the legwork but had nothing to show for it. But we weren't alone—Sam Solomon had experienced the same thing. Weeks of research, investigations, and stakeouts had produced zilch—not a shred of evidence. It was Episode #27—*The Bartlett Pair Caper.*

Josiah Bartlett, who was suffering from a terminal illness, hired Sam to help find his identical twin, Jeremiah. He just wanted to say good-bye. The two had been separated at infancy. Sam spent more than a month trying to track down the missing brother. He had spoken with dozens of sources and had spent endless hours on the case. He was just about ready to give up when he got a tip regarding the whereabouts of Jeremiah Bartlett. Not only was Sam able to locate the long-lost brother, but since he was Josiah's identical twin, a simple blood transfusion from this perfect match helped cure his ailing client. If Sam was patient enough to suffer through a series of dead ends to uncover the truth, then I was more than capable of doing the same.

As I had predicted, my mom was only too happy to welcome two extra guests for lunch. She was always pleased to see me with other kids. I think she worried about my ability to make friends—you know, because of the whole weight-challenged thing and all.

"So, Scarlett," she said, "I think I've met your mother before . . . at a school function maybe."

"I'm not sure, Mrs. Collier. But you probably have."

My mom winked at me while she threw two more grilled cheese sandwiches onto the griddle. I think she was happy to learn that I actually had a friend who was a girl. She must have thought I was moving up the social ladder at school. Sorry to disappoint you, Mom, but this relationship, unfortunately, was all business.

"Personally, I can't wait to dig my teeth into another one of your famous grilled cheese sandwiches, Mrs. Collier," Henry said. He always seemed to know when to turn on the charm. And a free meal was apparently one of those times.

My dad sat at the head of the table with his face buried in the newspaper. He didn't seem to notice, or at least pretended not to, when Grandma tiptoed into the kitchen and plopped herself down between Henry and me. She was wearing a tight-fitting, black bodysuit. Her face was painted white, and on her head was a black beret.

Henry leaned back and smiled. He had witnessed Gram's rather unconventional behavior before, and he was a big fan.

I was only sorry that Scarlett had to see what was coming.

Gram immediately began her best mime performance. She reached for an imaginary plate, then scooped spoonfuls of nothing into it. She began chewing heartily, then at one point seemed to choke on something. She grabbed her throat and pointed into her mouth.

I knew this was all part of the act, but I also knew that if someone didn't quickly become a willing participant in this performance, Grandma would continue until someone caved in. You should have seen the look on Scarlett's face. To spare the others any more drama, I leaned over, put my arms around my grandmother from behind, and proceeded to perform the Heimlich maneuver. She gagged, choked, then pretended to spit something onto the table.

My dad did his best to ignore Gram's theatrics. He didn't want to encourage her. Whenever she assumed a new identity, he would just ignore it and act like everything was normal.

"Mom," he said. "If you want me to get the muffler on your car fixed, I'm gonna need your keys."

Gram reached into an imaginary pants pocket, fished around for a minute, and pulled out an invisible set of keys. She set them down in front of my dad and smiled.

By the expression on his face, it was easy to tell that he was getting tired of the games. He let out a long sigh, leaned over, and flipped on the television next to the dinner table. The local noon news was in progress.

"Yesterday Mayor Wilde and council members unveiled an experimental rehabilitation program for young offenders in the area," the news anchor began. "And earlier today, the first group of teenagers held in Oak Grove's juvenile detention facility were taken to the Camp Phoenix compound, just northeast of the city."

I watched the news report as a long line of teens boarded a yellow school bus.

"Under the direction of Colonel Harvard Culpepper, the camp director, the young recruits will undergo a regimen of classroom instruction, manual labor, and what the colonel refers to as *suggestive meditation*," the newscaster said.

"Lunch is ready. Turn the TV off, please," my mom said.

My dad turned off the set but continued reading his paper. "Will you look at this," he said.

"What?" my mom replied.

"Someone else has been arrested at that fancy French restaurant in Clifton City. And for the same thing that happened a few weeks ago."

"Who was arrested? For what?" I said.

"It was a woman this time," my dad said. "She was picked up for disturbing the peace."

"What did she do, Mr. Collier?" Henry said.

My dad set the newspaper down. "She went into the restaurant kitchen and started screaming at the chef."

"Why?" Scarlett said. "What did the chef do?"

"Well, it seems that this particular restaurant serves a rather controversial delicacy—something called foie gras. I hope I'm pronouncing it correctly."

"What's so controversial about it?" I asked.

My grandmother slammed her fist on the table. "I'll tell you," she said. She started wiping the white makeup from her face with a napkin. "A lot of people don't like how they make it—including me."

I couldn't remember seeing my grandmother quite this upset before.

"Well, how *is* it made, Mrs. Collier?" Henry asked.

"It's not really the type of conversation we should be having at mealtime," my dad said.

My mom placed a plate full of grilled cheese sandwiches in front of us. "I agree," she said. "Why don't we table this discussion?"

"It's too important to put off," Gram said. "This is just the kind of thing these kids should know about."

My mom looked to my dad for support. He was not about to take on Grandma. He hid behind his newspaper.

Grandma scooted up to the table. "This is how they make this stuff. See what you think."

My mom made a face. She apparently knew what was coming. But it was clear from the looks on the faces of Henry and Scarlett that they felt differently. They were all ears.

"In order to make this stuff, workers ram pipes down the throats of geese and ducks."

"Ooooh," Scarlett squealed.

"Then they force-feed them huge amounts of grain and fat, which causes their livers to swell up to an enormous size. Then they kill them and sell the swollen livers as foie gras."

"And this is legal?" Scarlett said.

"In some places it still is," Gram said. "I just keep thinking of those poor, defenseless creatures."

I tried to picture what Gram had just described. It

was so creepy. It just didn't seem right. And then something hit me. Something that she had said.

"Gram, what did you just say? What did you call those animals?"

"The ducks and geese?"

"Yeah."

"Poor, defenseless creatures. Why? You don't think so?"

"No, I do. I do."

My mom set a bowl of potato salad on the table. "Okay, enough talk. Let's eat."

It was the second time today that someone had used that phrase. It suddenly got me to thinking about Josh.

"Dad, did you say that someone else had been arrested at that restaurant for doing the same thing?"

"Yeah," he said. "About three weeks ago, I think."

"Man or woman?" I asked.

"Actually, it was a teenage boy," he said. "Why do you want to know?"

"I was just wondering. That's all."

Henry, Scarlett, and I all looked at each other at the same moment. This couldn't be a coincidence. We were now officially on Josh's trail.

CHAPTER 9

The Died in the Wool Caper

The three of us sat at the table staring at the potato salad. Gram's story of how they made foie gras had caused us to lose our appetites.

"I don't know about anyone else, but I'm not really too hungry right now," I said.

"Me neither," Henry said.

"Scarlett," my mom said. "How about you?"

Scarlett held her lips tightly closed, almost as if she was afraid she was going to hurl right then and there.

"You see what you did, Ma," my dad said. "Everyone's too sick to eat after that story."

"Well, what was I supposed to do? They needed to know the truth," Gram said. "And come to think of it, you were the one who brought up the story in the first place."

As Gram and my dad continued their heated exchange, Scarlett, Henry, and I slipped out. I motioned to my mom that we were headed up to my room. She nodded her approval. As we headed up the stairs, Scarlett stopped in mid-stride.

"I may never eat again," she said.

"Yeah, right," Henry said. "You'll be hungry in ten minutes. Just wait."

I led the others into my room. I was so worked up about the foie gras story and the connection to Josh that I almost didn't realize that this was the first time a girl, other than my mom or grandmother, of course, had ever been in my room. Now that it had finally happened, it didn't seem like such a big deal. I was thankful that it was a Saturday. Before I left the house this morning, my mom had made me clean my room. I was glad there wasn't dirty underwear all over the floor.

"So that had to be Josh protesting at that restaurant a few weeks ago, right?" Henry said.

"It all makes perfect sense," I said. "First Zach tells us to look for him in a jail in one of the surrounding towns. Clifton City is just one town over."

"And then Deirdre tells us that Josh used the words 'poor, defenseless creatures' before he left," Scarlett said. "He had to be referring to the ducks and geese."

"And knowing the kinds of causes that Josh supports," I said, "this foie gras thing sounds just like something he would do."

There was a knock at the door.

"Come in," I said.

My mom walked in holding plate of grilled cheese sandwiches. "I warmed them up," she said. "Anyone interested?"

"I'll take one," Henry said.

"How can you eat anything right now?" Scarlett said.

I reached in and helped myself to a sandwich as well.

Scarlett glared at me.

"What?" I said. "It's lunchtime."

"Relax, it's not like we're eating goose liver or anything," Henry said.

Scarlett immediately grabbed her mouth. She looked pale. "Where's the bathroom?" She gagged.

"Follow me," my mom said. As she led Scarlett out, she looked back and made a face at us. "You boys are something else sometimes."

"What'd I say?" Henry mumbled. His mouth was full.

A few minutes later, Scarlett rejoined us. The color had now returned to her face.

"How do you feel?" I asked.

"Better," she said. "No thanks to you guys."

"Listen," Henry said. "If you want to be an official member of this agency, you're going to have to toughen up." Henry looked to me for support. "Right?"

"Well, I guess."

"You *guess*?" he said. "Aren't you the one telling me all the time about the kinds of scrapes Sam Solomon gets himself into and all the creepy stuff that happens to him? Just the other day, you said something about Sam and a dead body. What was that about?"

Henry was right. He was referring to Episode #30—*The Died in the Wool Caper.* It was the story of a sheep rancher who had vanished. Sam had been hired by his daughter to find him. This episode did not have a happy ending. Sam spent eight hours up close and personal with a decaying corpse. I didn't dare tell Scarlett about that one.

"Who's Sam Solomon anyway?" she said.

"Who's Sam Solomon?" I repeated in disbelief. I glanced at Henry. He had one of those *I-told-you-so* looks on his face. Now that Scarlett had insulted my hero, he was in his glory. He had to assume I'd join his camp. I didn't want to overreact. I had to relax. I had to tell myself that every person has his or her own passion. I didn't know what Scarlett's was. But I knew that if I allowed myself to be bothered by Scarlett's ignorance of the world's greatest literary detective—and I let her know exactly how I felt—then she might decide to bolt. And I didn't want that. So I decided to ignore the whole thing and instead get down to business.

"All right," I said. "We've got some work to do. I'm guessing that Josh is in the Clifton City jail. And since he probably refused to give the authorities his name or gave them a bogus one, he might still be sitting there."

"For weeks?" Henry said. "You're gonna keep a kid locked up that long for disturbing the peace? I doubt that, Charlie. Don't you think they would have released him by now?"

"If they did, then where is he?" Scarlett said. "He would either have contacted his mom or at least his girlfriend if he'd gotten out . . . and he hasn't done either."

I opened a desk drawer and pulled out a map of the area. I opened it up and laid it out on the bed.

"Okay, now," I said, pointing to the map. "Here's where *we* are." I then slid my finger all the way across to the other side. "And *here's* Clifton City."

"That's gotta be fifteen or twenty miles," Henry said. "Do you actually expect us to ride our bikes over there?"

"Well, it's not the distance I'm worried about," I said. "It's this." I pointed to a four-lane interstate highway. "There's no way we can cross that on bikes."

"Then how are we going to get there?" Scarlett said.

"By car, of course."

Henry looked at me skeptically. He knew that we'd never convince our parents to drive us over there. They'd been trying to thwart our little detective agency for some time now. Even if we came up with a story that sounded legitimate, they'd eventually figure it out. I had another idea in mind regarding transportation.

But before I could share it with the others, Scarlett chimed in.

"So, who can drive us? Your parents?" she asked. Her question was directed at me.

"Are you serious?" I said. "My parents would never be a party to this."

She turned to Henry.

"Don't look at me," he said. "Mine feel the same way. They'd like nothing better than to see this agency just go away. They think it's too dangerous."

Since Scarlett seemed so intent upon enlisting our parents, I decided to toss the ball in her court.

"What about your folks?" I said.

"Are you kidding?" she said. "They don't even know I'm here right now. They'd never agree to help us with any of this. And I have no intention of asking."

I began folding up the map.

"I guess we need a new plan then, huh?" Scarlett said.

I opened the desk drawer and slid the map in. "The old plan will work just fine."

"Huh?" she said.

"Be right back," I said.

I left Henry and Scarlett in my room, slipped into the hallway, down the stairs, and made my way to Gram's bedroom and knocked on the door.

"Enter at your own risk," she said in a muffled voice.

When I opened the door, I thought I had been transported into the center ring of the circus. Gram was dressed in a lion tamer's outfit. She was holding a chair in one hand and a whip in the other.

"Not too close, sonny," she said. "Sheba doesn't like strangers."

I smiled. Gram never disappointed me.

"Back . . . back in your cage, sweetheart. We have company." She appeared to be talking to an oversize pillow balanced on top of a lamp shade, which rested on her nightstand. Meet Sheba, the queen of beasts. Gram leaned over so as not to be overheard by the lioness. "I've never really used this thing on her," she said, referring to the whip. "It's just to get her attention." She set down the chair and took a seat. "So, what can I do for you?" she said.

"Gram, I don't mean to interrupt, but I have a favor to ask."

"Anything for a patron of the big top," she said.

I sat down on the edge of the bed. "You know we're working on a big missing persons case, right?"

She nodded.

"Well, we have reason to believe that our person in question may be in the Clifton City lockup, and we need a ride over there to confirm our suspicions. I know it's a long haul, and I wouldn't ask if there was any other way of getting there."

Her eyes narrowed. "You're sure about this?"

"I wouldn't say *sure*. But I am fairly confident," I said. "All the evidence points in that direction."

She got up and put her hand on my shoulder. "If it were in my power, I'd be happy to run you over there. But, right at the moment, my car's headed to the shop for some tricky exhaust work. Your dad just left with it a few minutes ago."

"When will it be done?" I asked.

She threw her arms up. "No one knows. The car's over thirty years old. The last time we took it in, they had to special order the parts. It took over a week. I wish I could help, Charlie. I'm sorry."

"That's okay, Gram. Thanks anyway."

She kissed me on the forehead and suddenly lunged for her whip. "Bad Sheba, bad girl."

Since Sheba was misbehaving, I thought it best to leave. When I returned to my room, I didn't know what to expect. I should have known better than to have left Henry and Scarlett alone. I half expected to find two lifeless bodies. Instead I found Henry at the computer and Scarlett texting a friend. No damage done . . . thankfully.

Henry lifted his eyes from the keyboard. "So, do we have a ride?" he said.

"No go," I said. "My grandma's car is in the shop."

"Well, then maybe she could borrow your parents' car," Henry said. "What do you think?"

It was hard to keep from laughing. "Are you joking?" I said. "My dad doesn't let her anywhere near that car. You know how she drives."

"Oh yeah," Henry said.

We were back to square one. It seemed that we had run out of options. There didn't appear to be anyone who might be willing to take us. And then all at once, it hit me. Of course! Why hadn't I thought of it sooner?

"Have either of you ever ridden in the back of a hearse?" I said.

CHAPTER 10

The Fools Rush Inn Caper

"Your money's no good here, sailor," Eugene said as he pulled the hearse onto the main highway and accelerated.

With the price of gas these days, and the fact that Eugene's car was anything but fuel efficient, I thought that the least we could do was to offer him a few dollars for his trouble, but he wouldn't hear of it.

"Anytime I can help out a fellow P.I. in search of the truth," he said, "I'm only too happy to lend a hand."

"We appreciate it, Eugene," I said. Henry, Scarlett, and I sat in the backseat of Eugene's hearse. It was one of the biggest and most comfortable backseats I'd ever been in. Since it was the place where the family of the deceased would sit during a funeral procession, I guess it was only fitting to make them as comfortable as possible while they mourned the loss of a loved one.

As we drove through the outskirts of Oak Grove, I explained to Eugene everything that had taken place since we had last spoken. I told him about the interrogations of Zach and Deirdre—and about how tidbits of those conversations, along with information provided by my dad and grandma, led us to the conclusion that Josh was being held in the Clifton City jail.

"Well, it sounds like you kids may just be on to something," he said.

Eugene sped up as we turned onto the entrance ramp and merged onto the interstate. We would only have to take it till the next exit. But even that short a distance on an expressway would have been far too dangerous to have negotiated on bikes—not to mention the fact that it was illegal to ride a bicycle on an interstate. This was our only option, and we knew we were lucky to have found someone available to transport us. And it was even better that it was Eugene since we didn't have to make up a story about why we needed to visit a jail in a nearby town.

The entire trip took about thirty-five minutes. Eugene pulled up right in front of the Clifton City Police Department. And as always seems to happen whenever people get a good look at Eugene's mode of transportation, there were plenty of stares. Henry, Scarlett, and I jumped from the car. This would be a good opportunity for Scarlett to watch a pro extract information from the authorities. There was a science to it. Hopefully she'd be paying close attention.

I poked my head through the passenger's-side

window. “Are you going to stay here, Eugene? Or should we look for you someplace else?”

“I’ll pull into that lot over there,” he said, pointing across the street.

“But that says *authorized vehicles only,*” Henry said. It was the official lot for police vehicles.

“They won’t bother me,” Eugene said. “You forget—I have special privileges at most of these places.”

“Oh yeah,” I said. I waved good-bye and joined the others as Eugene pulled away from the curb.

“So now what?” Scarlett said.

I pointed to a large set of doors. “Now we find out if Josh is somewhere in there.” We climbed the stairs and threw open one of the heavy steel doors.

Standing at the entrance was a uniformed officer. He motioned for us to proceed down the hallway.

We moved forward in silence and approached the front desk. “Excuse me, Officer,” I said.

A policeman who appeared to be in his mid-fifties sat up in his chair. He flipped over the crossword puzzle he had been working on and slid it to the side. Apparently we weren’t supposed to have seen that.

“We’re interested in finding out if you’re holding a particular individual,” I said.

He picked up the phone and dialed. A couple of seconds later, he pressed the receiver to his ear.

“I have three kids up here who need some help,”

the officer said. "Okay, thanks." He hung up the phone and pointed to a bench against the wall. "You can wait over there. Someone'll be here in a minute."

"Thank you. Thank you very much," I said.

As we made our way to the waiting area, Henry tapped me on the shoulder. "So who's our lead interrogator today?" he asked. He turned to Scarlett. "How 'bout you?" he said with a smirk. He was assuming she would pass.

"You don't think I can do it, do you?" she said. "Well, I have half a mind to say *yes*."

Henry wasn't prepared for that. His expression soured. "You're not qualified. Since Charlie talked to Zach and I questioned Deirdre, it's his turn anyway."

Scarlett smiled. "I'm fine with that. Just let me know if he needs any help."

"Yeah, right," Henry said.

I was about to step in and break up another potential war of words when a tall, rugged plainclothes officer appeared.

"So what can I do for you kids?" he said. His name tag read *Detective Thomas Morgan*.

I stood to greet him. "We'd like to find out if you arrested someone about a month ago and if he's still being held here."

"Why don't you come to my office, and we'll check the computer," the officer said.

We followed him around a corner, down a short hallway, and into a small, messy office. There were two desks pushed together. One was Officer Morgan's. Behind the other sat a rather unfriendly-looking fellow. The nameplate on his desk said *Detective Ray Berkland.* He didn't look happy to see us.

"You guys can sit right there," Officer Morgan said. He then noticed that there were only two chairs. "Hey, Ray, can I borrow one of yours?"

Detective Berkland lifted himself out of his chair as if he were half dead. He made a grunting sound and slid a chair over.

Officer Morgan pulled his keyboard closer. "Okay, what have you got?"

I sat forward in my chair. "About a month ago, there was some kind of disturbance at a French restaurant here in town and a teenager was arrested for disorderly conduct. Does that sound familiar?" I asked.

Detective Berkland sat up in his chair. He was suddenly interested. He glanced at the officer across from him.

"It seems to ring a bell," Officer Morgan said. He tried to appear nonchalant.

"Well, can you tell us if the name of that teenager was Joshua Doyle?" I said.

Detective Berkland cleared his throat. It seemed apparent that he was trying to communicate something to his partner. Berkland was stone-faced.

"Let me punch that in," Officer Morgan said. He stared at the screen for a few seconds. "We did pick up a young man at that restaurant about a month ago. He was initially charged with disorderly conduct. But it says here that the charges were eventually dropped and he was released."

"What was his name?" I asked.

Detective Berkland slid out his chair and stood up. "Since he wasn't prosecuted, I'm afraid we can't release that information."

"So, are you saying that it *wasn't* Josh?" I said.

"That's classified, son," Officer Berkland said.

"If we were newspaper reporters, you'd have to tell us," Scarlett said in an indignant tone.

"Well, honey, until you produce credentials proving that you're members of the press," the surly detective said, "I'm afraid you're out of luck."

This was going nowhere. These guys were hiding something. I knew it. And I had a feeling that we could sit here for the remainder of the afternoon and learn nothing.

Henry appeared frustrated. "I don't get it," he said. "Why can't you just tell us if it was Josh or not? What difference does it make? He happens to be a friend of ours."

Detective Berkland seemed to be losing his patience. "I just told you why," he said. "And if he's such a good friend of yours, why don't you go ask him?"

"We can't find him," I said. "That's why we came."

"Your friend isn't here," Berkland said. "Listen, kids, we have a lot of work to do. You need to go."

This was futile. For whatever reason, these officers were reluctant to share the identity of the individual who had been arrested that day. But the more I thought about it, the more I felt that it had to have been Josh. If it hadn't been, then all they had to do was say *no* when we asked if the suspect's name was Josh Doyle. If they had said that, we would have gladly gone away. But since they refused to confirm or deny the name of the suspect, it had to be Josh. The only question I had was why—why were they so tight-lipped about this case?

"Can you at least tell us the date you released him?" I asked.

"Sorry, no can do," Officer Morgan said.

It was time to go. I had hoped to have conducted a first-class demonstration of how to interrogate a member of law enforcement for Scarlett. That wasn't to be. She couldn't have been particularly impressed with my performance. She was probably wondering why she had teamed up with us in the first place. But I couldn't worry about that now. I had to concentrate on this case and stop thinking about my bruised ego. I tried to refocus. Based on what the police *hadn't* told us, I was fairly certain that Josh had been arrested and taken here, but then what? Where had he disappeared to? If he had been released, then why hadn't he shown up at home or at his girlfriend's? There was something else going on here. And if we could figure out why these officers seemed so uncooperative, then we might have a lead on Josh's whereabouts.

"Well, thanks anyway," I said.

Henry frowned. He was obviously disappointed that I was surrendering. If it had been up to him, we undoubtedly would have continued the verbal assault until we were physically removed from the premises. But that would have made no sense. We had gotten as much information as we were going to get. Belaboring the point would have accomplished nothing. And we might need to call on these officers in the future. Best not to burn a source.

"Sorry, guys," Officer Morgan said. "I wish we could have been of more help."

"Yeah, right," Henry said under his breath.

We were escorted to the entrance of the building. Officer Morgan pushed open one of the large metal doors but said nothing. We plopped down on the front steps and waited for Eugene to arrive. We could see his car parked in the lot across the street, but he wasn't with it.

"What a waste of an afternoon," Scarlett said.

"I apologize, you guys," I said. "It wasn't one of my better efforts."

"It's not your fault," she replied. "Even a seasoned professional would have had a hard time getting anything out of those two."

I was glad to hear her say that. Just when I was worried that Scarlett might think I was a hack at this job, she defended me. Even though we had learned little more than we had started with, I was feeling pretty good right at that moment.

"Charlie, are you thinking what I'm thinking?" Henry said.

"What?"

"By not telling us if it was Josh who was arrested, they basically confirmed that it *was* him."

"That's exactly what I was thinking," I said.

Scarlett sighed. "Then where the heck is he? And if he was released, why hasn't anyone seen him?"

Before we could ponder Scarlett's question, a familiar voice in the distance caught our attention.

"You kids all done?" It was Eugene. "So, what'd you find out?"

For the next few minutes, we told Eugene about what had happened. We mentioned the fact that we were fairly certain that both officers were withholding information. We also told him we were sorry that he had wasted his time and gas to drive us over here. We tried again to offer gas money—and once again he refused.

"Tell me something," Eugene said. "Do you know the names of the officers you spoke to?"

"Yeah," I said. "Morgan and Berkland. They were detectives."

Eugene smiled.

"You know them?" Scarlett said.

"I know *of* them," Eugene replied. "But more importantly, I know their boss. A couple of years ago, I turned him on to a smuggling operation that was taking place right under his nose. We have history, you might say." He checked his watch. "You guys still have a few minutes?"

"Sure," I said.

"Let me ask a few questions in there and see if I have any luck."

"Really?" I said. "You'd do that for us?"

Eugene climbed to the top step and turned around. "Charlie, we're all working together here. If I needed some help, I could count on you kids, right?"

"Of course," we answered in unison.

"Then just consider this a professional courtesy. Be right back." He disappeared behind the steel doors.

While we waited for Eugene, we each tossed out our own thoughts about what might have happened to Josh—but none of us was particularly confident in our theories. We discussed what we would do next if Eugene got the cold shoulder from his contact in the department. And we all agreed on one thing—we had no idea what to do next. We sat on the steps waiting for Eugene for a good twenty minutes. We figured that the longer he was in there, the better. At one point it got very quiet. And then, as happens at least once a day, Sam Solomon popped into my head. I remembered a time when a source at a local police station shared a tip with him that enabled him to solve a case. It happened in Episode #25—*The Fools Rush Inn Caper.*

In this particular story, Sam had been hired by a new bride who was worried about the couple's finances. Money was disappearing from their joint account at an alarming rate, and her new husband denied withdrawing it. A tip from a friend at the local police department shed some light on the subject. A longtime sergeant informed Sam that they were investigating an illegal gambling operation at a newly opened club, the Fools Rush Inn. Sam soon discovered that the new groom had been gambling away hundreds of dollars each night for some time at the club. The case had been solved thanks to an inside tip from a friend in the department. I was hoping Eugene would have the same experience.

"There he is," Henry said as Eugene emerged from the police station.

We all jumped to our feet to greet him.

Eugene was grinning. "It sure pays to have friends," he said.

"So you found out?" I said.

"Let's go to the car. I'll fill you in."

We raced down the steps and up to the street. We waited for Eugene to catch up. He waved for us to go ahead. Within seconds, we were all safely seated in the hearse anxiously awaiting the lowdown from Eugene.

"So, were we right?" Henry said. He could barely contain himself.

"You kids were right on the money," he said. "I couldn't be prouder of your stellar detective work." Eugene rolled down the driver's-side window. It was getting a little stuffy in the car. "Here's what we're looking at. The teenager arrested at that French restaurant here a few weeks back was indeed Josh Doyle."

"I knew it," I said. "Did it have something to do with that foie gras business?"

"It did. He was protesting there because that was one of the few restaurants in the area still serving it."

Henry sat forward. "Okay, then, so they arrested him and charged him with disturbing the peace, right?"

"Not at first," Eugene said. "Apparently Josh kept giving them bogus names. They didn't know who he was for a while. So they decided to take his fingerprints. When they couldn't find a match in their files, they sent the prints to other departments in the area. And it didn't take long to find a match."

"In Oak Grove, I'll bet. He was arrested there," I said.

"Precisely."

"And so *then* they charged him with disturbing the peace?" Henry said.

"Yep," Eugene said. He pulled a key from his pocket and started up the hearse.

"Wait a minute," I said. "So where is Josh now?"

Eugene turned the engine off. "The rest of this story is off the record. It was a private conversation between friends. You can't go public with any of it. Understand?"

We all nodded. This was getting better by the minute.

"They have no idea where Josh is," Eugene said. "He's disappeared. One minute he was there. The next minute he wasn't."

"You mean he escaped?" Scarlett said.

Eugene shrugged. "They tell me he couldn't have escaped. They say it's impossible. There's a uniformed officer stationed at every entrance."

"Then what do they think happened?" she said.

"They just don't know," Eugene said.

"So why all the mystery?" I asked. "Why couldn't they just tell us that he was there and then he wasn't there? I don't get it."

Eugene smiled. "That one's easy. It's called covering your butt. You see, it wouldn't look very good for a police department to have to admit that they lost a prisoner. It would be kind of embarrassing. And since this was a relatively minor offense, they just wiped it off the books. It's like it never happened."

As we sat in the hearse, a yellow school bus pulled up in front of the police station. On its side were the words *Camp Phoenix.* Seconds later a long line of teens paraded out the front door of the station and onto the bus.

"Eugene," Henry said, "how do *you* think Josh escaped?"

Eugene scratched his head. "He must have slipped out somehow. It's a mystery. Maybe he blended in with a group of people leaving the station. Normal folks go into police stations for any number of reasons—asking for directions, paying parking tickets, reporting a dog bite—you name it. It's the only thing I can think of."

I found myself watching the kids filing onto the Camp Phoenix bus. They were all teenage boys. And suddenly it got me to thinking.

"Wait a minute," I said, pointing to the bus. "I know exactly where he is."

CHAPTER 11

The Uncivil Marriage Caper

As we sat there, I could barely contain myself. My head was spinning. All the clues had been right there in front of me. It had taken until now for things to click.

"So, where is he?" Henry said.

"Don't you see? It all makes perfect sense. The police arrested Josh a month ago. He wouldn't give them his name. They took his fingerprints. No match. So they sent them out. Suddenly, a match—in Oak Grove. But while they were waiting for the results, Colonel Culpepper and his Camp Phoenix bus pulled up. The cops rounded up all the kids headed to the boot camp. In the process, Josh slipped into the line and blended in. Before they knew it, he was gone. I'm telling you—that's where he is."

Eugene started the car up and merged into traffic.

"So Clifton City must have cut the same deal with this colonel guy that Oak Grove did?" Henry said.

"They did. Don't you remember?" I said. "When we saw that press conference in town, Culpepper was telling the reporters that if they didn't think his methods would work, all they had to do was talk to the mayor of Clifton City. He's there, all right. He's gotta be."

We were approaching the entrance ramp for the interstate when Scarlett poked me on the arm.

"Okay, so let's say that Josh pretended he was part of some other group and managed to sneak out of the police station," she said. "What's to say he mixed in with the kids headed to Camp Phoenix? It could have been any group."

"I'll tell you why," I said. "Because we already saw him with Culpepper."

"What are you talking about?" she said.

"He was at that press conference. We saw him there."

After exiting the interstate, we could see the *Welcome to Oak Grove, Illinois* sign in the distance.

"Charlie, I don't get it," Henry said. "If you saw him at the press conference, why didn't you say anything?"

"Because I didn't realize it until now. Don't you remember seeing two kids on the stage? They were dressed in army fatigues. And they had on helmets and goggles."

"I remember them," Scarlett said.

"One of the kids had a limp. Does that sound familiar?" I said.

"Yeah . . . *yeah* . . . I do remember him," Henry said.

It was all coming together for him now too. "Of course, that was him. That was Josh. He's been there all this time."

As we pulled up to a red light and stopped, Eugene turned toward us. "Charlie, I have to give you credit. That was a great demonstration of deductive reasoning. I'm proud of you."

"So is that it?" Scarlett said. "We solved the case, right? We can tell Sherman and his mom where they can find Josh and we're done."

"Not quite," I said. "This is still a hypothesis. We can't share our findings with the client until we've confirmed his whereabouts. The next thing we have to do is contact Camp Phoenix and determine if Josh is really there."

"So, if they say that he is . . . then we're done, right?" Scarlett said.

"If the Camp Phoenix brass tells us that Josh is a resident at their compound, then we're only half done. Remember—we not only agreed to locate Josh, we promised to personally deliver him to Sherman and his mom. Once we've accomplished *that,* then our jobs are done. And then we can finally say, 'Case closed.'"

What a day. I was on top of the world. It felt so good to have figured things out. Whenever I managed to solve a case—even partially—it confirmed for me that I was destined to do this for the rest of my life. Running my own detective agency—for real—was a long way off, but I knew it was in my future. I wasn't even in high school yet, but I already knew what I'd study in college. I'd major in criminal justice. And I'd double minor in sociology and psychology. It was best to know what made people tick.

Eugene dropped us off about a block from my house. We thought it might be best. We didn't want my parents wondering about where Eugene had taken us. They trusted him and all, but they still would have been curious as to where we had been. As we piled out of Eugene's car, he stuck his head out the driver's-side window.

"Nice doing business with you today," he said. "And if you need any more help, you know where to come."

"Thanks," I said. "You're a lifesaver, Eugene."

We waved as he drove off.

"It's getting late," Scarlett said. "I'd better get going."

"So what's next?" Henry said.

"How does your schedule look tomorrow?" I asked.

Scarlett, with cell phone in hand, was busily texting. "Huh?"

"Tomorrow? Are you free tomorrow?" I said.

"Sorry, can't do it," she said.

"I'm out too, Charlie," Henry said. "My mom's having people over for a big Sunday dinner. I can't get out of it."

"Okay," I said. "We'll talk Monday at school, then. Good work, guys."

And with that, we each went our separate ways. As I walked home, I held my head up high. I was feeling pretty good right then. There was nothing in the world like it—when everything fell neatly into place. I recalled the moment that Sam Solomon finally put all of the puzzle pieces together in Episode #23—*The Uncivil Marriage Caper.*

This was the story of a devious group of beautiful but greedy housewives—or rather gold diggers, to be more precise—who banded together to frame their wealthy husbands for crimes that the wives had actually committed. When each husband was tried, found guilty, and sent to prison, the wives divvied up his fortune. Sam had been baffled by this caper for weeks, but when he was finally able to secure one valuable piece of evidence, he was suddenly able to see the big picture. Things had clicked for Sam the same way they had clicked for me moments ago. As for Sam's case—it wasn't long before he helped police corral this den of dangerous dames.

I spent the better part of Sunday in my room. Since it rained most of the day, I didn't feel as though I was missing anything. It would provide some valuable time to plan out our strategy for the case. We knew one thing for sure—we would contact Camp Phoenix tomorrow and find out whether or not our hypothesis was correct. Everything pointed to Josh being at the camp. We would soon confirm it. I sat back in my chair with my feet up on the desk. If I had allowed myself to, I could easily have dozed off. But I fought it. I wanted to come away from this weekend with even more information than we had discovered yesterday. I knew that I was being greedy. I should have been thrilled with the fact that we had determined where Josh might be, but I kept telling myself that if I had figured out that much, then I might be able to uncover even more evidence before I met up with Henry and Scarlett at school the next day.

I closed my eyes, clenched my fists, and tried to make something pop into my head. No matter how hard I squeezed, nothing would happen. I even tried holding my breath. After a few minutes, just when I was about to surrender, I suddenly sat up. My feet fell to the floor with a thud. Something *had* popped into my head. I remembered how I had felt yesterday when I figured out that Josh was being held at Camp Phoenix. It was the teenager with the limp at the press conference that gave him away. But what about the other time I had seen a kid hobbling around? A couple of days ago—on the news—I saw security camera footage of a teenage boy limping out of the fur store. And Gram said that he looked like the same kid she had seen in the beauty parlor when it was robbed.

Could it be a coincidence that there were two teenagers out there with bum legs? It had to be. Could the kid on the news and the one at the beauty parlor be one and the same? It was possible, but it couldn't have been Josh. There was no evidence to support it. And on top of that, the timing was impossible. Josh was arrested three or so weeks ago, and the cops had lost him a few hours later. If we were right—and he had been taken to Camp Phoenix that same day—then how could he have gotten out to pull off those heists? And why would he possibly have done so? I didn't know Josh particularly well, but from all accounts, he was basically an honest kid. He'd get a little carried away sometimes defending one of his causes, but he wasn't a thief. I had to dismiss the fact that Josh could have had anything to do with those robberies and instead assume it was another kid with a leg injury. That had to be it. At least, I hoped so.

But the more I thought about it, the more worried I was that my theory might be wrong. What if Josh had never been taken to the camp in the first place? What if he had simply wandered away from the Clifton City police station and was miles from here, fighting for another cause somewhere? What if the kid at the press conference just happened to be someone else . . . someone else with a limp? What then? A moment ago, I was on top of the world. But now my case seemed to be crumbling before my eyes. If my assumptions were wrong, then this entire investigation had been a huge waste of time, and we'd have nothing to show for it. I was beginning to seriously doubt my theory.

I decided that I needed some fresh air to think things through. As I made my way downstairs and into the living room, I found my dad with a bowl of potato chips filled to the brim along with a container of dip from the refrigerator. He was headed to his favorite easy chair in the corner of the room when something strange but fairly predictable occurred. Hiding in the front hall closet just a few feet away from her prey was Grandma. The closet door was slightly ajar. I could see that she was dressed in a referee's outfit—black-and-white-striped shirt, black pants and shoes—and she wore a whistle around her neck.

My initial instincts were to sneak past both of them and slip out, but like those people who stare at a wreck on the highway, I couldn't help myself. Just as my dad was about to plop down into the chair and devour his feast, Grandma sprang from the closet with the whistle held firmly between her teeth. A shrill, piercing sound followed. As you might guess, both my dad's bowl of chips and the dip were now airborne.

"Offensive foul," Grandma screamed.

My dad, chips and dip in his hair, dropped his arms to his sides and let out a long sigh.

"Are you happy now, Mom?" he said. "Is this the reaction you were hoping for?"

"Don't give me any lip, son, or I'll hit you with a technical," Grandma snapped.

I knew that a smile was beginning to form on my face. I did my best to fight it. I pressed my lips together and looked away. But it was no use.

"You think this is funny, Charlie?" my dad said.

"No. Not at all," I said. "I wasn't laughing." And then the worst-possible thing happened. I started laughing. And I just couldn't stop.

But before my dad could pass sentence on me, Grandma came to the rescue. She slapped him on the shoulder and pointed to the floor.

"Clean this mess up," she said. "How do you expect anyone to play on this floor with your garbage all over it?" As she walked away, she was still firing. "That's what you get for letting the fans sit courtside."

With Grandma running interference, I decided to make a hasty exit. I slipped by the combatants and into the kitchen, headed for the back door. I could only hope that my dad wouldn't reappear for a refill. I was just about to make my escape when I heard a sound coming from the hallway.

"Pssst, Charlie." It was my grandmother. "Come here, I want to show you something."

I tiptoed out of the kitchen, careful not to let my

dad see me fraternizing with the enemy, and snuck into Grandma's room.

"So, how are things going with your case?" she said.

"A minute ago, I thought I had everything figured out, but now I just don't know."

"Charlie, it's normal to doubt yourself," she said. "But you always seem to figure things out in the end. I wouldn't worry if I were you."

"But Gram, you don't understand. If our missing person isn't where we think he is, then we're back to square one. It's as if we've accomplished nothing."

She smiled and motioned for me to follow her. "I've got just the thing for you." She slid open the top drawer of her dresser, dug in, and emerged with what looked like some kind of little safe. "This is my strongbox," she said. "I keep all my really important stuff in it." There was a combination lock on the front of it. Grandma rubbed her fingers together and blew on them. She smiled as she spun the tumbler. She turned it left, right, and then left again. She tugged gently at the top of the box until there was a *click*. "I still got it," she said as she lifted the top. She reached in, pulled out what looked like a credit card, and handed it to me.

I immediately realized that this was no credit card. I spotted the words *Office of Naval Intelligence* along with its logo—the one with the eagle standing on top of an anchor. Then I noticed the name—*Constance Collier.*

"Gram, this is awesome. This is your official Naval Intelligence ID card?"

"One and the same," she said. "This little card got me out of a lot of tough scrapes."

I couldn't help but stare at it. "This card did? I don't understand."

She sat down on the bed and motioned for me to join her. "Charlie, there were times—plenty of 'em—when I was on a case, trying to crack a code, and just couldn't figure things out. Sound familiar?"

I nodded.

"I wondered if I was losing my touch—if maybe I wasn't cut out for this job. And then I would reach into my pocket or my purse, pull out this card, and just stare at it."

"Did it help?"

"I should say. When I saw my name . . . and that logo . . . it just made me think that there were people in Washington who were counting on me—people who had confidence in me and in my abilities to succeed. And then suddenly, I knew that no matter how baffling a case might be, I wouldn't be holding a card like this unless I was capable of solving that problem. And I always did."

"Wow, I can't tell you how many times I could have used a card like this," I said.

"I've been thinking the same thing," she said.

Gram placed the ID card back into her strongbox

and locked it up. She slid the strongbox back into its hiding place and closed the drawer. She then opened another drawer, reached in, and lifted out a small cardboard box. She pulled off the top. Inside were dozens of little business cards. She lifted one out and handed it to me.

"What do you think?" she said.

I couldn't believe my eyes. I was staring at a genuine Charlie Collier, Snoop for Hire business card.

"It's sensational," I said. "You had these made up for me?"

She nodded and grinned.

My own official business card. I couldn't believe it. I loved the design. The magnifying glass was a nice touch. There was no doubt about it—these cards would impress a lot of people. Just wait till Scarlett got a look at this. Then I noticed something at the bottom of the card.

“What’s with the e-mail address?” I asked.

“Well, I thought you needed an official-sounding e-mail address, so I secured the charliecolliersnoop-forhire.com domain and added an e-mail to it.”

“This is unbelievable,” I said. “Hey, does this mean that we have our own website too?”

“Uh-huh,” she said. “Nothing on it yet, but you kids should have fun designing it.”

“Henry is gonna love this. He makes fun of me all the time ’cause I like doing things the old-fashioned way—the way Sam Solomon did things. But maybe it’s time to modernize the agency a little bit.”

Gram snapped her fingers. She had apparently just remembered something. “Speaking of Henry—and Scarlett—get a load of these.” She pulled out two more boxes and opened them. She not only had gotten me a box of official business cards, but she had done the same for Henry and Scarlett.

“Oh, man, wait until they see these. They’re gonna flip.”

“It wouldn’t be right for only one of you to have your own calling card,” she said. “You guys are a team.”

I just kept staring at the new cards. They were so awesome.

“You know,” Gram said, “I wanted to put a phone number on that card for you, but I knew your folks wouldn’t let you have a cell phone—and I didn’t think it would be a very good idea to put the home phone on there . . . if you know what I mean."

"Gram, this is perfect just the way it is. I'm going to put this card in my pocket, and when I doubt my abilities to solve a case, I'll just pull it out, and I know that it'll inspire me the same way your card inspired you."

"Not so fast," she said. Gram lifted the new business cards out of the box, fished out one that was sitting on the bottom, and handed it to me. "Here's the one to keep in your pocket." It was the same card as the earlier one, but this one was sealed in plastic—hard plastic. "I got this one laminated so it'd hold up better."

Since Gram and I were the only ones in the room and I didn't have to worry about damaging my reputation, I threw my arms around her.

"I don't know how to thank you," I said.

"You just be the best detective you can be and help folks solve their problems. That's all the thanks I need."

I grinned. "I promise I will."

"And remember, Charlie," she said, "the next time you get into a jam, pull that card out of your pocket and take a gander. It just might open up a few doors for you someday."

CHAPTER 12

The Fresh Heir Caper

During our lunch period at school on Monday, Henry and I snuck off to the computer lab to find a contact number for Camp Phoenix. We planned to call them later to find out if Josh was there.

"That's it," Henry said.

Our search had taken us to the Camp Phoenix website. On the home page was a picture of Colonel Harvard Culpepper as well as photos of some of the campers. They were all smiling and seemed to be having a good time. We eventually found a tab marked *contact us* and clicked on it.

"There it is," I said as the number appeared onscreen. I jotted it down on a scrap of paper.

"See how easy that was?" Henry said.

"Yeah, so?"

"You're always telling me about how Sam Solomon solved all his cases without the use of modern technology—

and about how we should do that," Henry said. "But you didn't seem to have any problem with looking up that phone number on the Internet, I noticed."

I stuffed the paper into my pocket. "That's different," I said.

"What's different about it?"

We slipped out of the computer lab before anyone had noticed us and headed back to the cafeteria.

"Listen, I'm perfectly happy to use a phone book," I said, "but where are we supposed to find one at school? We had no other choice."

"I don't buy it, Charlie," Henry said. "I think I've finally converted you."

"No way."

"Well, then tell me why we just didn't wait until we got to your house after school and use one of the phone books there? Huh?"

Ever since Gram had given me that business card with an official e-mail address and website for the agency, I guess I was softening up—but I couldn't let Henry know that.

"I was just trying to buy us a little more time," I said. "And I wouldn't want my parents to see what we were up to. That's all."

"Yeah, right."

When we entered the cafeteria, I noticed Scarlett waving to us from across the room. She was actually waving to me . . . in public. The idea of something like that happening a few weeks ago was unthinkable. I almost felt like announcing it to the entire room. "Hey, gang, did you happen to see that? The most popular girl in the sixth grade needs *me.*" But instead of rubbing it in, I strolled past everyone with my head held high and just hoped people might notice. I decided to slow down a little as we got closer. I didn't want to seem too anxious.

When we arrived, Scarlett was busily checking something on her cell phone. "I just wanted to find out if there's anything going on this afternoon," she said. "My schedule's filling up fast."

I leaned in so that the others at her table couldn't hear. "Don't you remember? We're calling that boot camp after school to see if Josh is there."

She frowned. "Do you absolutely need me for that?"

Henry folded his arms and began tapping his foot. He was growing impatient with Scarlett. So what else was new?

"Well, I guess we could handle it ourselves," I said. "I just thought—you know, since you're a member of the agency—that you'd want to be included in everything we do."

"Does it really take three people to make a phone call?" she said.

I could tell that Henry was just about to give Scarlett

a piece of his mind when her friend Sarah, sitting across from her, chimed in.

"Why would you want to go with *them* anyway?" she said. "Come with us, Scarlett. My mom's gonna drop us off at the mall later."

"That's a great idea," Henry said. "Why don't you just go to the mall."

I could have predicted what was about to happen next. Once Henry had *uninvited* her, Scarlett would insist on joining us even though she had no interest in doing so.

"That sounds like fun, Sarah," she said, "but I'd better not. These guys need me."

"What?" Henry said. He was dumbfounded.

"Actually, they'd be lost without me," she said.

I watched as a series of blotchy red spots began to appear on Henry's neck. Within seconds, his face would be beet red. He was about to explode. I had seen this before. It wasn't pretty. Whenever he got like this, he always managed to say something he would later regret. I needed to save him. I needed to protect him from himself. I needed something that would distract him—but what? He was so zoned in on Scarlett right now that I couldn't think of anything that might divert his attention.

And then I had it. Of course. He wouldn't be able to resist. I dug into my pocket and pulled out the business card my grandma had given me yesterday.

"Hey, guys, did you see what my gram made up for me?" I said. "And would you believe it—we now have our own agency website."

As if on a turret, Henry's head spun around. "What did you say?" The verbal assault on Scarlett was now ancient history. "Let me see that."

I handed him the card.

"So let me get this straight," he said. "Charliecollier-snoopforhire.com is ours?"

I nodded and grinned.

"I gotta find a computer. I gotta see this thing," Henry said.

"Well, there's nothing there right now," I said. "All you'll find is a page that says *Under Construction*."

"And who's designing the website?" Henry asked.

"My gram suggested we do it ourselves."

Henry threw his arms into the air. "Yessssss. This is so awesome."

I didn't remember ever having seen Henry quite that excited before.

"Charlie, I am all over this," he said. "Let's get started immediately."

"Wait a minute," Scarlett said. "Let me see that card." She slid it out of Henry's hand and studied it for a moment. Then she looked up and pointed to something on the front.

"What's this?" she said. She was pointing to the line

that read *Charlie Collier, Proprietor.* "You want to explain that?"

"Well, sure," I said. "A proprietor is kind of like the owner—"

"I know what a proprietor is," she snapped. "I want to know how come *our* names aren't on there."

I expected this reaction. I decided to have a little fun with Scarlett.

"It doesn't have your name on there because it's *my* card," I said.

It was clear that Scarlett didn't care for my answer. And even Henry bristled a bit.

"I have to tell you, Charlie," Henry said, "I was wondering the same thing. How come you left us off?"

"*I* didn't leave anybody off," I said. "My gram had these made up. Did you expect her to buy business cards for you guys too . . . on her meager fixed income?" There it was—the guilt trip—and played effectively, I might add.

Scarlett stared at her shoes. "I guess not," she said.

Since I had gotten the reaction I had hoped for, it was time to surprise them. I dug into my pocket and pulled out customized cards for each of them.

"Here," I said with a chuckle. "My grandmother *did* make them up for you guys too. There's a whole box for each of you at my house."

"That was a dirty trick," Scarlett said as she examined her card. "But under the circumstances, I'll forgive you."

Henry stared at his card and smiled. "It's a beaut," he said. "You gotta thank your gram for me."

"Me too," Scarlett said. "Better yet, I'll write her a thank-you note."

From the corner of my eye, I could see Henry busily at work. His brain kicked into gear. He was so excited about his new card that he was ready to burst. He needed to let it out some way. And for Henry, that could only mean one thing. He was about to unleash a brain buster.

"Okay, fellow detectives," he said, "let's see if we've earned the right to carry these cards." He grinned. "What five-letter word becomes shorter when you add two letters to it?"

I wasn't sure I was ready to test out the old noodle. I had spent so much time on this missing persons case that I was a little out of practice at solving riddles these days. What five-letter word becomes shorter when you add two letters to it? I knew immediately that it was a trick question—if you add letters to a word, it will undoubtedly become longer. There was something else going on here. But what? I stood there for a good minute trying to figure it out.

"Give up?" Henry said.

"I'll get it," I said. "I just need another minute."

"Take all the time you need," he said.

Scarlett seemed to stare out into space for a moment, and then a smile began to form on her face.

"Wait a minute," she said. "I think I know the answer." She glanced in my direction. "Do you mind?"

"Be my guest," I said. Although I didn't really expect her to enlighten us.

"The word you're looking for is *short,*" she said. "If you add two letters to it—namely an *e* and an *r*—it becomes *shorter.*" She turned to Henry. "Is that it?"

Now, normally Henry would have stewed for a while after someone had solved one of his brainteasers, but this time it was different. This was a celebration brain buster.

"That's it exactly," he said, extending his hand to Scarlett. "Congratulations."

I couldn't believe what I was seeing. Henry and Scarlett, who had been at each other's throats for as long as I could remember, were actually shaking hands. Could a simple business card have produced harmony? Had their squabbles finally come to an end? Were my days as a referee over? Only time would tell. I called to mind a situation that Sam Solomon had once found himself in. It was Episode #28—*The Fresh Heir Caper.*

In this particular case, Sam had been hired by Reginald Worth, an arrogant, abrasive socialite who believed he was destined to inherit an industrial fortune. He wanted Sam to prove that he, and not his sister, was the rightful heir. Once Sam began his investigation, he soon realized that the details of the case were so complicated that even a team of lawyers would be lucky to unravel it. If the siblings continued to fight, their court battle would gobble up all of their resources and leave both of them penniless. Sam convinced them that they would live happy and comfortable lives if they learned to work as a team and share the proceeds of the company.

And that's exactly what I had been trying to do for as long as I could remember—end the feud between Henry and Scarlett. It was hard to believe it might actually be over. And I owed it all to Gram.

Henry and I met up at the bus stop after school as usual.

"I don't see Scarlett," he said. "I thought she was coming with us today."

"There's been a change of plans," I said.

"What's her excuse this time?" he asked.

The bus pulled up and we hopped on.

"At the last minute, one of her friends told her about a pedicure special at the mall," I said.

"A *pedicure* special?"

"I guess she couldn't pass it up," I said. "Ten toes for the price of eight."

Henry thought for a minute. "But what if you only have eight toes?" he said. "Then what? No freebies?"

Now, I would have expected any number of reactions from Henry at that moment, but this wasn't one of them. In a million years, I couldn't have predicted that response. I simply had no answer for such a bizarre question.

"Uhhhh . . ."

"Oh, never mind," he said. "On to more important things." He reached into his pocket and pulled out his new business card. "Let's talk about the website. So, who's the hosting company?" he asked. "And is this one of those sites where you pick from a bunch of website templates or can we develop our own from scratch? And how many gigabytes of disk space do we have available? And can we set up our own blog? And how many e-mail addresses will we have?"

"Um, I'm afraid you're asking the wrong guy," I said. "But I'm sure we can call and find out. I'll ask my grandmother for their number."

Henry was all smiles.

"But first things first," I said. "There's another call—a more important one—we need to make before that."

"Yeah, okay," he said, but that was just to shut me up. "I've been thinking about using some flash technology on the site. Now picture this—we'll have this magnifying glass that you can control with your cursor. And then wherever you move it on the page . . ."

And on and on he went for the entire ride home. Most of what he was saying could just have easily been in a foreign language as far as I was concerned. Henry was the techie—not me. He was certain that our presence on the web would drive business in our direction. He even had himself convinced that we would someday have a client on the other side of the globe.

When we got to my house, we encountered both good and bad news. The good news—my mom was baking cookies. The bad news—my mom was baking cookies. As tasty as her famous raisin-filled cookies were right from the oven, I would have preferred an empty house right at that moment. We had to call the boot camp, and the last thing we needed was an audience. Henry and I sat down at the kitchen table for an after-school snack, but I only managed to down three of the tasty morsels before my mom pulled the plug. She was counting calories for me. It was probably a good thing that one of us was acting in a responsible manner.

Minutes later Henry and I snuck down to the basement to use the extension phone.

"So do you want me to call or do you want to?" Henry said.

"I'll do it." I dug into my pocket for the phone number and began dialing.

"Do you know what you're gonna say?" Henry asked.

"Not really," I said. "I was just going to wing it and hope for the best." Within a few seconds, I heard the phone ringing on the other end.

"Camp Phoenix, may we help you?" a female voice said.

"Yes," I said, "I'm wondering if you can tell me if a young man by the name of Joshua Doyle is currently residing at your facility." I tried to make it sound as official as possible.

"Are you a relative?" she said.

"Well, not exactly," I said. "I'm a friend, you might say, a pretty close friend."

"I'm sorry, sir," the woman said, "but Camp Phoenix policy strictly prohibits me from divulging that sort of information to non-family members. I'm sorry."

I held the receiver so that Henry could hear as well.

"I don't need to talk to him or anything," I said. "I just want to know if he's there."

"I'm afraid I'm unable to share the identity of our residents with you," the operator said.

I somehow needed to convince this woman that I wasn't trying to be nosy or anything.

"You see, his mom is really worried about him," I said. "And she just needs to know where he is. That's all."

"Then have her call us," the woman said. "But I seriously doubt your friend is here. If he was, his mother would already know. Before any of the young offenders are brought here, their parents or guardians are informed. So the fact that his mother was never contacted tells me that he's not with us. Good day."

"Wait a minute. Don't hang up," I said. I couldn't let her blow me off like that. I needed to keep her talking. There had to be some way of finding out about Josh. "Would it be okay if we were to stop by the camp sometime and look around for ourselves?"

"Absolutely not," she snapped. "Unauthorized guests are strictly prohibited from entering the Camp Phoenix compound. If you came, you'd just be turned away at the front gate. Don't waste your time. Now . . . good day." And she hung up.

I glanced at Henry. "How do you like that?"

"Real friendly, huh?" Henry said. "So now what?"

I wasn't sure myself. I hadn't counted on this. "I guess all we can do for now is share our findings with Sherman and his mom," I said. "Then she'll have to call the camp."

"So that's it, then?" Henry said. "We've gone as far as we can? We're done?"

But for some reason, it just didn't feel like we were done. This whole thing had ended rather abruptly. Henry and I agreed that the only thing to do was to run over to Sherman's house and try to convince his mom to make the call. I slipped the phone number into my pocket and we were off. Twenty minutes later, we were approaching Sherman's house. We weren't in what you would call the safest part of town. The neighborhood was kind of run-down. I didn't plan on telling my parents where we spent the afternoon. But at least we were in familiar territory. Henry and I had actually been here last month when we were following Sherman to see if he had anything to do with the bird heist.

We climbed the front steps of his house and were just about to ring the bell when we noticed a sign that read *Doorbell out of order. Please knock.* Henry shrugged and rapped on the front door. We stood there for a good minute before the door opened. Sherman stood in the doorway.

"What are you guys doing here?" he said. And then something seemed to click. Sherman suddenly seemed hopeful. "Is it about Josh?"

"Yeah," I said. "You got a minute?"

From inside we could hear Sherman's mother. "Who is it?"

"Just a friend," he said. "I'll be right back." He stepped out onto the porch and pulled the door closed behind him. "So, what'd you find out?"

I pulled a pad of paper from my back pocket. It was blank, but I wanted to make it look like we had been taking notes throughout the investigation.

"Here's what we think," I said. "We have reason to believe that Josh was arrested in Clifton City for protesting at a restaurant that was serving . . ." I knew I was probably going to mispronounce that goose liver thing. "For protesting something."

"Sounds like Josh," he said. "Then what happened?"

"Then we think he slipped away from the police and was eventually taken to a place called Camp Phoenix. Ever heard of it?"

He leaned against the door. "I think so," he said.

"It's a place where they rehabilitate teenage hoodlums," Henry said.

Sherman didn't seem to appreciate the suggestion that Josh was a criminal. "My brother is no hoodlum."

"I didn't mean it like that," Henry said.

I decided to defuse the situation before things got out of hand. I flipped a page on the notepad just to look official.

"So we called over there to confirm his whereabouts, but since we weren't family, they wouldn't tell us if he was there or not. They did say, however, that if someone like your mom called, then they would tell her."

Sherman peeked through a small window in the door to see inside the house. He must be looking for his mom.

"So you want me to ask her to call this place to see if Josh is there?" he said.

"Precisely," Henry said.

Sherman sighed. "I was hoping not to have to bother her with any of this." He paused for a moment and seemed to be thinking. "But if it means finding Josh, then I'll do it," he said.

I reached into my pocket and pulled out the phone number. "Here you go."

Sherman turned and opened the door.

"We'll wait out here for you," I said.

Sherman nodded and disappeared. Henry and I plopped down on the front steps. We tried to imagine the scene taking place inside—where Sherman had to explain to his mom that he hired us to find Josh and how he needed her to call some camp that she probably never heard of. We were anxious to learn the results of the phone call. It could either mean that we were close to wrapping up another case or that we needed to go back to the drawing board. About five minutes later, Sherman reappeared. He looked frustrated.

"He's not there," he said.

"You're sure?" I asked.

"They said there was no one there by that name."

I shook my head. "I just don't get it. I was so sure." I didn't like the idea of failing a client.

Sherman sighed. "Well, thanks anyway, Collier. At least you tried."

I couldn't believe what I was hearing. He was acting as if I was about to give up. He apparently didn't know me very well. I would never throw in the towel.

"Sherman, what are you talking about?" I said. "The investigation has just begun. We still have a lot of leads. So . . . one didn't pan out. Big deal. We're not done by a long shot."

"Really?" he said.

"Of course. You forget who you're talking to—Charlie Collier, Snoop for Hire. And we won't rest until we deliver Josh to your front door. Got it?"

"Got it," he said.

I could see a smile slowly beginning to form on Sherman's face. Oh, how I loved a satisfied client. Now I only hoped I could actually keep my promise.

CHAPTER 13

The Write a Wrong Caper

"If he's not there, then where is he?" Henry said as we walked back to my house.

"Who *said* he's not there?" I said.

"Huh?"

The more I thought about it, the more convinced I was that we were still on the right track.

"I think Josh is exactly where we thought he was," I said.

"So, what are you saying?" Henry replied. "You think that lady from the camp lied to us? And to Sherman's mom?"

We stopped walking. "Not necessarily," I said. "She might have been telling the truth."

Henry shook his head. "Now I'm completely confused."

"Have you forgotten? Josh doesn't always tell people his real name. He could have given them a phony one."

I smiled. "There's only one way to know for sure. We're going to have to go over there ourselves."

"Ourselves?" Henry said. There was a nervousness in his voice. "Why can't we get someone like Eugene to go over there?"

We resumed our walk back to my house. "Don't you remember what that woman told us? That no unauthorized guests are permitted on the compound? They'll never let Eugene in. But they just might let *us* in." I smiled. "And they might not even know they did."

"What do you mean?"

I felt the wheels spinning in my brain. "All we have to do is figure out a way to get into that camp. Once we're there, we can blend in with the other kids. Then we can find out, once and for all, if Josh is there."

"How exactly do you expect us to get into that place to look around?" Henry asked.

I found myself trying to think of some type of disguise that might help us gain access to Camp Phoenix. But nothing was popping into my head.

"Well, I guess we could just break the law and get thrown in jail. That's one way," Henry said with a chuckle.

I was only listening to Henry with half an ear. I kept trying to think up a plan that might get us into that boot camp. It had to be good—really good. And we had to make sure that we could get in and out of there safely. The last thing we'd want would be to get caught while searching for Josh. I kept racking my brain with the hopes of . . . Wait a minute . . . wait just a minute.

"Henry, what did you just say?"

"Um . . . I don't know."

"Something about going to jail?"

"Oh yeah. I said if we get ourselves arrested and thrown in the clink, then when the Camp Phoenix bus pulls up, we can just climb on board with the other delinquents. That's one way to get in."

"That's a brilliant idea," I said. "That's exactly how we're gonna do it."

"Wait a minute. I was only kidding," he said.

I patted him on the back. "Kidding or not, you nailed it." I put my arm around him. "Who would have believed it? You and me—a couple of jailbirds."

"Charlie, you're absolutely crazy," he said. "You're not really thinking about getting yourself arrested just to get into that camp, are you?"

I was a little disappointed in Henry. By now, he had to have known that every once in a while, a good P.I. was forced to take desperate measures.

"Why not? It's the only way," I said. "Have you got a better idea?"

"But consider the downside. If you think your parents get on your case when they find out you've been taking on clients, just imagine what they'll do if you get arrested."

It was time for a bold move. I couldn't worry about

being grounded. I had to think about solving this caper no matter what.

"I've made up my mind," I said. "I somehow have to break the law, get caught, get tossed in jail, and get picked up by the Camp Phoenix bus."

Henry was beside himself. "I can't believe what I'm hearing. Who in his right mind would go to jail just to solve a case?"

"I'll tell you who," I said. "Sam Solomon—in Episode #29—*The Write a Wrong Caper.*"

I proceeded to enlighten Henry. I told him about this reporter who was subpoenaed to appear in court and who was eventually thrown in jail for refusing to identify one of his sources in a newspaper story. Most people believed that the source in question was an organized crime kingpin, but there was no proof. And here's where Sam fit in. He had been hired by the daughter of one of the victims of the unnamed Mafia chief. Sam desperately needed to talk to this reporter, but since he was locked up, no one had access to him. That's when Sam decided that the only way to get to the newsman was to get tossed in jail himself. He threw a punch at a police lieutenant one day and got his wish. While incarcerated, the master detective questioned the reporter, who reluctantly gave up the name of his source.

"Charlie, don't confuse fiction with real life," Henry said. "You do what you want to do, but I don't want any part of this. It's crazy. Do you want to go around with a record for the rest of your life?"

"Once I get into the camp and solve the case, I'm sure they'll drop the charges."

"And what if they don't? If I'm not mistaken," Henry said, "you can't get your private detective license if you've been convicted of a felony."

"Who said anything about a felony? I'm thinking misdemeanor at best. I just need to make a nuisance of myself, that's all."

"What do you have in mind?" Henry asked.

"I don't know yet. I need some time to figure things out," I said. "Hey, you're with me on this, right? Partners? Till the end?"

Henry folded his arms. He had a stern look on his face. He was about to take a stand.

"Charlie, you can risk your future if you want to, but I want no part of it. I may want to go into law enforcement someday—the secret service, the FBI, or maybe even the CIA. I can't afford a blemish on my record. They'd never take me."

We continued walking. It had suddenly gotten very quiet. Henry seemed bothered by all of this jailbird business.

"All right," he said. "Let's just say that you somehow manage to pull this off. Aren't your parents going to wonder where you've disappeared to? Who knows how long it'll take once you're in there? And what if you can't get out?"

"You know, Henry, I appreciate your concern. But instead of telling me how dangerous this might be, can't you just help me figure out a way to pull it off?"

Henry shook his head as if he were clearing the cobwebs. "Okay, I just want to go on record that I think this is a really bad idea. There, I've gotten it out of my system. Now we can figure out how to make this happen. I'll give it some thought tonight. We can compare notes tomorrow at school. Are you happy now?"

I smiled. I knew he'd come around. And even though I planned to do the dirty work myself, I would need an accomplice on the outside just in case something went wrong. The more I thought about what was ahead, the more I realized that Henry was probably right. This *was* real life, and it *was* a little crazy and maybe dangerous to boot. But I had made up my mind, and since no one else had an alternate plan, I was now destined to become a juvenile offender.

The next day at school, I waited for recess to drop the bomb on Scarlett. Like Henry, she was completely opposed to my idea of getting arrested and incarcerated.

"Are you crazy?" she said.

"That's exactly what I told him," Henry said. "But he's too stubborn to listen."

"My mind's made up," I said. "And I'd appreciate a little help from both of you . . . but if I have to do this thing myself, I will. Tell you what—let's meet in my garage after school. My mom's headed to the supermarket today. All right?"

"I don't think I can," Henry said. "We're having a new couch delivered, and I got to be there when the guy comes 'cause my mom won't be home."

Since when was a new couch more important than solving a case? Where were Henry's priorities anyway?

"What time is the guy coming?" I asked.

"Between four and five."

"Perfect," I said. "You can come over for a little while."

"Ten minutes—tops," he said.

I turned to Scarlett. "How about you?"

"All right," she said impatiently. "But I might be a little late. You can start without me."

As Scarlett walked off, I began to wonder just how badly she really wanted to be part of our little agency. In the past few weeks, I had become convinced that she did indeed have something to offer, but it just didn't seem that her heart was in it.

"Why the long face?" Henry said. "Trust me, we are more than capable of thinking up some way to get you into that camp. We don't need her."

"But she should be there—and on time," I said. "She's

an official member of the agency now, and she can't treat it like some minor inconvenience." I wasn't sure if I was more upset about the fact that she didn't take the agency commitment as seriously as I did or just that I was losing out on spending some quality time with her.

"If you want her there, I can make that happen," Henry said. "And I can't believe I just said that."

"Well, of course I want her there."

"Okay, then, watch this," Henry said. "Hey, Scarlett," he yelled out to her.

She was just about to enter the front door of school when she stopped.

"Don't worry about this afternoon," Henry said. "Charlie and I can figure this thing out by ourselves. You don't need to rush. We'll see you tomorrow."

Scarlett was now marching in our direction. "I'll be there, okay? And I'll be on time. Are you happy now?" She spun around and headed back to the front door.

Henry smiled at me and raised his eyebrows. He was pretty proud of himself at that moment. And he should have been. For a long time, Henry had been the bookkeeper, business manager, and muscle at the agency. But it now seemed that he was being underutilized. This guy was a great psychologist.

And just as she had promised, Scarlett met us in the garage only minutes after Henry and I had gotten there.

"All right," Henry said. "So, here's the plan. Whatever you decide to do to get yourself arrested, it would be best if you did it on Friday afternoon."

"Why?" Scarlett asked.

"Because we have no idea how long Charlie will be gone," he said. "If we can come up with a great excuse to give his parents, it buys us time."

"I was actually thinking about what I could tell them," I said. "It's got to be a lot better than a simple sleepover. Let's tell them that you invited me on a camping trip this weekend with your family."

"A camping trip? Are you serious?" Henry said.

"What's wrong with that?" I said. "It's the perfect way to kill a weekend. My parents would buy it."

"It's a bad idea, and I'll tell you why," he said. "My mom is not what you'd call a *nature lover*—if you know what I mean. She's allergic to anything that's green—leaves, grass, shrubs, moss. Heck, she's even allergic to leprechauns."

"Yeah, but she's not really going camping. What difference does it make?"

Henry held up his hand. "Charlie, don't you think that *your* mom will call *my* mom and talk about what we should pack? It won't work. We'll get busted."

He was right. He was absolutely right. Our moms talked to each other all the time. I think they compared notes on what we were up to each day.

But before we could continue the debate, there was a knock at the door.

"Who's that?" I said. "Henry, did you book someone?"

He grabbed the clipboard from the workbench. "Nobody," he said.

"We're too busy for a walk-in today," I said. "See if you can get rid of them."

Henry shuffled over to the door and threw it open.

Standing in the entryway was Bethany Nesmith. Bethany was a classmate of ours. She was in one of the inner circles at school. You know the type—dressed to the nines, not a hair out of place, and a killer smile. She was also Scarlett's biggest rival. The two were polite to each other in public, but when no one was around, the gloves came off.

"Hi, Bethany," I said.

Scarlett didn't say a word. She just stared. Better make that glared.

"Charlie, have you got a minute?" Bethany said.

"Well . . ." I wasn't sure how to answer.

"Bethany, we're kinda busy," Scarlett said. "Big case and all."

"Oh, this should only take a minute—for Charlie, that is." And then she flashed that smile.

Henry, never one to miss out on landing a new client and collecting a fee, slid in between us.

"I'm Charlie's partner," he said. "What can we do for you?"

"I have a little problem I'd like to talk to him about," she said.

"It'll cost you," he said.

"It's just a *little* problem," Bethany said. "I'm sure Charlie wouldn't charge me for it . . . would you, Charlie?" Another smile. Boy, did she have straight teeth.

"To tell you the truth," I said, "I usually let Henry handle all of the money matters."

Henry crossed his arms and grinned.

"How about if I just tell you about it," she said, "and then you tell me if it'll cost anything. What do you say?"

"Sorry, Bethany, it's just not a good time," Scarlett said.

Bethany turned to me and pouted. I knew that we should just reschedule her. It would certainly make Scarlett happy. And we only had a few minutes before Henry had to leave. But I have a really hard time saying no to a girl—especially one like Bethany. Sam Solomon and I were both victims of the same curse. We were suckers for a pretty face. I can't tell you how many times Sam got himself into trouble whenever he let his emotions do the talking. And yet, knowing all of that, I still caved in.

"I guess it wouldn't hurt just to listen, right?" I directed my comment to both Henry and Scarlett.

Scarlett rolled her eyes and looked away. I knew she didn't approve.

"We'll just find out what her problem is," Henry said. "But if she wants a solution, it's gonna cost her."

"Fair enough," I said. "Okay, Bethany, what's up?"

"There's a thief on the loose," she said. "And I need you to find him."

"A thief?" Scarlett said. "What are you talking about?"

"It's true," Bethany said. "And I know who it is. Well, actually, it's one of two people. I guess I don't know for sure who's the culprit."

"When and where did this happen?" Henry asked.

I opened up a lawn chair and set it down next to Bethany. "Please, have a seat," I said.

"It was in the school library this afternoon," she said. "I was sitting at a table with Sean Morrison and Jeremy Guthrie. And one of them is the thief. I know it."

I pulled the card table down from behind a ladder. "Henry, can you help me with this?" We proceeded to open the table and then set up chairs around it for the rest of us. This was starting to get interesting. "Go on," I said to Bethany.

"Well, I remember opening my purse and seeing if I had enough money for the snack machine. I took out a five-dollar bill and a single and set them down on the table. Then I checked to see if I had any change. But since I didn't have enough, I grabbed the bills and went into the lobby to buy a bag of chips. When I got there, I discovered that I only had the one-dollar bill. By mistake I had left the five on the table."

"You're sure about that?" I said.

"I'm positive."

"Okay, so what happened next?" Henry said.

Bethany leaned forward in her chair and lowered her voice. "When I went back into the library, the money was gone, and so were the boys."

"So, did you try to find them to see if they remembered seeing the money?" Scarlett said.

She nodded.

"What'd they say?" I asked.

"Sean said that he remembered seeing the five-dollar bill on the table but assumed that I'd be coming back for it, so he just left it."

"And Jeremy?" Scarlett said.

"He told me that he saw it too. But he was afraid to leave it there, so he stuck it in a book for safekeeping."

I slid my chair out, stood up, and began to pace. It always helped me think things through when I was on the move.

"Did he remember which book he put it in?" I asked.

"Yeah," Bethany said. "He said he looked for the bookshelf closest to the table and found a book called *Nineteenth Century Russian Literature.*"

"He remembered that specific title?" Henry said skeptically.

"Not only that," she said, "he even told me he put it between pages sixty-three and sixty-four."

"Did you go and try to find the book?" Scarlett said.

"Of course. Duh," Bethany said. "But when I found it, the money wasn't there."

There was something about what Bethany had just said that bothered me. But what was it?

"I'm afraid your money's gone," Henry said. "Somebody else obviously picked up that book, paged through it, found the money, and kept it." He stood and began folding up his chair. "And that's about as much help as you're going to get without paying."

"Somebody else *in our school* picked up a book called *Nineteenth Century Russian Literature*?" Scarlett said. "What are the chances?"

"It's possible," Henry said.

"Wait a minute," I said. I leaned over and grabbed my backpack from the floor. I unzipped it and pulled out a few of my books. I then began to page through each one. "I knew it." I set the books on the table, each one opened to page 63. "Bethany, you're absolutely correct. The thief *was* one of the boys sitting at the table with you—and I know which one." The others all stared at me. "It was Jeremy."

"How do you figure that?" Henry said. "How do you know he didn't put it between the pages of the book like he said?"

I sat back down and smiled. "Because it's impossible."

"Huh?" Bethany said.

"Look at these books," I said. "Look at how the pages

are laid out. When you open a book and lay it flat, the even-numbered page is always on the left and the odd-numbered page is on the right. That's the way that all books are printed."

"I never knew that," Scarlett said.

"It was physically impossible for Jeremy to have stuck that five-dollar bill between pages sixty-three and sixty-four—because they share the same page—sixty-three is on one side of the page, and sixty-four is on the other." I turned to Bethany. "You better go have a long talk with Jeremy."

"That rat," she said.

Henry made a beeline for the cash jar on one of the shelves. He returned shaking it for Bethany's benefit.

"Now, that's gonna cost you," he said.

"I don't have any money," she said. "But when I get my five dollars back from Jeremy, then I'll be sure to stop by and pay up." She smiled, flicked her hair, spun around, and disappeared.

When I turned back around, I noticed that Henry and Scarlett were both scowling at me.

"I thought you were the one in a hurry," Scarlett said.

"Well . . ."

"And you knew darn well she wasn't going to pay," Henry said. "You just couldn't help yourself, could you?"

"Well . . ."

"What a complete waste of time," he said. "And we're no closer to a solution than when we got here."

Scarlett's phone dinged and she glanced at it. "Listen, I gotta go," she said.

"Me too, it's almost four o'clock," Henry added.

"Wait, guys," I said.

But a moment later, they were gone. I suppose I had that coming. We had assembled here to accomplish a task. Henry and Scarlett weren't fans of my plan to get arrested—and yet they still made it a point to show up. And what had I done? I had managed to forget all about that and let my emotions get the best of me. Apparently it was now up to me to figure out a way to get myself tossed in jail. It couldn't be that hard, right? I mean—people seemed to do it every day. But then I realized that I had another problem—I had to reconnect with my partners first. I had to bring them back into the fold and convince them that I wouldn't flake out, no matter who walked through that door. They knew my track record—especially Henry. This wasn't going to be easy.

CHAPTER 14

The French-Made Caper

Before I left the house for school the next day, I decided that I had better approach my mom and bring up the topic of this camping trip. I had ruled out the idea of a weekend in the wilderness with Henry's family. We'd never get away with that one. But what if I picked another classmate—someone my mom didn't know very well—and someone whose mom never talked to mine? It didn't take long to identify a likely candidate. It was a little radical, but it just might work.

That morning my mom was in the basement doing laundry. It was as good a time as any to drop the bomb.

"Mom, do you have a minute?"

"What are you still doing here?" she said. "You're going to miss your bus."

"Don't worry, I'll make it," I said. "Listen, I have an opportunity this weekend to go on a camping trip, and I just wanted to make sure it was okay."

She poured detergent into the washer and closed the lid.

"A camping trip? Where to? And who with? Henry?"

"No. Do you remember the kid that helped us get out of Olsen's basement last month?"

Her eyes widened. "You mean the boy who stole those birds?"

"Mom, he was cleared of that," I said. "Sherman's a good guy. Really."

"We don't know anything about his family," she said.

She wasn't making this easy. It always seemed that whenever I stretched the truth—and even if she didn't know that—I was in for a battle.

"Mom, it's gonna be a lot of fun. A bunch of kids are going."

She picked up the empty basket. "Do I know any of them?"

"No, I don't think so. But they're all good kids. Please. I don't want to miss it. And if I can't go, what are the chances that you and Dad'll ever take me camping?" There it was—the dagger. I knew my parents were anything but outdoorsmen, and a little guilt trip was the perfect weapon.

"Your father and I are not campers. You know that." She sighed. "Oh, all right. But I want a phone number where I can reach you in an emergency."

"Absolutely, Mom, I'll be sure to get that for you." I

peeked at the clock on the wall. "Hey, I gotta run. See you later." Yessss! I had done it. Sam Solomon would have been so proud.

The days that followed seemed to drag by. Every day at recess, Henry, Scarlett, and I would meet up to discuss the case. Then if everyone's schedules gelled, we would hook back up in the garage after school. By Friday afternoon, we still hadn't come up with a strategy that would place me in a jail cell at the police station. My brain seemed to have shut down. There was nothing percolating up there. I had set a deadline for myself, and it was now looming. I would have expected a little more help from my associates, but knowing how they felt about my plan, it wasn't surprising that they weren't offering any suggestions. It did occur to me that by appearing stumped, Henry and Scarlett just might be playing out their own strategy—if there was no plan in place, then I couldn't very well go through with it.

Time was running out. As we entered Mrs. Jansen's science class, the last period of the day, we were only a couple of hours from our self-imposed deadline. I guessed that the worst thing that could happen would be for us to delay our plan for another week, but I just hated the thought of that. It was time to make our move, and I was determined to do so. I kept trying to think of a way to get myself arrested but not end up with any sort of criminal record. I was worried about something Henry had said earlier. What if he was right? What if it would be impossible to get my private investigator's license someday because of a blemish on my record? How could I end up in the slammer and then have all the paperwork mysteriously disappear?

"Find your seats, everyone," Mrs. Jansen said. "I'd like to start off class today with a murder mystery."

And suddenly I had forgotten all about the pending case. It was time to concentrate on something more important—one of Mrs. Jansen's brain busters.

"Okay, here's the scenario," she said. "The police are investigating an unsolved murder, and they need your help. It seems that an elderly coin collector, Mr. Watkins, was found dead in the kitchen of his home. He was found by his best friend, Mr. Tolbert, who was also fond of rare coins. Mr. Tolbert told the police that he was taking a stroll one night when he passed by Mr. Watkins's house. He wanted to stop in and say hello, but it was late and he didn't see any lights on. So he went around to the back of the house and noticed a light on in the kitchen, but he couldn't see in because it was winter and there was frost on the windows. So he told the police that he wiped the frost off one of the windows and spotted his friend lying dead on the kitchen floor. That's when he went into the house and called the police." Mrs.

Jansen smiled. "End of story," she said. "No more clues. Who can solve this murder for us?"

Sherman raised his hand.

"Yes, Sherman," she said.

"There's gotta be more," he said. "We need more clues to solve it."

"You have everything you need in order to identify the murderer," she said. "Who'd like to take a crack at this?"

The room went quiet. Some kids just shook their heads. A few others were shrugging. Some threw up their arms. Everyone was stumped.

I kept repeating the lines she had spoken. I knew that the answer was hidden somewhere.

Henry, seated directly behind me, tapped my shoulder. "You have any idea?" he said.

I shook my head.

"Now, think really hard about everything you just heard," Mrs. Jansen said.

I began scribbling on a piece of scratch paper. I jotted down the facts of the case. Then I drew a picture of the kitchen window with frost on it . . . and suddenly I knew the identity of the murderer. It had taken only seconds. It was good to know I still had it. I looked around to see if anyone else had figured it out. The room was quiet. I started to raise my hand . . . then I froze. This was what always seemed to happen—I'd figure out the problem . . . desperately want to answer it . . . talk myself out of it . . . then eventually spit out the solution. Since I knew how things would ultimately turn out, I decided to act. I didn't even wait for Mrs. Jansen to ask me. I threw my hand into the air. There was no sense wasting time. But what I hadn't noticed was that Scarlett's hand was also raised.

"Well, let's see here," Mrs. Jansen said. "Whose hand went up first?"

Scarlett and I stared at each other. Our hands were both still airborne. I had a bad feeling that Scarlett had actually raised her hand a split second before mine. I knew that the fair thing to do would be to let her answer it, but I didn't want any of my classmates to think I was losing my edge. Then again, what was I worried about? What were the chances that she'd be able to solve a mystery—one that would require someone with expert problem-solving powers—before I could? It was unlikely. But anything was possible, I guess. And lately, she *had* shown signs of being able to compete on my level.

I wasn't quite sure what to do. Should I do the right thing and withdraw? Should I be a gentleman and back off? It might actually help our relationship. I tried to imagine her thanking me after class for pulling out of the competition. Now, that would be worth it. But then I caught myself. Who was I kidding? I was thinking the unthinkable. I had a tendency to do that. Whether I pulled out or not, Scarlett and I would never be more than just casual friends. I had to accept that.

"Well, I guess I'm just going to have to pick one of you," Mrs. Jansen said.

Should I just let Mrs. Jansen choose? And then all at once I remembered when Sam Solomon had to make a similar decision. It was in Episode #35—*The French-Made Caper.*

Sam had been hired by Parisian scientist Gilles Benoît, who had invented the first prototype ballpoint pen. Benoît feared that the blueprints for his new invention had been copied by his maid and sold to a competitor. But he had no proof. To solve this one, Sam teamed up with French police, and during the investigation, he got chummy with a rookie officer by the name of Pierre Duprée. When the time came for the evidence to be presented to the client and the police chief, Sam decided to let the young officer take credit for uncovering the plot, which, as you might guess, did indeed implicate the maid. And thanks to Sam's unselfishness, the young officer soon earned the respect and admiration of his coworkers, and he and Sam became lifelong friends.

I slowly lowered my arm. "Now that I think about it, Mrs. Jansen, I think Scarlett had her hand up first."

"Oh, okay," she said. "Scarlett, can you give us the identity of the murderer and tell us how you came to your conclusion?"

Scarlett stood up sheepishly. You could tell she was unaccustomed to being in the spotlight—at least when it came to solving brainteasers.

"Here's how I see it," she said. "The murderer has to be the victim's friend, Mr. Tolbert. And here's why. Now unless I'm mistaken, frost forms on the *inside* of windows in the winter, not on the *outside.* Since Mr. Tolbert told the police that he wiped the frost off the outside of the kitchen window, it is clear he was lying. He obviously killed his friend, probably for some rare coin, and then made it look like a home invasion of some kind. It was the friend. I'd bank on it."

Mrs. Jansen smiled and looked in my direction. "Since you're the resident authority on brain busters in this class, Charlie, would you like to add anything?"

"Nope," I said. "Nothing to add. She nailed it."

"She nailed it indeed," Mrs. Jansen said. "Well done, Scarlett."

By the looks on the faces of other kids in class, most seemed surprised that Scarlett had beaten me to the punch. If called upon, I would have answered the question in the same manner, but for some reason, I wasn't upset about someone else receiving kudos—as long as it was Scarlett or Henry, that is. I could now see why Sam allowed his friend Pierre to take the credit. It felt really good. For the remainder of the period, I noticed Scarlett glancing at me and smiling. This was truly a win-win.

• • •

Scarlett, Henry, and I met up at the bus stop after school. Henry seemed anxious to know where things stood with the case.

"So, have you figured out something yet or do we put this crazy plan of yours on hold?" he said.

I had gotten so wrapped up in the brain buster in Mrs. Jansen's class and watching Scarlett in action that I had completely forgotten to think up a way to get tossed in jail. But I wasn't going to let that stop me. I had no intention of delaying things just because I was stuck. I would just proceed and force myself to concoct a plan before time ran out.

"Meet me in front of the police station in an hour," I said. "The Camp Phoenix Caper is on."

"What do you plan to do?" Scarlett asked.

I guess that I could have just told them the truth—that I had no idea—but it seemed more fun to add a little drama.

"You'll see when you get there," I said.

"Okay," she said. "See you in an hour." Scarlett immediately began looking for her mom's car and was off.

Henry and I waited another couple of minutes for our bus in silence. I knew he probably wanted to ask me about my plan, but he knew I'd never tell. When the bus eventually pulled up, we hopped on board and talked about things unrelated to the case until we reached Henry's stop. Once I was finally alone, I put the old noodle to work. In the time it took to reach my house—ten minutes or so—I was determined to have mapped out a strategy. But minutes later I realized I had failed.

"Collier," a voice rang out. "This is your stop. Let's go."

I awoke from my trance, grabbed my backpack, and exited the bus. As I trudged the last two hundred yards to my front door, instead of working on a plan, I now found myself trying to think up an excuse to tell Henry and Scarlett as to why we would need to reschedule. This was going to be embarrassing. I had hoped that Mrs. Jansen's brainteaser would awaken something in me. I reached into my pocket and pulled out the business card that my grandmother had given me. Here I was, the proprietor of my own detective agency and unable to devise a plan of attack. I didn't deserve to be a member of my own firm.

When I walked into the house, I noticed my mom sitting on her bed with dozens of papers spread all over.

"Charlie," she said. "Come in here. I want to show you something."

"I'm in kind of a hurry, Mom. Can we do this later?"

"No, we can't," she said. "This'll only take a minute."

I reluctantly joined her in the bedroom.

She picked up one of the papers and smiled. "Look

at this. How old do you think you were when you did this?" She was holding a drawing that I had done when I was a kid. I took a closer look at the other papers on the bed. They were all pictures I had drawn or painted when I was small.

"I don't know," I said. "Maybe six."

She flipped it over. "You were only four," she said. "Imagine a four-year-old drawing a picture of his family with such detail." She sighed. "I have to be honest. There was a time when I thought you might grow up to become a commercial artist or a famous painter maybe."

I smiled back. Were we done here? I needed to go.

"Remember that old milk crate," she said, "the one you kept all of your art supplies in?"

"Yeah, I guess."

"It's still downstairs somewhere. I should pull it out sometime," she said. "Wouldn't that be fun to look through?"

"Oh yeah," I said sarcastically. And then something on the corner of the bed caught my eye. I walked over and picked it up. "Of course. This just might work," I said under my breath.

"What?"

"Oh, nothing."

My mom glanced at the clock on her dresser. "You'd better hurry," she said. "Are you all packed?"

"Packed? For what?"

"For your big camping trip with Sherman's family. Don't tell me you forgot?"

Oh, brother, I had forgotten. I was starting to get careless. "No, no, I didn't forget."

"Well, listen," she said, "I put some clean underwear and socks on your bed."

"Okay, thanks." I turned to leave.

"You know, I'm still wondering if I should call Sherman's mother and introduce myself."

No. She couldn't do that. It would ruin everything. "Mom, you can't call. It'll make me look like a baby. Nobody else's parents have called."

"Now, how would you know that?" she said.

"I just know."

She shook her head. "Oh, all right. But don't forget to leave me a number for Sherman's mom before you go."

"You got it," I said. "Hey, I'd better go finish packing." I smiled and exited. But before I went to my room, I ran downstairs. I had to find that milk crate with the art supplies in it.

For the better part of twenty minutes, I nearly ransacked the basement. And just when I was about to give up, I noticed something under some of the Christmas decorations next to the furnace.

"Eureka," I yelled. I pulled out the crate and began rummaging through it. As soon as I found what I was looking for, I slid it into my back pocket and headed upstairs. On the way to my room, I grabbed yesterday's newspaper off the living room coffee table. Things were finally falling into place, but I was running out of time. When I got to my room, I spotted the clean underwear and socks my mom had left for me. I stuffed them into a drawer. I was certain I wouldn't be gone long enough to need them. Then I dumped the contents of my backpack onto my bed and started crumpling up sheets of newspaper and stuffing them in. The backpack needed to look like it was full of clothes and stuff, but I didn't actually want to carry around anything heavy.

"Looks like you'll be catching up on current events this weekend, huh?" a voice said. My grandmother was standing in the doorway.

"Oh, hi, Gram." I nonchalantly zipped the backpack closed. I tried to appear as innocent as possible, but it was clear that she had seen what I was doing.

"Now, it's none of my business, Charlie, but something tells me that you'd need to pack a lot more than some old newspapers for a weekend camping trip."

My shoulders slumped. "Gram, please don't tell Mom and Dad."

"I can keep a secret," she said. "But I need to know what's going on."

"It's a long story," I said.

She pushed my schoolbooks to the side, sat down on

the bed, and folded her arms. "This has something to do with your case, doesn't it?"

I knew that my grandmother was probably the only person I could talk to about this caper without fear of getting into trouble. But I also knew that if she thought my plan was too dangerous, she was more than capable of ratting me out—for my own safety, that is. At this point, however, I was out of options. She knew that I was trying to deceive my parents. I had no choice but to spill it.

"Gram, I think I know where Josh Doyle is. He's the missing person we've been trying to find. But I can't confirm it." I pointed to my backpack. "This is the only way I can think of finding out."

"I think you've left out some parts," she said.

I took a deep breath. "We're almost positive that he's being held at the boot camp on the edge of town—a place called Camp Phoenix."

"I've heard about it on the news," she said.

"That's the one. It's a place where they rehabilitate teenagers who get into trouble with the law."

"So what's stopping you from calling them or just going over there?" she asked. "Either Eugene or I would be glad to take you."

I sat down on the bed next to her. "I'm afraid it's not that easy. It's impossible to get information out of them. They're not talking. And they won't let anybody past their front gates. Sherman's mom even called, and they wouldn't give her any information either."

"I have a bad feeling you're going to tell me that you plan to break in there."

I stared at the floor. "Not exactly. I'm gonna get myself arrested, and then when their bus comes by the jail to pick up kids, I plan on sneaking in with the others and joining them."

Gram sighed and made a face. It was clear she wasn't a big fan of my idea. "Sounds dangerous," she said. "You sure there's no other way?"

"I haven't been able to think of one," I said.

"Maybe Eugene or I could figure out a way to get into that place."

"Even if you could, Gram, a couple of strangers—especially adults—would stick out like a sore thumb. But a kid—a kid could blend in with the others and go undetected. Plus, if Josh is there and hiding his identity, there's more of a chance he'd talk to me. I'm afraid it's the only way."

She got up, walked over to the window, and stared out for several seconds. "All right," she said. "I can't say I like it, but it's your case and I'll support you. Go ahead and follow through on your plan, and I'll cover for you. But there's one thing I want you to do."

"Name it," I said.

"I want you to have some way of contacting either

Eugene or me if you get in over your head. Can you promise me that?"

I wasn't sure exactly how I could make that happen, but I knew that I had to agree to it or Gram would never sign off on our deal.

"I promise. I'll just borrow a cell phone from one of my friends."

"Okay," she said. "Be careful." She kissed me on the forehead and went back downstairs.

On occasion I've been known to have told my parents a white lie while in the process of solving a case. I didn't like doing it, but I always felt an obligation to the client, and that helped me justify my actions. But I really didn't like the idea of lying to my grandmother. She had been an ally for as long as I could remember. I didn't want to betray her confidence. Somehow I had to keep the promise that I had made—even if it meant asking a favor of someone who would probably rather die than grant me this particular request.

CHAPTER 15

The Bizarre Bazaar Caper

When I arrived at the police station, Henry and Scarlett were waiting for me. They had their game faces on. It was apparent that they had sensed the gravity of the situation.

"I was afraid you weren't gonna show," Henry said.

"No. Just ran into a little complication. That's all," I said.

"What sort of complication?" Scarlett asked.

I shuffled my feet for a moment. I knew that both Henry and Scarlett would be unhappy to hear that I had told someone else about our plans. But what was I supposed to do? They needed to know.

"I . . . er . . . had to tell somebody about my plan to get arrested."

"You told someone?" Henry said. "Who?"

"My grandmother."

"And she's still letting you do it?" Scarlett said.

"Well, she wasn't too happy about it," I said. "But she agreed to let me go through with it on one condition." I pointed to a park bench across the street from the police station. "Let's talk about it over there," I said. We made our way to a wooden bench with peeling paint and sat down.

"So what's the catch?" Scarlett said.

"She told me that I couldn't go unless I had a way of communicating with either her or Eugene at all times. She's worried that something might go wrong."

"What'd you tell her?" Henry said.

"I said *okay*. What else could I say?"

"What are you gonna do now?" Scarlett asked.

I glanced down at the cell phone that Scarlett held tightly in her hand.

She immediately jumped off the bench. She pressed her phone against her heart.

"Don't even think about it. There is no way you're using my phone."

It was the reaction I had expected. But Scarlett was my only hope. There was no one else I could ask.

Henry smiled. "I can't believe that Charlie Collier, Snoop for Hire, a student of the great Sam Solomon, would ever consider using a cell phone. I need to write this down."

"Well, he's not getting mine," Scarlett said emphatically.

"It would only be for a day or two," I said.

Scarlett was beside herself. Her face reddened. Her body tightened. She could barely speak.

"You're not serious?" she shrieked.

Henry leaned against the back of the bench and grinned. "Sure seems like the kind of thing that one associate would do for another," he said.

Scarlett was speechless.

"If you want to be part of the agency," Henry said, "then I'm afraid you're gonna have to part with your little friend there. That's all there is to it."

Scarlett plopped back down on the bench and folded her arms tightly. "You never told me I'd be asked to make sacrifices like this," she said.

I sat down next to her. "Listen, I'll be real careful with it. I promise."

She closed her eyes and held out her hand. She had yet to release her death grip on the phone. A moment later, her fingers relaxed and I was able to slowly pry it from her hands.

"Charlie Collier, if I find as much as a smudge on that phone, you're buying me a new one. Do you understand?"

"Don't worry," I said.

"And it's only to be used for emergencies," she said.

"Absolutely."

"And don't go poking your nose into anything on

the phone—names, numbers, notes, pictures, anything. You got it?"

"Scarlett, I'll just use it to call my grandmother or Eugene if I get into trouble. You can trust me."

She let out a long sigh.

I stared at the phone in my hand. I couldn't believe she had let me have it. This was one for the ages. I glanced at Scarlett. Right at that moment she seemed incomplete. It was if she had lost an appendage or something.

"What are you looking at?" she snarled.

"Nothing."

"Well, don't just stand there," she said. "Aren't you gonna go break the law or something?"

I slipped the phone into my pocket and nodded. I set my backpack on the bench and unzipped it. I reached in and pulled out a long tray of paints that I had found in the basement with my other art supplies.

"What's that for?" Henry said.

"You'll see," I said. I slid the backpack over to Henry. "Can you keep an eye on this?"

"I guess so." He zipped the backpack closed and set it in his lap. "You're really gonna do this, huh?"

"Yep. Wish me luck," I said. I checked for traffic and then jogged across the street. Parked directly in front of the police station was one of their squad cars. It read *Oak Grove Police* on the side. I sat down on the sidewalk next to the car and opened up my tray of paints. There were twelve colors to choose from. I proceeded to spit into what was left of the black paint. I worked it in with my finger until it was nice and moist. Then I took the brush, still good and hard, dipped it into the black paint, and stopped. Wait a minute, I hadn't thought about the words that I planned to paint on the side of the car. After a few moments, I had it. I decided to make the kind of statement that Josh might make.

By that time, Henry and Scarlett had crossed the street and were hiding behind a tree a few feet away. They apparently wanted to witness the criminal act in person.

I took a deep breath and got to work. I painted *Save the* and hesitated. I wanted to choose something that people naturally would want to save, but I also wanted to be original. I thought for a moment—and then I had it. I added the last word and then leaned back to admire my handiwork. Now all I had to do was wait to get caught. Fortunately, it didn't take long. A minute or so later, I heard the front door of the police station open.

"Hey, what are you doing over there?" a voice called out.

Just for effect, I decided to give my artwork a second coat. I could hear footsteps behind me. And as I was about to paint over the *t* in *the,* someone reached in and grabbed the paintbrush from my hand.

"You got a lot of nerve, kid," a uniformed officer said. "Defacing police property—in front of a police station. It's almost as if you wanted to get caught." He took a close look at the side of the car and scratched his head. "Save the *eels*?"

At least it was original. I rose from a crouched position and turned to face my accuser. I put my wrists together and extended them outward. I was waiting to be handcuffed and hauled away.

"Do your duty, Officer," I said.

The policeman shook his head. He bent over, picked up the tray of paints, and pointed at the front door of the station.

"Follow me," he said. "Let's go call your parents."

What was the meaning of this? I was a desperate criminal. No handcuffs? No pepper spray? No whacks with a baton? No stun gun? What kind of law enforcement was this anyway? I demanded to be treated like the criminal I was.

I winked at Henry and Scarlett as I followed the officer into the station. We walked down a narrow hallway and entered a small cubicle. He pointed at a folding chair next to his desk. I sat down and stared forward.

The officer dropped into his chair, opened a side desk drawer, and pulled out a piece of paper with writing on it.

"Name," he said.

I locked my jaw. There was no way I would divulge my name. I didn't want a criminal record to ruin my chances for a P.I. license someday.

"Oh, so that's how it's going to be, huh?" the officer said. "I don't suppose you're going to give me your address or phone number either, are you?"

I avoided eye contact.

The officer sat back in his chair and sighed. "Well, I hope you realize what kind of trouble you're in, son. Do you have any idea what it's gonna cost to get paint off that car?"

Now, I had told myself earlier that under no circumstances would I utter a word while in police custody. But he was all wrong about that paint. Someone had to set him straight.

"It won't cost anything," I said.

"Oh, so you *can* talk," he said. "Well, just how do you figure that?"

"Look at the paints. They're watercolors. They'll come off with a wet rag."

The officer sat up and examined the paints. He looked in the direction of the hallway.

"Hey, rookie, get in here."

A moment later a young officer in uniform appeared.

"Get some wet paper towels from the washroom and see if you can get the paint off the side of the squad car parked out in front."

The rookie nodded and disappeared.

The first officer appeared confused. "I don't get it. Why would you use watercolors to make some sort of political statement?" He leaned forward. "That *was* some kind of political statement, wasn't it?"

"Sort of, I guess."

"So, what exactly are you trying to accomplish?"

I thought for a minute. "You see, I just wanted to get people's attention about this cause, but I didn't want to vandalize anything. It didn't seem right."

"I like the way you think," he said. "By the way, is somebody killing off all the eels? I never read anything about that."

Before I could respond, the rookie officer reappeared. Since I had no answer on the plight of the eel, his timing couldn't have been better.

"Well?" the veteran cop said to his young assistant.

"It came right off, sir," the rookie said. "It's like it was never there."

"Thanks," he said, and waved off the rookie. He looked at me and smiled. He then picked up the piece of paper on his desk, crumpled it up, and tossed it into a nearby wastebasket. "Why don't we say this never happened?"

What? How could this be? He was supposed to throw the book at me. He couldn't just let me go.

"Listen, Officer," I said, "if you want to throw me in

the clink for a couple of hours to teach me a lesson, I'd be perfectly fine with that."

"The clink?" He chuckled, stood up, and motioned for me to stand. "You look like a good kid," he said. "You're just a little misguided, that's all." He leaned into the hallway and pointed to the front door. "Can I give you a little advice?"

I nodded.

"Why don't you stop by the drugstore, pick up some poster board, and make up a sign about the eels? Then stand on a street corner and share your views with the public. It's all perfectly legal."

"But—"

He gave me a little shove in the direction of the front door. "Get out of here. I have work to do," he said.

When I stepped out onto the front steps of the police station, I noticed that Henry and Scarlett were perched on the park bench across the street. They jumped up when they saw me. Tail between my legs, I dropped my head and moved slowly in their direction.

"What happened?" Henry said.

"They let me go," I said.

Showing little to no interest in the story of my release, Scarlett held out her hand, palm up.

"My phone. Now," she demanded.

I reached into my pocket and returned her prized possession.

"I told you it was a bad idea," she said.

"It was a *good* idea," I said. "I just did it badly."

"So now what?" Henry said. "Do we think up another crime for you to commit or figure out a different way to get you into that boot camp?"

"I don't know," I said. "If I could only have hung around in there long enough, I might have been able to sneak on the Camp Phoenix bus when it came."

"Well, you didn't," Scarlett said as she slipped the phone into her back jeans pocket. "I don't know about either of you, but I've had enough excitement for one day." She turned and left.

"I guess I'd better get going too," Henry said. "We'll touch base tomorrow. Don't worry, partner, we'll think of something." Henry had traveled less than thirty yards when he spun around. "Hey, Charlie, what are you gonna tell your parents about the camping trip? Won't they wonder why you're back so soon?"

I had completely forgotten about the camping trip scenario. "I'll just tell them it got canceled. Don't worry," I said. "Go ahead. I'll call you tomorrow."

With that, Henry waved and was off.

I sat down on the park bench to lick my wounds. Today had been a complete bust. I was starting to wonder if my next plan—whatever that might be—would blow up in my face as well. What I needed right now was a confidence boost. I needed to remind myself that sometimes things don't go as planned. It could happen to anyone. Even the best private detectives on the planet had bad days, right? Even Sam Solomon had failures. Like in Episode #33—*The Bizarre Bazaar Caper.*

Sam had been hired by wealthy socialite Eunice Peppernell to track down the disappearance of several thousand dollars. Each year Eunice held a charity bazaar for starving artists. Local merchants were invited to sell their wares at the event, with fifty percent of the proceeds going to charity. It had always been a wildly successful affair, but the amount raised this year was rather disappointing. During his investigation, an informant revealed to Sam that the merchants had been forced to pay protection money to a local strongman and therefore were unable to contribute to the charity. The P.I. decided to go public with his information, and just when he was about to produce the witness who would corroborate his findings, his source vanished. Sam no longer had the proof he needed. He had jumped the gun, and worse, he had failed his client. Mrs. Peppernell was just about to remove him from the case and hire another private eye when Sam was finally able to track down the missing snitch and redeem himself.

So there—Sam had failed—just like I had. But then he rebounded nicely—just like I would. At least I hoped it would turn out that way.

I spent the next half hour on the bench in deep

thought. Somehow I had to figure out another way to get into that boot camp. It wasn't going to be easy. I was guessing that the place was well guarded and probably had a secure perimeter. Breaking in would not be an option. I managed to come up with a few new ideas, but then just as quickly as they popped into my head, I dismissed them for one reason or another. This wasn't going well. When I had exhausted nearly every plan of attack, I decided that I needed a change of scenery. Maybe new surroundings would jog something in me.

I threw my backpack over my shoulder and had prepared to leave when I heard the sound of a motor in the distance. Roaring down the street and coming to an abrupt stop in front of the police station was the Camp Phoenix bus. Oh, great. Now I felt even worse. Had I successfully managed to have gotten myself arrested, I would have been a passenger on that bus. But it wasn't to be. I waited around for a few minutes, and then right on cue, a parade of teenage boys marched out the front door of the station. If I just could have convinced that officer to let me spend even an hour in the big house, then I'd be one step closer to finding Josh. It just wasn't fair. I had concocted a perfect strategy that . . . Wait a minute. Wait just a minute. Maybe it wasn't too late after all. Maybe I could still pull this off. All I had to do was casually blend in to the line of kids. I could do it. I *would* do it.

And then I thought about the deal I had made with my grandmother. I had given her my word that I wouldn't proceed unless I had some way of communicating with her. I couldn't just ignore that. How could I get my hands on another cell phone in time? But I had also given my word to Sherman. Was my obligation to the client stronger than my allegiance to my own family? I wasn't sure. But I knew one thing for certain—there was no time to debate the issue. It was now or never. I immediately thought about what Sam Solomon might do in this situation, and I had my answer.

If I was somehow able to sneak on that bus, I would need to let Henry know where I was. I unzipped my backpack and looked for something to write on. Since I had dumped out all of my school supplies earlier, the only paper available was the crumpled-up pieces of newspaper I had stuffed into it. I reached in and fumbled around for something to write with. Nothing. Not a pencil—not a pen—not even a crayon. All I did find was an old glue stick, stuck to the bottom of the backpack. I couldn't very well write with that.

I glanced at the long line of boys boarding the bus. How could I leave a message for Henry with nothing to write with? Then I got a brainstorm. I began unfolding the pages of newspaper and searched for large headlines. I started tearing out individual letters one by one until I had enough to form the words I needed. I used the glue stick to spread adhesive on the back of each letter and pasted them on one of the pieces of newspaper. I decided to stick them to a large photograph where they would stand out better. I had written

O-N T-H-E B-U-S

and just hoped that Henry would find the note and figure out what I was up to. I folded up the page, with the letters showing, and placed it on top of the others in my backpack. I then zipped it up and left the entire backpack on the ground behind the park bench.

I crossed the street and noticed that the last kid had just boarded the bus. I ran up to the door, as if I belonged there, and was just about to step on board when a man wearing army fatigues and holding a clipboard grabbed me by the arm.

"Wait one minute, son," he said. He glanced at a paper on the clipboard. "What's your name?"

Oh no, I hadn't planned on that. I needed to think fast.

"Um . . . you won't find it there," I said. "I just got booked a few minutes ago. The cop told me to run out here and get on board. He said he'd fax the paperwork over."

The Camp Phoenix rep made a face. He apparently didn't like my answer. He glanced back over his shoulder at the police station. He was probably considering going in there himself to pick up the paperwork. But, of course, it didn't exist. A few moments passed. Then he sighed and motioned for me to board the bus.

Phew. I had done it. I had actually done it. A new chapter in my life as a professional P.I. was about to begin.

CHAPTER 16

The Suite and Sour Caper

I was grinning when I stepped onto the bus. I was pretty proud of how I had talked my way past the guy with the clipboard. Sam Solomon would have approved. That smile, however, quickly faded when I got a good look at the other kids on the bus. They all seemed to be staring at me. And they all looked really mean. Some of them looked like they wanted a piece of me right then and there. I was wondering at that very moment what I had gotten myself into. I had always managed to use my brains to get out of tough scrapes. I was hoping that my intellect would somehow protect me from this bunch.

I searched for an open seat. There were none. It appeared that I would have to share with one of the other offenders. I tried to find a seat next to someone who didn't look as if he wanted to do me harm. I slowly made my way down the aisle, careful not to make contact with anyone. That soon became impossible when the bus suddenly started up and darted forward. The jolt sent me flying. I had become a human pinball, bouncing off seats, metal rails, and bodies.

"What do think you're doing, you idiot?" one of the teens yelled out.

I was now flat on my back in the middle of the aisle. I slowly lifted my head. "Sorry," I said as I attempted to stand. Before I had gotten back to my feet, I felt a shove from another unfriendly type. I was once again on my butt. This was getting ridiculous.

"Hey, fat boy, watch your step," some kid said. He was laughing. As were many of the others.

I was wondering if Colonel Harvard Culpepper knew what he was doing by bringing these troublemakers to his camp. They might destroy the place. I got back up for a second time and looked for a place to sit. The stares continued. I didn't feel welcome. If I ever did manage to solve this case, I was just hoping to come out of it alive.

I worked my way to the back of the bus. There was a kid with a crew cut and glasses in the last seat. He was staring at the floor. He seemed to know I was standing there but said nothing. He wasn't overly friendly, but at least he didn't look threatening. I thought it best to ask permission to sit.

"Is this seat taken?" I asked.

The kid just shrugged.

I took that as an invitation to join him. After I had plopped down next to him, he slid over a few inches. I guess I did take up a full seat and then some. I tried to give him as much space as possible. The ride for the next few minutes was fairly uneventful until we got stopped by a freight train and were stuck in traffic for what seemed like forever. It was at that point that I decided to take a chance and start up a conversation. I was just about to extend my hand and identify myself when I abruptly stopped.

Wait a minute. I wasn't supposed to be a nice guy. I was supposed to be like one of these kids—a troubled youth. I needed to make it seem like the world was against me—like following rules was for suckers—like anyone who got in my way might not live to talk about it.

I slapped my seatmate on the shoulder. "So, how ya doin'?" I said. I tried to sound tough.

"Not so good," the kid replied.

"So whatcha in for?" I asked.

"I'd rather not talk about it, if you don't mind," he said.

I cracked my knuckles. "Would you believe it?" I said. "They got me for breaking and entering." Out of the corner of my eye, I looked for a reaction from the kid. There was none. Apparently I hadn't convinced him I was an actual juvenile delinquent. He obviously needed more persuading. I nudged him in the ribs with my elbow. "Oh yeah, I almost forgot. They also pinched me for assault with a deadly weapon." That seemed to do the trick.

The kid suddenly looked at me as if I were an ax murderer. He slid over as close to the window as possible.

I leaned toward him and whispered, "Let me tell you something, pal." I looked around to make sure no one else was listening. "I intend to break outta this place. You can join me if you want."

The reaction I got was totally unexpected.

"Listen, I don't belong here," the kid said. "I'm not like you or any of these other—" He stopped in midsentence. He apparently didn't want to offend any of the others. "Please just leave me alone. Okay?" He closed his eyes and buried his head in his hands.

Whoa. I didn't mean anything by it. I was just trying to fit in. I wasn't trying to stir things up. This kid had nothing to worry about from me. Actually the two of us were probably more alike than he realized. I wasn't like any of these other kids either. In any event, I decided to respect his privacy. I put my head back against the seat and kept my mouth shut for the remainder of the trip.

About twenty-five minutes later, we pulled up in front of a long iron gate. It was connected to a chain-link fence that seemed to go for miles on either side. On top of the fence, four strands of barbed wire ran along the entire length. A sign hanging over the gate read, in large letters, *Camp Phoenix.* And beneath it, the words *You enter here as boys. You will leave here as young men.* An attendant dressed in army fatigues stepped out of a small guardhouse and walked up to the bus. He stopped at the driver's-side window. There was a brief, inaudible exchange with the bus driver.

A moment later, the gate slowly opened and we proceeded into the compound. I leaned in the direction of my new friend to see out the window. He pulled away from me as I tried to get a better look at things. The estate was filled with thick green grass and hundreds of tall maple trees. Since we had two maples in our yard at home, I was able to recognize them. As we continued on, I could see two rows of buildings on either side of the road. The ones to our left were gray and drab with peeling paint and broken windows. The grounds around them were filled with weeds and patches of brown grass. The buildings to our right, however, had a brilliant redbrick facade. Sculpted bushes and colorful flower beds surrounded them. There were even statues and fountains. What a contrast.

The bus turned left and headed in the direction of the older, run-down buildings. This wasn't a good sign. We pulled into a driveway with potholes everywhere. The bus and its contents bounced in every direction.

I grabbed a nearby handrail to avoid falling out of my seat. Some of the kids started yelling at the bus driver.

"Hey, jerk, are you trying to kill us?" one of them said.

"Drive much?" another added.

"Back up. You missed one of them potholes," a third one chimed in.

From where I was sitting, I could only see the back of the driver's head. I was waiting for some kind of reaction. It didn't take long. The bus screeched to a halt at the front entrance of a building with a sign that read *Repentance Hall.* The driver jumped from his seat and stood in the aisle with his arms folded.

"You boys got a lot to learn about respect," he said. "Now, I want you to exit this vehicle in an orderly fashion. I don't want to hear a peep. When you get out there"—he pointed to a spot right in front of the building—"I want you to line up single file, and remember to keep your mouths shut. And if I hear even a sigh, you'll spend the next week in the sweatshop. You got it?"

If the driver was attempting to intimidate us, he had done an excellent job. There were plenty of scowls on the faces of the passengers, but as instructed, no one made a sound. A minute later we had assembled in front of Repentance Hall. The driver was the last one off the bus. He waited for the group to fall into place.

"My name is Sergeant Stanley," he said. "Remember

that. Sergeant Stanley." He cocked his head to the side. "Now, let's see what kind of soldiers we have here." He turned his back to us and then spun back around and yelled out, "Attention!" with the accent on the last syllable.

Some of the kids just stood there. Most stood perfectly erect with their arms at their sides. I'm happy to say that both my friend and I were in the latter group. And then in military fashion, the sergeant placed his arms behind his back and began a formal inspection. He walked past us and made eye contact with each one of his new recruits. Noticing that one of the boot campers was slouching, Sergeant Stanley grabbed him by the shoulders and pulled him up, nearly lifting him off the ground.

When he had completed his rounds, the sergeant stood in front of the group. "At ease," he said.

Again, most of the kids responded appropriately. But a few seemed confused by the order.

"I can see we have a lot of work to do," he said. He pointed at Repentance Hall. "That, gentlemen, is your home for the next few weeks."

Next few weeks? Oh no. I was expecting to locate Josh and finish up here by the end of the weekend. If I didn't show up at home on Sunday night, my mom was sure to call Sherman's mother and this whole thing would blow up in my face—although I had conveniently forgotten to leave her a phone number.

"I intend to turn every one of you into a new man. Before we're done, you'll become contributing members of society. It may take some of you a little longer than others, but that's completely up to you."

"You can't keep us here," one of the older teens shouted out. He was taller than most of the others. He probably weighed in at close to 250 pounds. Now, I was certainly big for my age—or rather round—but I didn't tip the scales at anything close to that. By the tone of this bad boy, there seemed to be very few people he was afraid of.

My seatmate from the bus, standing to my left, mumbled something under his breath.

"What'd you say?" I whispered.

"I said—what am I doing here?"

Sergeant Stanley was now nose to nose with the smart-mouthed recruit. "We can't keep you here?" he said. "Oh yes, we can." With both hands, he grabbed the kid by the collar and head-butted him.

The tall teen fell backward and grabbed his forehead. As you might guess, the sergeant now had our complete attention.

"Anybody else with a problem?" he said.

There was complete silence.

"I thought so," he said.

If that hadn't been disturbing enough, a bullhorn then sounded. Some of the kids jumped. Seconds later, groups of teens filed out of Repentance Hall. They were dressed in orange prison jumpsuits. Each one seemed to be holding some kind of yard tool—shovel, rake, pitchfork, broom, hoe, hedge clippers, watering can, you name it. Others were pushing wheelbarrows. Still others carried large plastic bags. They followed a member of the camp staff, dressed in fatigues. He led them to an area overrun with weeds and other debris.

"Get to work," he yelled out.

Sergeant Stanley cleared his throat. "Take a good look, gentlemen. Tomorrow you'll be joining those poor suckers." He smiled. He seemed to enjoy seeing the frightened looks on our faces. "You see, fellas, Colonel Culpepper believes that the only way to rehabilitate you is to introduce you to organized physical labor. Each day you'll work until you drop. And then you'll work some more. And in a few weeks, when we've purged all the toxins from your pathetic carcasses, then you just might be worthy enough to re-enter civilized society."

I glanced down the line at my new band of brothers. I hadn't committed the kinds of offenses that some of them had, but I was beginning to feel sorry not just for myself, but for all of us. This just didn't seem like the right way to turn these kids around. Intimidate them? Work them to death? And it certainly wasn't the way to treat someone like Josh Doyle. He wasn't a criminal really. A little misguided maybe, but not a criminal. The sooner I found him and we got out of here, the better.

"But there *is* a way to avoid all this," the sergeant said.

We all looked up.

He looked at his watch and seemed to be counting down the seconds. Suddenly, the bullhorn sounded again.

"Take a good look across the road," he said, pointing at the beautifully manicured grounds and the shiny redbrick building with the sign *Resurrection Hall*.

A group of teenage boys soon began pouring out of the building. But this group was nothing like the others we had just seen. These kids were in street clothes. They were laughing and joking with one another. Some were wearing baseball gloves. They began playing catch. Others threw a football around. Still others tossed Frisbees. What exactly was going on here? Everyone seemed so happy and content. I just didn't get it. None of this made any sense.

And then all at once, I felt a sensation in the pit of my stomach. I couldn't believe what I was looking at. It was him. It was Josh Doyle. I was sure of it. He was standing around talking with some of the other kids from Resurrection Hall. And then as soon as he started walking, my suspicions were confirmed. He was limping. It was definitely him. I had been right about him being here all along.

There was something, however, that seemed odd—Josh was smiling. He appeared to be happy and having a good time. I had only seen him a few times before in my entire life, but never once had I seen a smile on his face. He was always so serious. I was beginning to wonder if I was doing the right thing. Was I about to rescue him, or was I denying him a chance at happiness?

"Play your cards right, fellas, and you could end up there," Sergeant Stanley said. "Once you make it to Resurrection Hall, then you've really made it. If you end up there, you never have to leave. You can stay there as long as you like. You don't have to go back to jail or back home to your dysfunctional families. Everything that you could ever want is provided for you. What do you think of that? Looks pretty good, huh?"

I wasn't sure if I'd get into trouble, but I decided to speak up anyway. I raised my hand just to be safe.

"Yes, Private," he said.

"Sergeant, how exactly do we end up over there?"

"Now there's a bright young man," he said. "With that attitude, you just might make it, son."

I noticed some of the other guys staring at me. I wasn't sure if they were glad I had asked the question or wondering who the sap was.

"Well, let me tell you how you can go from this side of the road to that side," the sergeant said. "All you gotta do is buy into the program. You need to do everything that the colonel says—even if you don't like it. But there'll be plenty of time to discuss all of that. Right now we need to get you processed and assigned to rooms." The sergeant motioned for us to follow him.

While we made our way to wherever, I glanced across the road again at Josh. He was now sitting on the grass in a small circle with some of the other boys. They were holding paper cups. Someone from the camp was pouring what looked like lemonade into them. One of the kids in his group patted Josh on the back. Both grinned. This wasn't at all the scenario I had expected. I had assumed that every kid at this camp would be miserable and would welcome a chance to escape. My plan to get myself arrested and end up here had seemed like the perfect strategy. Now I was worried that I had made a big mistake. I began to wonder what Sam Solomon might have done in a situation like this. At first I couldn't recall anything similar, but then it came to me. Of course, Episode #34—*The Suite and Sour Caper.*

Sam had been hired by a wealthy couple whose teenage daughter had been kidnapped and was being held for ransom. Sam trailed the kidnappers across six states before discovering the missing girl in a hotel suite in Miami Beach. But when he got there, the young captive was angry that he had tracked her down. It seemed she didn't want to be rescued. She wanted to stay with her kidnappers. The girl was suffering from what we now call Stockholm syndrome, where hostages begin to bond with their captors and have positive feelings toward them. Sam knew in his heart that this girl was confused, and although she resisted, he still returned her to her parents.

I thought about Josh. I started to wonder if this case would end up the same as Sam's and what I would do if it did. Would Josh be happy to see me? Would he even know who I was? Would he agree to go with me? Would he want to leave the camp? I wasn't necessarily suggesting that Colonel Culpepper was a kidnapper or anything. It's just that something was odd about this whole arrangement. Why were there two completely different groups of kids here? How did someone actually make it from one side of the road to the other? I decided right then and there that my mission here would now be twofold: I would somehow find a way to talk to Josh and try to convince him to leave, and I would also investigate the mysterious way that some kids made the transition from pauper to prince.

CHAPTER 17

The Prose and Cons Caper

The line of new recruits snaked through the lobby of Repentance Hall. It was almost my turn to be processed by camp personnel. The friend, or rather acquaintance, I had made on the bus was directly in front of me. He was now first in line. When they called him, I intended to get close enough to the desk to listen in and find out what types of questions they were asking. Within a few seconds, one of the camp employees, also dressed in military garb, motioned the boy in front of me to proceed forward. As he approached the desk, I inched closer in order to overhear their conversation.

"The name is Corporal Waters. Who are you?"

The boy stared at his feet. "Evan . . . Evan Wright," he said.

"And what brings you here today?" the corporal said.

He looked up. "Huh? What do you mean?"

Corporal Waters shook his head disgustedly. "Why do all you guys come here with attitude?"

"Wait a minute, sir," Evan said. "I don't understand the question. I'm not trying to cause a problem."

The corporal smiled, but it was anything but sincere. "What'd you do to get your keister thrown in jail?"

"Oh," Evan said. He looked at the floor again. He seemed embarrassed and a little ashamed. "I . . . I was arrested for stealing a car."

The corporal sat back in his chair and grinned. "A joyride, huh? And see where it got you. You kids'll never learn."

"It wasn't like that," Evan said. "You see, I didn't know—"

"Yeah, yeah, yeah," Corporal Waters said. He began mimicking a whiny teenager. "'I didn't know it was stolen, Officer.' 'I don't know how those drugs got in there, Officer.' 'That's not my knife, Officer.'" He made a face. "I've heard 'em all, kid. A few weeks here and you'll start to take responsibility for your actions." The corporal grabbed a towel from a tall pile on the desk in front of him and shoved it at Evan. Then he reached for a bar of soap.

"Catch, kid," he said as he tossed it to him.

The soap slipped through Evan's hands, hit the floor, and bounced away.

"Nice grab." Corporal Waters pointed to a hallway

over his shoulder. "Room one fourteen," he said. He looked in my direction. "Next."

Evan looked up at me as he retrieved the bar of soap. He seemed lost. He was probably right—he didn't belong here.

"Name?" the corporal said.

"Char—" I froze. What was I doing? I couldn't give him my real name. My plan was to get in and out of this place as quickly as possible and without being noticed.

The corporal slammed his pen on the table. "The questions are gonna get tougher, kid."

"Chase . . . Chase Cunningham." It was the first thing that popped into my head. I hoped Henry wouldn't mind me borrowing his name, but I needed something fast.

The corporal ran his finger down the page of names. "Cunningham . . . Cunningham . . . you're not on my list," he said.

I repeated my initial story. "I just got arrested about an hour ago. They must still be processing the paperwork or something."

Corporal Waters leaned back in his chair and stared at me quizzically. It was almost as if he didn't believe me. He seemed to think for a moment, and then he sighed.

"All right. *Chase,* is it?"

"Yes, sir."

"So what brings you to our friendly abode?" he said.

"I guess you might call it vandalism," I said.

"You guess?" the corporal said.

"I spray-painted a police car. Only it wasn't spray paint. And it wasn't permanent. And—"

The corporal rolled his eyes. "I know. I know. You're just some mixed-up, misunderstood kid. Right?"

"Well, not exactly," I said. "You see—"

"Spare me, kid." He tossed a towel and bar of soap at me and pointed at the stairwell. "Room two twenty-two. Next."

Although I hated to pass up another chance to engage in sparkling conversation with Corporal Waters, I thought it best to go look for my room. And anyway, it was about time to begin my investigation of this place. I climbed the stairs leading to the second floor and soon came upon a long hallway with dozens of rooms on either side. The carpeting was faded and filled with what looked like cigarette burns. The lighting was dim, but I still managed to notice the walls were in desperate need of a paint job. The Ritz, this was not.

Room 222 was near the end of the hallway. The door was open. I crept in slowly, not sure what I'd find. The first thing I noticed was the boarded-up window. It gave me sort of a claustrophobic feeling. The room was about eight feet square. A cot was pushed up against one wall. A beat-up dresser sat on the opposite wall. And that was about it. I opened up the top dresser drawer and placed my towel and soap inside. I was careful to keep them away from the spiderweb filled with dead bugs in the far-right corner of the drawer. Apparently this was going to be an adventure. I could see why the residents of Repentance Hall would want to keep their stay here as short as possible.

I decided to stretch out on the cot for a few minutes to think things through. I had to figure out a way to break away in order to talk to Josh. Since I had no idea what sort of schedule we'd be on at this place, it was hard to plan out anything. I closed my eyes for just a moment. The next thing I remembered was waking up to the sound of doors being slammed—one after another. Before long, a kid no more than eighteen, dressed in army garb and combat boots, appeared in the doorway. He had a handful of orange prison jumpsuits over his arm. He tossed one over to me.

"Put this on," he said. He grabbed the doorknob. "And keep this door closed at all times. Understand?" And with that, he pulled it shut.

Well, it was nice to meet you too, I thought. One thing was for certain—people around here sure weren't too friendly. I guess that was their tough love approach in action. I got up off the cot and changed into the jumpsuit. If I had ever wanted to know how it felt to be a convict, seeing myself in this outfit definitely answered that question. I had a little trouble zipping it up. The fit was snug. So, what else was new?

I decided to look out into the hallway to see if it was

clear. No time like the present to make my move. But when I turned the doorknob, I realized it was locked. Hey! What was going on here anyway? Doors aren't supposed to lock from the outside. There was a mistake of some kind.

I thought for a minute. And suddenly things began to make sense. There was no mistake. I wasn't just a new member of the boot camp, I was a prisoner, and I suspected that every kid in this building was too. I examined the door more closely. When I realized that the hinges were on the outside of the door, then I knew for sure what was going on. If the hinges had been on the inside, an enterprising individual, with something as simple as a screwdriver, could just remove them and escape. Well, this was just great. If I couldn't sneak around to ask a few questions and conduct an investigation, then what was the point of coming here in the first place?

At that moment I needed some real inspiration—and I knew exactly how to get it. I picked up the pants I had tossed onto the floor, dug my hand into the front pocket, and pulled out the laminated business card that Gram had given me a few days earlier. I stared at it. I was half expecting something magical to happen. But there was nothing. No bells or whistles or lights or anything. Right then I didn't feel much like a successful private detective—and especially not like one who ran his own agency. I was getting sloppy. Lately I seemed to be making a series of bad decisions. Then I remembered what Gram told me when she handed me the card: "The next time you get into a jam, pull that card out of your pocket and take a gander. It just might open up a few doors for you someday."

What could she possibly mean by that? I took a second look at the card. It was actually kind of fun to look at. When Gram first gave it to me, I remembered that it made me feel important. But I wasn't feeling very important right at that moment—or inspired for that matter. I slid the card into the front pocket of my jumpsuit and stared at the boarded-up window. Even though we were on the second floor, maybe that was a way out. I started pulling at the pieces of plywood, but they wouldn't budge. The building itself might not have been well constructed, but whoever had nailed these boards to the window had done a professional job.

I sat back down on the bed and sighed. And thought about Sam Solomon. Sam had gotten himself into jams like this all the time. I pulled the business card from my pocket again and stared at it. "You don't deserve to call yourself a private detective," I told myself. "You're no Sam Solomon. You're nothing but a fraud." I tried to recall a time when Sam was totally baffled—when he had exhausted every conceivable idea. I couldn't think of one. That sure would have helped me deal with these feelings of incompetence. And then all at once, as if someone had flipped a switch, I remembered something. How could I have been so dense? Episode #46—*The Prose and Cons Caper.*

This particular case had Sam so frustrated that he actually considered hanging up his fedora. Sam had been hired by the warden of a maximum-security prison to uncover a leak. Apparently, some of the Mafia bosses housed in this institution were somehow still able to run their operations from inside the joint. Sam spent weeks investigating the case. At one point, he was ready to give up. He even considered closing his doors. Then he discovered that a volunteer English professor from a local community college who was teaching a creative-writing class to some of the prisoners was the actual leak. When the teacher collected assignments from his pupils at the end of each writing session, he was holding papers filled with marching orders from the Mafia bosses to their street crews.

Had Sam given up and closed the agency, the mystery series would have ended right there. But like the fighter he was, he persevered and once again proved himself to be the master detective. Thinking about that case had suddenly awakened me. I felt rejuvenated and inspired. I knew that I would rebound the same way that Sam had. And then all at once, something clicked. It's funny—when you find yourself on the lowest rung of the ladder—at that point of total despair—that's when you find out what you're really made of. I thought about my grandmother's words and suddenly realized that her message had a *literal* meaning to it. "It just might open up a few doors for you someday."

I scooted over to the locked door and inserted the business card between the door and the frame. I could feel the card up against the latch. I knew that if I could push it really hard, I should be able to move the latch just enough to open the door. I pushed the card as hard as I could until I felt the latch move slightly. It was starting to slide back into the door. With one hand still holding the card in place, I grabbed doorknob and pushed. Nothing yet. My hand was starting to get sore. I knew I was running out of time. I decided to give it one last thrust. I leaned into the door and put my oversize body to work. Sometimes those extra pounds actually came in handy. And just when I was about to give up, I felt the card inch forward. I quickly grabbed the doorknob and pushed. Yes! It opened. I had done it.

I stuck my head out into the hallway. It was clear. It was time to sneak out and look for Josh. I didn't know how much time I had before someone from the camp came strolling by. I was just about to close the door behind me when I suddenly thought of something. If I closed this door, how would I be able to get back in? Based on how the latch was slanted, I knew that I wouldn't be able to use the business card to open the door from the outside. What I really needed right at that moment was a piece of tape. Then I could put it over the latch to keep it from locking the door behind me. But there wasn't any tape. I scooted back into the room and began rummaging through the dresser drawers. They were empty. Now what? How could I possibly keep that door unlocked?

Then it hit me. I opened the top drawer and grabbed the bar of soap that the corporal had given me. I broke off a corner of the bar and started jamming it into the hole where the latch would go. I kept breaking off little pieces until I had completely filled the hole. I closed the door to see if it would work. Eureka! I had done it—again. The door now opened and closed with ease.

I closed the door behind me and tiptoed down the hallway. It was pretty quiet. I made my way down the stairs to the first floor. I immediately spotted a boot camp employee stationed at the main door. I wasn't expecting that. I needed to find another exit—and quick. I casually walked down the first-floor hallway. It was best to look as if I belonged there. I was hoping there was another door somewhere in that direction.

When I reached the end of the hall, I noticed a second exit—but I also noticed a second guard. Now what? These folks certainly didn't want any of their guests—or rather, inmates—vacating the premises. Right at that moment, I was really missing Henry. He and I had tackled problems like this in the past. Whenever we found ourselves in a similar situation, one of us would manage to create a diversion while the other slipped by undetected. We had done it countless times. What I really needed right now was an accomplice. But who? Who did I know at this place besides Josh? I couldn't very well try to recruit a complete stranger. I didn't know anything about these kids. And what I did know was a little scary. Most of the kids here wouldn't be in the circle of friends my parents would want for me.

Wait a minute. What about that Evan kid? The one I sat with on the bus. He didn't seem like a hardened criminal or anything. He kept saying that he didn't belong here. I wondered if I could trust him. It was worth a shot. Maybe I could tell him that I'd help him escape from this place if he joined forces with me. It might just work. I remembered that Corporal Waters had given him room one fourteen. I decided to pay a little visit to one Mr. Evan Wright.

His room was on the other end of the hallway. I examined the door before knocking. It was just like mine—locked from the outside. I wondered if he knew he was a captive of the colonel. I knocked lightly.

"Pssst, Evan," I whispered. "Are you in there?"

Seconds later I heard a weak voice from the other side. "Yeah, who is it?"

"It's me. I met you on the bus. Remember? We sat together."

"What do you want?" he said.

"I gotta talk to you," I said. "It's important. Can I come in?"

"I don't know. I don't think we're supposed to let anybody else in our rooms."

This kid wasn't making it easy. How could I convince him that I was one of the good guys?

"Have you tried opening this door yet?" I asked.

"No. Why?"

"Because you're locked in. That's why." I heard him turn the knob. He pushed and pulled at it with no luck.

"Hey, what's going on here?" he said.

"If you haven't noticed it yet—we're prisoners," I said. "And if you'd like to get out of this place, I can help. But you gotta let me in first."

"Well, how can I let you in if the door's locked?"

"Listen," I said. "Look down at your feet. I'm sending something your way." I pulled the business card from my pocket and slid it under the door. For a few seconds, I heard nothing. "Did you find it?" I asked.

"Yeah," he said. "Who's this *Charlie Collier* guy?"

"That's me. I'm Charlie Collier." I kept glancing down the hallway, fearful that someone might see me.

"*You're* a private detective? I don't believe it. You're just a kid . . . like me," he said.

"If you let me in, I'll explain everything."

"But how?" he said.

He seemed skeptical, but I was confident that I could convince him to cooperate. At least, I hoped so. "I want you to slide that card between the edge of the door and the frame—right where the latch is. Can you do that?" Within a few seconds I could hear the card being inserted and pushed up against the latch.

"Nothing's happening," he said.

"You gotta push really hard. You have to force the latch back into the door. Tell you what—you push the card and I'll pull from this end." Right at that moment I heard voices. They were coming from the exit at the end of the hallway. "Hurry, Evan," I said. "Push . . . as hard as you can." The voices were getting louder. At any moment, someone was sure to turn the corner and show his face—and if he spotted me, I was a dead duck.

"It's moving a little," he said.

I put my foot up against the door frame and yanked. I'd pull this thing off its hinges if I had to. "Push," I said. My voice was strained. *C'mon, Evan, you can do this.*

And then suddenly, the door gave way. I fell backward onto my butt. I didn't waste time getting to my feet. I scampered into his room on all fours and pulled the door closed behind me. I sat up against the back of the door and let out a long sigh.

CHAPTER 18

The Rack on Tour Caper

Evan was staring down at me. He appeared confused. "I don't understand what's going on here," he said. "Why are we locked up?"

I got to my feet. "If you've been following the news lately, you know that this Colonel Culpepper character made a deal with the city. He's supposedly trying to rehabilitate us."

"I understand that," he said, "but I didn't think this place was a jail."

"He must have left that part out," I said.

"Tell me something," Evan said. "How do you fit into all of this?" He handed my business card back to me. "Now I can see why you got arrested for breaking and entering."

"What?" I had to think about what he had said. "You got it all wrong. I didn't do any of the things I told you before."

"I don't get it," Evan said.

"I snuck on that bus to get here."

"Why in the world would you ever want to come to a place like this if you didn't have to?"

I sat down on the cot. "I was hired to find a missing person. And I found him. Or, at least, I *saw* him. Now I just have to figure out a way to get him—and me—outta here."

Evan joined me on the cot. "And me. Can you help me get outta here too?"

I smiled. That was just what I was hoping to hear. "I don't see why not," I said. "If you can help me run some interference, then I'll gladly help you escape from this place. Deal?" I extended my hand and we shook on it. Before we mapped out a strategy for locating Josh, I needed to find out a little more about my new partner. "Tell me a little something about yourself," I said. "What did you mean back there when you said you didn't belong here? Did you steal a car or not?"

"Of course not," he said. "Heck, I'm only thirteen. I can't drive. This whole thing is a big misunderstanding."

"Then what happened?" I asked.

Evan got up and walked to the window—or rather where a window was supposed to be. His was boarded up as well.

"I have this cousin—Tommy—who's always getting into trouble. He lives in Ohio. He got suspended from school about a week ago, so he and his mom—my aunt Penelope—came to visit us for a few days. I guess she figured a change of scenery might do him some good." He forced a laugh. "Yeah, right. The kid's a loser. He's only sixteen, and he's been in jail a half dozen times."

"Let me guess," I said. "*He* stole the car, and you were just along for the ride?"

"I didn't even know it was stolen," he said. He slapped at one of the boards on the window. "So, get this—a couple of nights ago, Tommy disappears. An hour later, he drives up to the house in this red Mustang convertible."

"And you weren't suspicious?"

"I guess I should have been," he said. "But he told me he had just come from a car dealer and he was test-driving it. That was possible, right?"

I wasn't sure if Evan was dumb or just naïve. "Listen, what dealer in his right mind is gonna let a sixteen-year-old kid drive off the showroom floor in a new car? Alone?"

"I know," he said. "It sounds bad now. And I guess I knew something wasn't right. But, for Pete's sake, it was a *Mustang*. And it was a *convertible*."

"And so that's how you got here, huh?"

"Well, yeah, but I'm not a thief or anything," he said.

"I guess the only crime you're guilty of is . . . poor judgment," I said.

Evan sat back down on the bed. "I can't argue with that—but I don't belong in a place like this, that's for sure."

"So where's your cousin now?" I asked. "Is he here too?"

Evan shook his head and sighed. "Nope. When the cops ran his name through the computer, they found an outstanding warrant for him back in Ohio. They're holding him until the Cleveland police come to pick him up. I told you he was bad news."

"Don't worry about that now," I said. "Let's just focus on finding a way for all of us to get out of here . . . safely."

Evan smiled and nodded. "I'm for that." It was the first time I had seen him smile since I had met him.

"Okay," I said. "I need you to help me get past those guards out there. First I want you—"

Evan grabbed my arm and squeezed it. There were sounds—voices—coming from the hallway. I pressed my ear up against the door to try to make out what was being said.

"What is it?" Evan said.

"Shhh," I said. I recognized the voice. It was the same guy who had given me the orange jumpsuit an hour or so ago. I heard him opening doors and saying something to the residents. He was getting louder, and he was headed this way. I needed to disappear—and fast. "You have to hide me," I told Evan.

Evan looked around the room. "Where?"

This was going to be a challenge. I couldn't hide behind the door because it opened up the other way—into the hallway. There was no closet. And with my physique, I knew that I'd never be able to fit under the cot. We could now both hear the voice coming our way. He had to be at the room next to us. I grabbed the cot and dragged it across the room and up against the dresser. That created a small spot in the corner. I climbed over the cot and crouched down in the corner.

"Do me a favor," I said. "Throw your towel and anything else you've got over me."

Evan grabbed his towel and laid it on top of me. He did his best to cover my entire body. Then he picked up the clothes he was wearing when he came here and tossed them on top. I could only hope it would just look like a pile of dirty clothes.

I could hear a key being inserted into the lock and the door being opened. I held my breath.

"Evan Wright?" the voice said.

"Yes, sir," Evan replied.

"In a couple of minutes, you'll hear a loud buzzer. When that happens, leave your room and proceed—in complete silence, I might add—out of Repentance Hall, across the field, and over to the mess hall for dinner. At no time will you speak to anyone. Is that understood?"

"Yes, sir."

I didn't hear anything for a few seconds. I was praying that the camp guard wasn't standing there looking in my direction and getting suspicious. I closed my eyes and remained perfectly still.

"Charlie?" Evan said. "The coast is clear. He's gone. You can come out now."

"Just to be safe," I said, "since that door's open, I think I'll stay right here until the buzzer goes off. If I come out now and that guy walks by again, it's all over."

"You're probably right."

Less than a minute later, this long, loud, annoying, shrill-pitched buzzer signaled that dinner was being served.

"Hey, Evan," I said from underneath the towel and clothes, "can you look in the hallway and make sure it's safe for me to come out?"

"Okay," he said. And then seconds later, "Looks good, c'mon."

I threw off the covering and stood up. I had a pain in my back from bending over all that time. A minute later, Evan and I emerged from the room. I couldn't help but notice a couple of the other kids looking at us funny. They were probably wondering why two people had come out of the same room. I just hoped that no one would get nosy and decide to speak up.

As we strolled down the hallway, I made it a point to act in a nonchalant manner. I couldn't draw any attention to myself. We walked out the main entrance and began to cross a large field. I was beginning to feel fairly confident that none of the officials at the camp had detected that I had come out of Evan's room. We slowly merged into a group of kids headed to the mess hall. We were blending in beautifully now. I was feeling a little cocky at that moment. And who wouldn't? I had made a successful escape on my own and was on the verge of solving yet another case—or so I thought.

I soon felt these large, bony fingers digging into my shoulder. It was the guard who had released us from our rooms minutes before.

"Cunningham? Chase Cunningham?" he said.

I almost didn't recognize the alias I had used. "Um, yes, can I help you?"

He pulled me to the side away from the others. "You're in big trouble, fella. You weren't in your room when I came by. Where were you? And how did you get out?"

"Whoa, wait a minute," I said. "You got things all wrong. I didn't sneak out or anything. Another guy, dressed just like you, came by and opened it up. He told me to come down for dinner."

The guard appeared skeptical. "Another guy? Impossible. I'm the only one who unlocks those doors."

"Well, then you better check with the rest of the staff," I said. "'Cause somebody else was doing your job for you."

The young guard scratched his head. I wasn't sure if he actually believed my story, but I could tell that he was at least considering my version of it.

"All right, get in there with the others. But I plan to check with some of the staff members. And if I find out you're lying to me, I certainly wouldn't want to be in your shoes. The colonel knows how to handle deceivers."

I didn't like the way that sounded, but I figured that if I could wrap up this case before camp personnel found out what really had happened, then maybe it wouldn't matter. I worked my way through the crowd and looked for Evan. Apparently the chosen ones, the kids from Resurrection Hall, weren't finished eating yet. They were still seated at tables waiting to be released.

Evan pointed at the kids sitting in the mess hall. "Get a load of that meal," he whispered. "It looks like steak, a double-baked potato, and sweet corn." He looked around to make sure he wasn't overheard. "Maybe this place isn't so bad."

A minute later, the buzzer sounded and the kids from the first shift got up and carried their trays to a conveyor belt on the far wall.

I carefully watched the group as they exited. They weren't in orange prison jumpsuits like the rest of us. They were in normal clothes—but really nice normal clothes. Most wore designer jeans and had on expensive-looking boots or running shoes. I wondered what a person would have to do to make it into that group. Was there some test you had to pass? An obstacle course maybe? Or just put in hours and hours of hard labor? I was anxious to make the transition but figured I wouldn't be here long enough to find out.

And then, near the end of the line, I spotted Josh. I worked my way over to where the line was passing by us. I was no more than about four or five feet away from them. I tried to make eye contact with him. I wasn't really sure if he'd recognize me since he had only seen me a couple of times before today, but I hoped he might. When it was clear that our eyes would not meet, I decided to break one of the camp commandments.

"Josh," I said under my breath as he approached me.

He glanced up and stared at me for a few seconds, then looked away. A bunch of the kids began to move away from me. Apparently no one wanted to have anything to do with someone who dared to speak.

I was certain that Josh had recognized me. But for whatever reason, he refused to acknowledge me. I had to do something. I couldn't waste this opportunity. I got as close to him as I possibly could and tried to keep pace with him as he passed through the lobby.

"Josh, it's me, Charlie Collier. I'm a friend of Sherman's."

With the mention of his brother, Josh stopped abruptly but still maintained his silence.

"I've been sent here to find you and bring you home," I said. "Your family's really worried about you."

Josh looked around nervously. He seemed uncomfortable about having a conversation with so many people around.

"Listen," he said under his breath. "I can't talk to you right now. I have to go."

"But wait," I said. "What should I tell Sherman? And your mom?"

"Tell 'em I'm fine. Tell them that I'll get in touch with them when I have a chance." Josh hesitated. "Just tell 'em not to worry." And with that, he was gone.

I thought it best not to try to follow him. The camp authorities already had a reason to keep an eye on me. I couldn't give them another one. The group from Repentance Hall began to move from the lobby into the mess hall. Kids were grabbing the first seats they saw. There apparently were no seating assignments. I spotted Evan and made my way over to his table. There was an open spot next to him.

"What were you doing out there?" he said. "Are you crazy?"

"That was the guy I came here to find. I had to talk to him."

"Well, you'd better not let anyone catch you doing that again," he said.

Clearly Evan was the cautious type. He seemed like someone who didn't like to make waves. I, on the other hand, was on a mission. When I took on an assignment, I had an obligation to do everything in my power to guarantee a successful outcome. Private detectives like Sam Solomon didn't have time to worry about the consequences. The same applied to me. We had made a commitment to the client and nothing, including bodily harm, would stop us. If the colonel or any of his storm troopers got tough with me, I was prepared. It was all part of the job. Like in Episode #31—*The Rack on Tour Caper.*

In this particular mystery, Sam found himself *stretched* a bit too thin—literally. Sam had been hired by a museum curator who asked him to investigate the recent disappearance of several rare artifacts from the museum. Following his investigation, Sam discovered that an antiques collector who had brought a traveling exhibit to the museum was the real culprit. The suspect was demonstrating a torture device used in the Middle Ages—the rack. When Sam confronted him, the private eye wasn't expecting a tussle, but that's exactly what he got. He was overpowered by his enemy and soon found himself a permanent part of the exhibit—strapped to the rack. I won't give away the ending, but let's just say that following his escape, Sam discovered that he was two inches taller than he had been before the adventure.

So, if Sam could withstand a little discomfort, why should it be any different for me? If things were to get a little physical, then that would be just fine. I'd been around the block a few times. If trouble was lurking around the corner, just let it show its ugly head. I wasn't afraid of—

I stopped in mid-thought. I listened to myself for a minute. What the heck was I saying? I had to be completely honest with myself—a confrontation was the last thing on my wish list. If I somehow managed to locate Josh and convinced him to leave the compound with me and if I could do so without any physical altercations, I would be thrilled. I was Charlie Collier, Snoop for Hire. I wasn't Sam Solomon. Who was I kidding anyway?

CHAPTER 19

The Lyin' Tamer Caper

It wasn't long before we were all seated and our dinners were placed before us. Unfortunately the meals we were now staring at in no way resembled the feast that the last group had enjoyed. The steak, double-baked potato, and sweet corn had been replaced by soupy mashed potatoes, cold green beans, and a piece of tough, fatty mystery meat. Appetizing, this was not.

"I take back what I said earlier," Evan muttered under his breath. "The sooner you can get us out of here, the better."

The expressions on the faces of the other dinner guests ranged from shock to disappointment to outright disgust. The colonel had made a real statement with this menu. And it was loud and clear—we were anything but camp favorites. Some of the kids played with their food, others pushed it away, but amazingly, a few devoured it.

I guess it had a lot to do with how hungry you were—and what you were used to at home. I don't ever remember thinking that my mom was a master chef, but after this experience, I made a pledge right there and then to appreciate her cooking and to let her know it.

Our attention was suddenly drawn to a commotion at the far end of the hall. I stood to see what was happening. I spotted about a dozen or so camp personnel dressed in army fatigues making their way into the mess hall. Positioned directly in the middle of the group was Colonel Culpepper. You couldn't miss him. He was decked out in full military dress blues—with a chest full of ribbons and medals. He marched to the center of the room, where someone handed him a microphone.

"Good evening, gentlemen, and welcome to Camp Phoenix. I hope you're finding the accommodations satisfactory."

I wasn't sure if he was actually serious or if he was just toying with us. It was hard to tell. He was expressionless.

"I suggest that you get a good night's sleep," he continued, "because tomorrow promises to be a day you will never forget."

"What's that supposed to mean?" Evan whispered.

I shrugged.

"Our goal," the colonel said, "is to break you of your bad habits and to reintroduce you into society as contributing members of your community. When you leave Camp Phoenix, you will no longer be referred to as thieves, thugs, vandals, or the like. You will be welcomed back with open arms."

Considering the fact that the room was filled with undesirables—*the bad kids in town*—I found it was amazing just how quiet everyone had become. Colonel Harvard Culpepper had either earned the respect of the group or he had instilled fear in them. I wasn't quite sure yet which it was.

"You may have noticed," he said, "that the living quarters here at the compound are in what we might refer to as a *dichotomous* state."

"Huh?" Evan said.

"He means that there's a big difference between this hall and the one across the road," I said. Besides Evan, I noticed a bunch of the kids had confused looks on their faces. Every so often, I was thankful that I had religiously studied my vocab words each week.

"This is," the colonel said with his arms raised, "Repentance Hall. The name says it all. You are here to pay for your sins. And, so, beginning tomorrow, you will start off with a regimen of toil and travail befitting the *miscreants* you are."

Evan tapped me on the arm and shrugged. He needed another translation.

"You don't want to know," I said.

Culpepper spun around, put a finger to his lips, and smiled. "But there is another way," he said.

The mess hall became eerily quiet.

"You *could* find yourselves on the fast track to Resurrection Hall and avoid all of these unpleasantries. But in order to do that, you'd have to have the right stuff. You'd have to have character and initiative. And you'd have to pledge your allegiance to this institution. Is there anyone in this room willing to make that sacrifice?"

Nearly every hand in the room shot into the air.

"That's what I was hoping to see," the colonel said. "But it's not as easy as just wanting it. You'll have to earn it."

As I sat there and listened intently, I realized that I knew very little about this man. I wasn't sure how he had gotten to where he was today, but there was something fascinating about him. I thought back to what Eugene had said about Colonel Culpepper a few days earlier—that he couldn't be trusted. But here he was, trying to give these troubled kids a second chance—and trying to make it as painless as possible for them. Maybe Eugene just didn't understand the guy.

I was beginning to see why Josh had reacted the way he had earlier in the day. Maybe he really was happy here. The colonel had obviously won him over. After all, the man was dynamic. He was the sort of fellow you'd want to follow. And he had this group eating right out of his hand. Colonel Harvard Culpepper was either a con man, like Eugene thought, or he was the real deal. And right at that moment, it was sure looking like the latter.

"And so each evening at dinnertime," the colonel said, "my staff and I will walk down these aisles and decide which of you will advance to a special program of rehabilitation and enlightenment. So, if you're still interested, keep those arms raised high, and you just may be fortunate enough to join the winning team."

It was starting to get a little crazy. Kids were muscling each other in their efforts to be noticed by the colonel and his team. Evan and I kept our hands raised and waited patiently for our chance.

The colonel and company strolled down each aisle and began choosing candidates for the program. It was critical that I be picked—for a number of reasons. First, the idea of more meals like this one was starting to give me a knot in my stomach. Second, the accommodations at Resurrection Hall would be a definite upgrade. And the third and most important reason—it would make it much easier to locate and talk to Josh.

As the colonel's party turned the corner and headed for our table, most of the kids on either side of Evan and me went out of their way to be noticed. They extended their arms so high up into the air that I wouldn't have been surprised if a few had actually hurt themselves. The colonel was now only a few feet away. Whenever his assistants would point to a kid, the colonel would either nod or shake his head. And every so often, he would make a comment to them. The moment of truth was now upon us. When one of the assistants pointed to Evan, the colonel put his finger to his lips. He was in deep thought. Then he smiled and nodded.

"He has an innocent face," he said. "That could come in handy."

Evan was in. It was now my turn. When another assistant in fatigues pointed in my direction, the colonel just shook his head. He leaned in to the others to avoid being overheard, but I could hear him loud and clear.

"Are you joking? Look at him. He's obviously too slow. He won't be able to outrun anybody."

Outrun? I wasn't sure what he was talking about. What difference did that make? I didn't know why I had even gotten my hopes up in the first place. I had been through this before—a million times. When you have a physique like mine, you're always the last one picked on the playground. Why should this be any different?

The selection process continued for several more minutes. Evan seemed to avoid eye contact with me. I knew he felt bad, but he had to be thrilled about being chosen. He was now on easy street. Whatever paces he would be put through in the days to come had to be less painful than what was in store for the rest of us. I was upset with myself. I wasn't sure what I could have done to have brought about a different outcome, but I knew that I had blown an opportunity that would have made it easier to solve this case. What if I never got another chance to talk to Josh? I needed a plan—a new plan—and fast.

A minute or so later, the buzzer sounded. The staff immediately started breaking us up into two groups—those lucky enough to be headed to Resurrection Hall and those destined to return to the slums of Repentance Hall. Evan smiled weakly at me and followed his new team members. I was still angry. Why couldn't it have been me? I had to get past this. There was no sense beating myself up. I never had a chance.

We were soon corralled and forced to march in single file back to our rooms. As I plopped down on the cot, one of the building guards stood in the doorway.

"There's always tomorrow, kid," he said. "But to be perfectly honest, unless you get yourself in shape, you ain't going nowhere. This place is gonna be home sweet home for quite some time." He pulled the door shut.

Now, normally a comment like that would have bothered me. But I had proven, more times than I could remember, that I was capable of handling myself in situations like these. I was determined to make him eat those words.

I decided to lie down and think things through. It was probably best to make my move after dark, so I needed to kill a couple of hours anyway. I started thinking about people back home. I wondered what my parents would do to me when they found out that I wasn't with Sherman and the other kids on a camping trip. I'd be grounded for sure. But since Gram knew what I was up to, maybe she could soften them up a little for me. Then again, I had given Gram my word that I wouldn't come here unless I had a way to communicate with her. She wouldn't be happy when she learned that I had broken my promise.

Eugene had made himself very clear about his dislike for Colonel Culpepper. I had a feeling that he wouldn't be pleased about my decision to come to the boot camp. I wondered if Henry or Scarlett would find my backpack in the bushes and discover the note I had left for them. But they really had no reason to look for it. They were under the impression that I had gone home. I could only hope Henry didn't call my house looking for me. Then my parents would know for sure that something was up.

I put my hands behind my head and closed my eyes. I hadn't intended to fall asleep, but at about nine thirty, I was rudely awakened by the sound of slamming doors in the hallway. I decided to see what was going on. I didn't need to use my business card to open the door since the soap that I had jammed into the hole in the door frame was still doing its job. I slowly opened the door and poked my head out. I could see some of the boys returning to their rooms. I immediately recognized a couple of kids that the colonel had chosen for his fast-track program. That probably meant Evan would be coming back too. I hadn't expected to see them back here. I would have thought they'd be permanent residents of Resurrection Hall by now. One thing was for sure—I was dying to know where they had been taken and to find out what had happened.

It was time to make my move. The first thing I did was to change out of the orange jumpsuit and back into my street clothes. That way I would be less obvious and might just be able to blend in with the kids from Resurrection Hall if necessary. The plan was to go downstairs and see if Evan was back yet. He'd fill me in on what was going on. I stuck my head out the door. The coast was clear. I pulled the door closed behind me and tiptoed the length of the hallway. I stopped at the stairwell to make sure no one had seen me. When I was certain I was alone, I ran down the stairs and up to Evan's door. I knocked lightly.

"Evan, it's me, Charlie. I gotta talk to you."

There was no sound from inside. I wondered if he had returned to his room yet, but his door was closed. I had noticed earlier that most doors were left open when the rooms were vacant. I decided to knock a second time.

"Go away," a voice said.

It was definitely Evan's voice, but he didn't sound too happy to see me.

"It's Charlie Collier. Can I come in?" I said. "Here, I'll slide the card under the door." I pulled out the laminated business card that Gram had given me and slid it under his door. Seconds later, it reappeared. Evan had kicked it back out.

"What's wrong?" I said.

"I can't talk to you anymore," he said.

"Why? What happened? Don't you want to get out of here with me and Josh?"

"No."

I wasn't sure what had changed. What had happened to Evan in the past couple of hours? I needed to find out.

"I just need two minutes—tops—I promise," I said.

"Charlie, please, just leave. It's better this way."

"I don't understand."

"I'm going to sleep. Good night," he said. And that was it.

I heard something coming from the exit right around the corner. It sounded like a door opening and closing. I crept to the end of the hallway and peeked out. There was no one there. The guard who was usually manning the door was gone. This was my chance. Then I noticed what looked like a tiny orange light outside moving ever so slightly a few yards from the door. I wasn't sure what it was at first, but I soon realized that the guard had stepped outside for a cigarette break. Apparently the colonel condoned a few bad habits.

The exit had six doors with push handles on each one. There was a small window, maybe eight inches square, in each door. I scooted to the doors and crouched down. Then I straightened up and peeked out. The guard was about fifteen feet from the door on the extreme left. I might just be able to sneak out the door on the right if I was really quiet. Once I made it outside, I was certain I would be able to sneak around. It was really dark out there. I decided to take a chance.

I got down on all fours, reached up for the handle, and pushed. I felt the door open. So far, so good. I used my hip to open it wide enough for me to slip out. I glanced at the guard. His back was to me. Perfect. I crawled all the way out and reached back to ease the door closed softly. But it slipped out of my hand and slammed shut. Oh no.

"Who is that?" the guard yelled out. "Who's there?"

I wedged myself between a bush and the building wall. I was afraid to move. For a second, I considered getting up and taking off, but this fellow appeared to be in pretty good shape. I was worried that he'd be able to outrun me, so I decided to stay put for the time being. When I heard footsteps coming toward me, I held my breath. From the corner of my eye, I could see his feet. He was wearing military boots. He tossed the cigarette to the ground, barely missing me, and stamped it out. Then I heard the door open and he was gone. A perfect escape. Sam Solomon would be so proud. It was almost as smooth as Sam's getaway in Episode #32—*The Lyin' Tamer Caper.*

In this mystery, Sam had been hired by the owner of a traveling circus to locate funds that had disappeared. Sam began interrogating some of the circus performers. Soon he identified his chief suspect—the lion tamer. When Sam pressed him, the handler released his big cat and instructed the animal to make quick work of the nosy detective. What the lion tamer was unaware of, however, was the knowledge that Sam possessed from a previous case. A few months earlier, Sam had been hired by the game warden in a remote section of eastern Africa to help thwart a band of poachers who were killing lions. It was from this experience that Sam learned not only how to survive a lion attack, but also how to hypnotize the lion. And so, while this oversize cat was catching a few z's, the police were tossing his handler into the deep freeze.

With my successful escape, I was starting to feel as though I actually had earned the right to hand out the business cards that my grandmother had given me.

CHAPTER 20

The Whine and Roses Caper

I moved along the outside wall of Repentance Hall as quietly as possible, careful not to step on twigs or dried leaves or anything that might make a sound and alert camp guards that I was on the loose. There were lights on in most of the rooms in Resurrection Hall. The mess hall was dark, but another building was brightly lit. It was about a hundred yards away and looked like some sort of auditorium. Since I was in street clothes, I decided to work my way over to Resurrection Hall and try to blend in with the other kids. I wanted to take another stab at locating Josh and trying to convince him to leave the compound with me. If not, maybe I could at least find out why he wanted to stay here so badly.

I scanned the general vicinity for activity. Seeing none, I was ready to make my attempt. I counted to three, put my head down, and ran across the road in the direction of the other hall. The darkness was providing perfect cover. I snaked my way through the elaborate landscaping and made it to the side of the building. I took baby steps as I moved in the direction of the front door. When I was no more than twenty yards away, I heard voices. I pressed my back against the wall and held my breath.

I couldn't make out what the kids were saying, but it seemed as if the entire building was emptying out. I watched quietly for a few minutes. I soon realized that they were headed in the direction of the building that looked like an auditorium. I inched closer to the front door and waited for my chance to slip in undetected. When I noticed a break in the crowd, I decided to take the plunge. I emerged from the bushes and headed for the front sidewalk. As I looked back, I could see more kids coming down the front steps, but it didn't appear anyone was aware that I had just infiltrated their ranks.

This was going perfectly. I slowed down and allowed a few of the kids to catch up to me so I didn't stand out as a loner. When three other boys were walking alongside me, I decided to take action—to do what I had come here to do.

"Hey, have any of you guys seen Josh around?" I said. "We were supposed to walk together."

All three of them looked at me as if I had two heads or something.

"You know . . . Josh *Doyle*?" I said.

"What are you talking about?" the middle boy said. "We don't use names here. You should know that. We all have numbers. If you know your friend's number, then maybe we can help you."

"Hmm, let me think," I said. I was stalling, but I didn't know what else to do. Maybe if I described Josh . . . maybe then they might know. "I just can't seem to remember his number. But he's sixteen, about your height, and he's got a bad leg. He has trouble walking."

The boy on the end tapped the middle kid on the shoulder. "He must be talking about the guy with the limp. I think he's the only one with a problem like that."

"You must be mean number one nineteen," the first boy said.

I slapped my forehead. "That's it, of course. Now why couldn't I remember that?"

"He left after us. I remember seeing him," the middle boy said as he pointed behind us. "He's gotta be back there somewhere."

"Thanks. Thanks a lot," I said. I quickly excused myself and began moving against the flow. I scanned the area for Josh. It was pretty dark, although there were lamps in the ground about every twenty feet lighting our way. I was getting a lot of stares from the others. Walking in the opposite direction as everyone else will do that. I had traveled about fifty yards when I spotted him. He was walking by himself. He appeared to be split off from a group of kids all heading this way. I waited for him to catch up to me and then conveniently slipped in next to him.

He seemed startled. "Oh no, not you again," he said.

"Josh, I gotta talk to you."

"I have nothing else to say."

"Just tell me what's going on here," I said. "Why don't you want to go home? I don't understand."

He stopped and grabbed me by the shoulders. "Listen, Charlie, this is my home now. I'm making a difference here. Some people may not approve of our tactics, but I'm making this planet a safer place for all of us. You're just going to have to accept that and leave me alone. If I get caught talking to you—" He stared right at me with these piercing eyes. "Hey, how'd you manage to get out here? You're not one of us yet."

"You can't tell anyone," I said. "I escaped from Repentance Hall. It was the only way to get to you."

Josh shook his head. "Oh, that's just great. If they catch me with someone from your group, we could both end up in the brig."

"The brig?"

"It's a military jail. They've got one here somewhere," he said. "At least, that's what they tell us."

"What can I say to convince you to leave here with me?" I said.

"Nothing." He pulled away. "Now just leave me alone."

I watched Josh merge into the crowd and disappear. This wasn't going well. I was thinking about just ending the investigation right here and figuring out a way to get out of this place. At least then I'd be able to report to Sherman that I had found his brother, even though I hadn't delivered him. That was better than nothing, right? I wondered how easy it might be to break away from the group and locate an exit somewhere. But the more I thought about giving up, the more I realized just how disappointed Sam Solomon would be with me. Sam wasn't a quitter—and neither was I. At least, I didn't think I was.

As I watched the crowd file into the auditorium, I knew I had to make a decision. I wasn't sure if I should stick it out. I had hit a speed bump. And I was beginning to feel like a failure. Then I began to think about everything I had accomplished up to this point. I had figured out where Josh was. I had managed to sneak onto this compound. I had successfully escaped from my quarters, and I had found Josh. Heck, I had actually talked to him. I *had* accomplished something. I wasn't a failure. I might be a little frustrated with the current state of affairs, but that was no reason to give up. I would see this through. I had to.

I followed the group into the building. If I was ever going to be able to convince Josh to leave with me, then

I had to find out what kind of hold Culpepper had on him. This was a kid who wanted to save the world. How many animals or trees or whatnot could he save while stuck in this place? There was something strange going on here, and I was determined to find out what it was.

I followed the others into a large theater and found a seat in the last row. I wanted to remain as inconspicuous as possible. Maybe it was my imagination, but it seemed that a few of the other kids were staring at me. I needed to make it look as though I belonged here. I smiled and tried to appear confident. There were probably about two hundred kids in the hall. We were obviously waiting for some kind of presentation, although I had no idea what to expect.

A moment later, the lights dimmed. It triggered a buzz from the crowd. Everyone seemed to know what was coming. The sound of beating drums soon followed. The room began to vibrate. Then a musical fanfare of deafening proportions could be heard. I held my ears. Crowd members started cheering. A spotlight fell on an empty stage. Then a trapdoor on the stage floor slid open and out of it rose a figure dressed in a brilliant white uniform—it was Colonel Culpepper. Before I knew what had happened, I was in the midst of a standing ovation. I jumped to my feet. I had to appear to be a member of this elite group.

As the music faded out, the colonel motioned with

his hands for us to be seated. You couldn't help but be impressed with this presentation. The colonel obviously knew how to put on a show.

"Good evening, my friends," he began. "It's so good to be with you—my chosen ones—once again."

The audience members sat on the edges of their seats in anticipation of the colonel's next words. It was as if they were in some hypnotic trance.

"In a few moments, you will leave this auditorium and make your way to the adjacent conference rooms, where you will receive your next assignments," Colonel Culpepper said. "But before that, I would like to tell you about some upgrades that we are making here at Camp Phoenix."

Every eye in the room was glued to the speaker.

The colonel reached into his pocket and pulled out a shiny silver object. "Tonight you will each receive your own . . . smart phones."

Thunderous applause followed.

"We want to be able to stay in contact with you at all times. But that's not all." The colonel motioned to someone offstage. Sergeant Stanley ran out and handed him something. The colonel immediately held the object over his head. "Following your next successful assignment, each of you will receive your own . . . computer tablet—the latest model from Magnatech."

Audience members jumped to their feet and

applauded loudly. I found myself thinking about Henry. He would kill for some of these toys.

"And there's more," the colonel said with a grin. "We will soon be removing the fifty-inch LCD TV from the Resurrection Hall lounge and will replace it with a *seventy-inch* LED screen."

The kids were having a difficult time containing themselves.

"And now our last bit of good news," Colonel Culpepper said. "As soon as we are able to reach our next fiscal goal, we will begin construction on a new coffeehouse here on the compound. And like everything else at Camp Phoenix, all of the mochas, lattes, and cappuccinos will be, of course . . . free of charge."

The kids in the audience cheered uncontrollably and began stomping their feet.

The colonel calmly held up his hands and motioned for everyone to quiet down and take their seats again.

"There is one more bit of news—disturbing news—that I must share with you," the colonel said. "A few minutes ago, following bed check, I was informed that one of the residents from Repentance Hall is missing." His voice became deadly serious. "This young man disobeyed orders and left his room. He will face severe consequences for his actions."

My heart suddenly began to race. I could feel it beating right through my chest. I was fairly certain that he was talking about me. I had to remain calm. If I looked even the slightest bit guilty, one of these kids would figure out that I didn't belong here and turn me in.

"If any of you have information about this individual," the colonel continued, "it is your sworn duty to inform the proper authorities. Failure to do so would place you in a very precarious position. Trust me—you don't want this to happen."

Most of the kids started looking around the auditorium trying to spot the intruder. I kept feeling that many of the stares were directed my way. In an effort to avoid suspicion, I decided to join the others. I glanced in all directions, as if I was also looking for the uninvited guest.

"Here are the rooms in which you are scheduled to meet immediately following this forum." The colonel pointed to a large screen that was in the process of descending from above. "Look for your number and room location." On the screen was a series of numbers under room names.

I looked for Josh's number—one nineteen. I decided that I would try to slip into the same conference room he was headed to. I assumed I would learn a lot by watching the campers receive their various assignments. After a few seconds, I spotted Josh's number under the Fort Dearborn conference room. I just needed to stay as cool as possible in order to pull this off.

"And one more thing," the colonel said. "Because of the security breach, as you enter each meeting room, be certain to show your Camp Phoenix ID card. We just want to make sure that our *friend* is not in this very room with all of us."

Once I heard that, I knew there was no way to follow Josh into his meeting. I would have to kill time some other way and then wait to talk with him after the meeting had ended. As the crowd emptied out of the auditorium, I couldn't help but think of Sam Solomon. I seemed to remember an episode where Sam had become the hunted one, like me tonight. Which one was it again? Oh yeah—Episode #36—*The Whine and Roses Caper.*

In this story, Sam had been hired by a man whose sister had mysteriously died a day after her thirty-fifth wedding anniversary. A coroner's report found that she had been poisoned. The brother suspected her husband, who would endlessly whine and complain about his wife, but the police were unable to tie him to the murder. Sam soon determined that the woman had been poisoned after having pricked her finger on a thorn from a bouquet of roses. Sam found traces of arsenic on each of the thorns in the vase. But before he was able to inform his client or the police, Sam discovered that the husband had become the hunter and he was the prey. The P.I. soon found himself running for his life. But in time, Sam got the drop on his suspect and was able to bring him to justice.

Is that what I was in for tonight? I wondered. Although I was hoping to maintain my deception, I had to prepare myself for the worst in the event that my cover was blown. I watched the others file into conference rooms adjacent to the auditorium. And as badly as I wanted to know what was happening in those rooms, I knew that without a camp ID card, there was no way I would dare venture anywhere near that area.

I slipped down one of the hallways to look for a hiding place until the meetings ended. Then I figured I would just blend in with the crowd and head back to Resurrection Hall—and a rendezvous with Josh, I hoped. Most of the doors in the main hallway were closed up tight. Even the doors to the restrooms were locked. The overhead lights were bright. If anyone came by now, they'd spot me for sure.

Then I heard a door open about thirty feet ahead. A man carrying a broom and pushing a large trash basket on squeaky wheels emerged. He soon disappeared around a corner. The man was obviously a member of the cleaning staff. This was my chance. The janitor had left the door open, so there was a good chance he'd be back. But since it was the only room available at the moment, I decided to proceed. I slipped in and looked for a place to hide.

The room turned out to be a huge, plush office. The desk, in the center of the room, was massive. The walls were floor-to-ceiling bookshelves. There was a long, glass conference table on one end with cushy chairs all around it. The person who belonged to this office was certainly living large. When I heard the squeaky wheels from the trash can right outside the door, I scrambled for a place to hide. I ducked down behind a large copy machine and hoped for the best.

I could hear the workman sweeping up and moving trash around in the room. The area behind the copy machine was filled with dust. I held my nose, fearful that I might sneeze and give myself away. A few minutes later, the room went dark, and I could hear the door close. At first I was afraid to move. The colonel had sounded pretty serious about the consequences if the person at large—namely me—were caught.

I counted to one hundred before standing—and even then, I was nervous. The light under the door from the hallway allowed me to tiptoe over to the light switch and turn it on. My first instinct was to search the place, but I didn't exactly know what I was looking for. I figured that if I could convince Josh to talk to me, then I'd find out everything I needed to know anyway. Then I thought about calling Gram. I had promised that I'd stay in contact with her. It might be a good idea to bring her up to speed on the investigation and ask her to update Eugene. I plopped down in one of the cushy chairs and reached for the receiver. I had my hand on the phone when I found myself admiring the room. *Pretty sweet digs,* I thought. I tried to imagine an office like this in the future. It sure put our garage, or Eugene's office for that matter, to shame. Who knew—maybe someday I'd have a successful practice and be able to furnish an office in a similar fashion.

I was just about to lift the receiver when I heard voices in the hallway and a key being inserted into the door lock. I ran over to turn off the light and slipped back behind the copy machine. I was hoping it was only the cleaning staff. But when I realized who had entered the office, I knew that I had bigger problems on my hands than being discovered by a janitor.

CHAPTER 21

The Quiche of Death Caper

I closed my eyes and dared not make a sound. Now I knew why this was such a glitzy office. It belonged to the Man—and if he found me, my days on this planet were numbered.

"Colonel," a voice said, "should I put this in the safe?"

I peeked around the copy machine to see Colonel Harvard Culpepper and his man Friday—Sergeant Stanley.

"Did you count it?" the colonel asked.

"Yes, sir. It's a little over twelve hundred dollars."

"That's it?" the colonel said. "The boys are slipping. Go ahead and lock it up."

The sergeant carried the sack of cash to the far wall and set it down on a file cabinet. Then he reached up and removed a large painting of General George Patton, which had been covering up a wall safe. He fingered the tumbler and had it open in seconds.

It was a large safe—at least a foot and a half square. From my vantage point, I could see that it was nearly full. The sergeant reached in and pulled out what looked like a mink jacket.

"Colonel, do you think it's safe now to fence these furs? We're running out of room in here."

The colonel walked over and took the mink from the sergeant. He rubbed his fingers across it and smiled.

"This is prime stuff," the colonel said. "I forget—who got this for us?"

"Don't you remember?" the sergeant said. "It was one nineteen."

"One nineteen?"

"The kid with the limp. You know, Colonel, he's probably our best earner."

"You don't say."

Oh my God. They were talking about Josh. Their *best earner*? What did they mean by that?

"Well, let's be sure to keep him happy, then," the colonel said.

"Not a problem. The kid'll do anything we say," Sergeant Stanley said, "as long as he thinks he's saving the planet." He chuckled. "Steal the furs, kid, and you'll stop the senseless slaughter of minks and chinchillas and whatnot. Steal from the pet stores so they can't buy any more animals from the puppy mills. And my favorite," the sergeant said with a grin, "rob the beauty salon so they stop using chemicals that'll eat through the ozone layer."

The colonel laughed. "That kid is such a sap."

"Speaking of saps, what about the mayor and council members?"

"They're even dumber," the colonel said.

And all at once, everything became crystal clear. Colonel Culpepper wasn't rehabilitating these boys. He was assembling his own personal army of thieves. It was the perfect cover. All the recent robberies in the area had to have been his doing. He must have sent his troops out into the streets to steal for him, and then he rewarded them with smart phones and computer tablets and big-screen TVs and whatever else they wanted. What a life. What kid could pass it up? And if any of his troops got caught, the police would arrest them, and then the next day the Camp Phoenix bus would pick them up—and the whole cycle would start all over again. I had to give the colonel credit. His plan was sinister, all right, but it was brilliant. And poor Josh was just an unsuspecting pawn in this chess match. He'd do anything to help save the environment, and the colonel just happened to have figured out how to make it work to his benefit.

As I crouched behind the copy machine, fighting off the dust bunnies, I thought about what had occurred a minute earlier. I was excited about uncovering the colonel's scheme, but I was also angry with myself. I should have figured this out before—after the first robbery. As was usually the case, Gram was right. When she witnessed the beauty shop heist, she had noticed that one of the robbers had a limp. I now knew for certain that it was Josh all along. And Gram was right about something else—she somehow knew that I would inevitably be drawn into this case and would eventually get to the bottom of these unsolved burglaries.

I now knew exactly what had to be done. Once the colonel and the sergeant left, I would use the office phone and call Gram and Eugene. I was sure they'd run on over. And then, while waiting for them to arrive, I would somehow try to sneak out of here and blend in with the other kids one more time. I'd try to find Josh and explain to him how he had been duped by the colonel. Armed with new information, I was certain that he would want to leave the camp now. But for some reason, I knew that rescuing Josh just wasn't good enough. I had been hired to find him and bring him home, but I now had an even bigger assignment facing me—I needed to somehow thwart Colonel Culpepper's scheme and bring down his evil empire. It was my duty as a law-abiding citizen.

At that very moment, I knew exactly how Sam Solomon must have felt. There were a number of times when Sam not only solved the case for his client, but also reported his findings to the police. He hadn't been paid to do so, but Sam was a law-and-order guy. Take, for example, Episode #37—*The Quiche of Death Caper.*

In this mystery, Sam had been hired by a woman whose husband had become violently ill one night after dinner. The woman asked Sam to determine the cause of his illness since doctors were baffled. The master detective soon discovered that a recipe the woman had followed on that fateful night was to blame. Sam immediately sought out the author of the cookbook. But upon further investigation, he learned that a disgruntled employee—the cookbook's editor—and not the author was the real culprit. Before the book had gone to press, the editor had altered the recipes just enough to produce deadly results. The spiteful editor had apparently been passed over for promotion and was determined to seek revenge against the publisher. Sam eventually brought his findings to the authorities—a gesture he considered to be his civic duty.

And now it was my obligation to report my findings to the police. I kept still, just waiting for an opportunity to escape. Seconds later, I knew I'd have my chance.

"Colonel, the boys should have received their next assignments by now," the sergeant said. "Should I release them?"

"I'd like to do it myself," the colonel said. "I want to see the looks on their faces when they receive their new phones."

A minute later, the lights went off and the door slammed shut. It was now time to get to work.

I ran over to the phone on the colonel's desk and picked up the receiver. But just as I was about to dial, I was stopped in my tracks.

"Did you want to place a call, Colonel?" an operator said.

I immediately hung up the phone. I had underestimated the security at Camp Phoenix. There was no way I'd be able to call out from any of the phones here. The operators apparently placed each call. I had to think of another way to arrange for reinforcements. I turned the lights off, opened the door, stuck my head out, and glanced down the hallway. I could see some of the kids milling about in the lobby. It appeared that the meetings had ended. It was now time to slip in with the others.

I casually strolled into the lobby, all the while oozing confidence. I had to look as if I was a bona fide member of this group. Since they were all now on the lookout for an intruder, I couldn't take any chances. I circulated for a few minutes but was unable to locate Josh. I decided it would be best to head back to Resurrection Hall and try to track him down there. I followed the others out of the auditorium and across the field. The footlights in the grass guided us back to the hall.

When I reached the front steps, I hesitated. I wasn't

sure which room Josh was in. I noticed a kid standing a few feet away.

"Hey, I'm looking for one nineteen," I said. "Would you happen to know what room he's in?"

The kid made a face and folded his arms. "One nineteen?"

"Yeah."

"Duh," he said. "Why don't you try *room* one nineteen? How long have you been here? Any idiot knows that."

I shook my head and smiled. "I *am* an idiot." I patted the kid on the back. "Sorry, thanks again."

I knew I had played that badly. I proceeded up the stone steps. When I glanced back over my shoulder, I noticed that the same kid was now standing with two other campers. He seemed to be pointing at me and telling them something. That wasn't a good sign. I scooted down the first-floor hallway and searched for Josh's room. I found it near the end of the hallway. I doubted that he'd be happy to see me, but it was important that I find him. I had to tell him how he had been deceived by the colonel. I knocked lightly. A few seconds later, the door opened slowly.

"Collier!" Josh cried. "What the heck are you doing here? I can't be seen talking to you. You have to get out of here right now."

"Josh, I gotta talk to you. It's really important. It'll only take a minute."

"Are you crazy? Do you know what'll happen to me . . . to both of us . . . if we're caught together? These people don't mess around." He slammed the door shut.

So now what? What could I say that would convince him I just wanted to help? I knocked again—this time more forcefully.

The door opened. Josh appeared nervous *and* angry. "Just go, Charlie. Please. There's a ton of people looking for you."

"Josh, this place isn't what it appears to be. The colonel's a thief. Can't you see that?"

"You don't know what you're talking about," he said.

"Oh no? I know for a fact that you robbed a fur store, a pet shop, and a beauty salon."

Josh grabbed me by the front of the shirt, pulled me into his room, shut the door, and pushed me down onto his bed.

"I don't know how you found that out," he said, "but there was a reason—a legitimate reason—for doing it."

"That's what he wants you to think. But he's been tricking you."

"I don't believe you," Josh said.

"The colonel wants you to think that you're helping save the environment, but it's all a sham. Trust me. I was hiding in his office. I heard the whole thing."

Josh squeezed the sides of his head. "I don't believe

any of this. The colonel is just like me. He cares about this planet."

"All he cares about is lining his pockets," I said. I got up off the bed. "One of these days, you're gonna get caught. And they're gonna throw your sorry butt in jail—not for a few days, but for a few years."

"Good," he said. "I'd welcome that. It'll give me a chance to study our flawed penal system."

Oh, brother. This guy was something else. Was there any cause he wasn't fighting for?

"I heard Colonel Culpepper, with my own ears, call you a *sap* because you were so naïve," I said.

"I refuse to believe that. You're making all of this up."

I wasn't sure what else to tell him. I was arguing my case the best I could, but I was right back where I had started. If I couldn't win Josh over, then I was all alone. I needed to think of something to at least save my own neck. I immediately noticed a phone—a shiny new smart phone on Josh's desk. I walked over and picked it up.

"I have a friend who has a phone just like this," I said.

"Put it down," he said.

I tapped the screen and stared at the keyboard. "You know, I've never really figured out how to do that texting thing. Seems awfully complicated." I then began feverishly tapping letters.

"What are you doing?" he said as he tried to grab it back.

I turned away and continued punching the tiny buttons.

A moment later, Josh had managed to wrestle it away. He angrily wiped the screen clean on the front of his shirt.

"I want you out of here right now," he said.

"I'm not leaving until—"

Josh abruptly covered my mouth with his hand. "Did you hear that?" he whispered. "There's someone out there. We have to hide you."

But before either of us could react, someone out in the hallway threw a shoulder into Josh's door, breaking it open. Splintered wood from the door frame littered the floor.

We found ourselves staring at Sergeant Stanley and at least a dozen members of his goon squad, all in riot gear.

The sergeant crossed his arms and shook his head. "Number one nineteen, what do you have to say for yourself?"

Josh pointed at me. "He forced his way in. I couldn't stop him."

"Do you know what the penalty is for harboring a fugitive?"

"But I didn't do anything," he argued.

The sergeant reached over and grabbed the cell phone from Josh's hand. "Give me that," he said. "You won't be needing this where you're headed. Let's go."

"Where are you taking us?" Josh asked.

"Oh, didn't I tell you?" the sergeant said. "Congratulations are in order. The two of you have won the grand prize—a private audience with the colonel."

CHAPTER 22

The Dead See Caper

Sergeant Stanley and his posse escorted us to a familiar place—Colonel Culpepper's office. Josh and I sat in a pair of hard-backed chairs awaiting our fate. The colonel hovered over us while at the same time examining my business card.

"This Charlie Collier character. Is that who you work for, young man?" he asked me.

At that very moment I knew exactly what I should have done. I should have kept my mouth shut and denied everything. But I couldn't help myself. This guy was so arrogant. Someone had to put him in his place. I guess my ego got the best of me.

"Hardly. Charlie Collier is yours truly," I said. "And for your information, I happen to be a professional private investigator."

The colonel threw his head back and laughed. "That's the best joke I've heard in a long time."

"It's no joke," I said.

The colonel's expression suddenly soured. "Listen, kid, whatever it is that you came here to investigate, I'm afraid you won't find it."

"I already found out what I was looking for," I said confidently.

"And that would be?" the colonel asked.

"Well, initially I was hired to find Josh and bring him home. But then I stumbled upon something far more intriguing."

"Oh?" the colonel said.

"You might be interested in knowing that I had the opportunity to listen in on a conversation between you and one of your staff members. And I now know everything."

"You know nothing," he snapped.

Now, right at that point, if I had learned anything from Sam Solomon, it should have been to shut my trap and refuse to continue. I knew I had piqued the colonel's curiosity, and I should have left it at that. He would think that I was bluffing and might be inclined to let us go just to get us out of his hair. But that wasn't the case. Apparently I hadn't learned a thing. The next words out of my mouth would seal our fate. It felt really good to say them, but I had badly misplayed my hand. I had revealed my cards far too early.

"I know how your little scam works, Colonel," I said.

"You send your bus out to the various jails in the area to pick up teenage offenders and claim that you can rehabilitate them. But you have no intention of doing that. You're just recruiting a new batch of thieves. You send them out to rob and steal from local businesses . . . and in return, the kids live here in plush quarters with every electronic gadget they could ever want. And if they get arrested, they're sent right back here, and the dirty little cycle continues."

"You have quite an imagination, Mr. Collier," Colonel Culpepper said. "Just try proving it."

"That's the easy part," I said. I pointed to the portrait on the far wall. "Once the police look in the safe behind General Patton over there, they'll have all the proof they need."

Colonel Culpepper and Sergeant Stanley exchanged nervous glances.

"By the way, Colonel, you might want to have the cleaning people vacuum up all the dust bunnies behind the copier. It made for a good hiding place but could use a little tidying up."

"Why, you nosy little brats," the sergeant said. "What should I do with them, Colonel?"

Josh jumped up. "Wait a minute. Wait just a minute. Colonel, tell this kid he's all wrong. Tell him he doesn't know what he's talking about. Tell him how much you love the environment and how you just want to protect it—like me."

"Boy, you are dumb," the colonel said. "Do me a favor and just shut up." The colonel pushed Josh back down into his seat, walked around to the front of his desk, and smiled at me. He was still holding my business card. "Well done, Charlie Collier, Snoop for Hire. It's just too bad that you won't be around to share any of your findings with the authorities." He turned to the sergeant. "Make our little friends disappear."

"What if anyone comes here looking for them?" the sergeant asked.

"Sergeant Stanley, I'm counting on you to remove all traces of these infidels. Make it seem as if they never existed."

The sergeant saluted. "Any suggestions, sir?"

"Throw them in the toolshed for tonight," the colonel said. "We'll discuss our options in the morning."

Now, most sixth-graders upon hearing those words would probably have cried out for their mommies, but not this one. I immediately thought—been there, done that. Just ask Rupert Olsen, who happened to be serving a lengthy prison sentence, thanks to me and my associates. When he held us captive in his basement a couple of months earlier, he planned to stuff us like all of his exotic birds. But he never got the chance to carry out his threats. So, the colonel's tough talk didn't scare me. I had been in jams like this before and managed to escape. There was no reason to believe this would be any different—at least, I hoped so.

Josh and I were placed in the back of a military jeep and driven off. We traveled what had to be at least a couple of miles before stopping. When we arrived at what the colonel had referred to as the *toolshed,* we found ourselves in a desolate area in the middle of nowhere. It was pitch-black, and there were no signs of civilization.

Sergeant Stanley, who was at the wheel, hopped out and motioned for us to follow. He pointed to a small steel structure about thirty feet away.

"So, how do you like it, fellas? Home sweet home. And by the way, if you get any crazy ideas about calling out for help, forget it. You could scream your lungs out, and no one—and I mean *no one*—will hear you."

He led us to the front door of the building. It had a thick padlock on it. The sergeant slipped a key ring off his belt, fumbled for a key in the dark, and unlocked the door.

"Right this way, gentlemen," he said as he shoved us inside.

A second later, the door slammed shut behind us. It was a solid steel door. We could hear the padlock being put in place and clamping shut.

I looked around. It was a typical toolshed, filled with what you might expect. Lawn tools—shovels, hoes, rakes, brooms, and the like—hung from hooks on the walls. I looked up. There was a skylight in the roof. It was at least ten feet off the ground. We were lucky that it was a clear night and the moon was nearly full. It provided enough light to keep us from tripping over each other.

"Nice going, Collier," Josh said. "We're both gonna get killed, thanks to you."

"I've been in tougher scrapes than this and survived," I said. "We just need a plan, that's all."

Josh plopped down onto the dirt floor. "You couldn't just leave things the way they were, could you?" he said. "You had to poke your nose into something that was none of your business. Everything was going just fine. I was making a difference."

Josh was fooling himself. He knew it, and I knew it.

"Boy, you've got a short memory," I said. "Do I have to remind you that you were nothing more than a rent-a-robber for Culpepper? He could care less about the environment. He tricked you, and the sooner you accept that, the better."

Josh didn't want to hear the truth. He got to his feet, grabbed a rake off the wall, and tried to break it over his knee . . . unsuccessfully.

"Listen," he said, "I would have eventually figured that out. And I would have left on my own."

"Do you actually think he would have let you leave?" I said. "You were one of his best earners. If you had tried to walk out of here, with what you know, you would have ended up right here in this same place."

Josh pounded his fist on the wall. "Just shut up. Shut

up. We're never gonna get out of here," he said. "And I don't even want to think about what they're gonna do to us tomorrow. So just leave me alone, okay?" He moved to the far corner of the shed, dropped down to the dirt floor, rolled up into a fetal position, and closed his eyes.

I thought it best just to leave him alone. I was certain that once he had time to think things through, he'd come to his senses. As for me, I now needed to come up with an escape plan. I couldn't count on help from Josh. If I ever needed a protester, he'd be my man, but this sure wasn't his specialty. What I needed was someone who could get himself out of a tough scrape—someone like Sam Solomon. In nearly every story, Sam would find himself locked up somewhere. I had to think about some of the ways he had managed to free himself. As I tried to recall each episode, I was remembering that Sam always seemed to find some gadget that he'd use to pry open a door or jimmy a lock or something. I looked around at the tools on the wall and wondered if any of those might help. But when I thought about the thickness of the door, and the even thicker padlock, I realized that none of them would work.

I began to rack my brain in an effort to recall the various escape plans that Sam had employed over the years. When I was just about to give up, I realized I was staring right at it. Sam had been in the exact same predicament in Episode #40—*The Dead See Caper.* All

I needed to do was to follow his instructions. It would work beautifully.

In this particular story, Sam was investigating a psychic who claimed to have the power to communicate with the dead. Unsuspecting clients, usually wealthy widows, would pay for the privilege of speaking to their dearly departed husbands. Each elderly woman would bring a picture of her late spouse to each séance, which was held in an old farmhouse. It didn't take Sam long to discover that the psychic was a fraud. Her accomplice, a former Hollywood makeup artist, would take on the appearance of the deceased husbands and would reappear to the distraught widows. When Sam confronted the pair, he was overpowered and taken prisoner. They locked him up in an old barn with a dirt floor, just like this toolshed. It didn't take long for him to devise a brilliant escape plan.

And if it had worked for Sam, it could work for us. I looked up at the skylight in the ceiling. That would be our passage to freedom. I was sure of it. I glanced at Josh, who had fallen asleep. I would have to do this on my own. I grabbed a shovel off the wall and began digging. I dug furiously for the better part of an hour. When the hole was about three feet deep, I hopped out and began digging in another location. It was right about then that Josh woke up.

"Hey, what are you doing?" he said.

"What do you think? I'm getting us out of here."

He stood up and walked over to where I was digging. "Are you trying to tunnel your way out or something?"

"Nope," I answered. "We're going out that way." I pointed to the skylight.

"But we'll never be able to reach it," he said.

Without making eye contact with Josh, I continued to dig. "In a few more hours, we'll be able to reach it. Trust me."

Josh scratched his head. "If we're headed *that* way," he said as he pointed skyward, "then why are you digging *that* way?" He motioned to the hole. "And why dig more than one hole? I don't get it."

If Josh had spent more time reading mystery novels instead of saving the earth, he'd know exactly what I was up to.

"If you dig a hole," I said, "the dirt has to go somewhere, right?"

"Yeah," he said.

"So if we keep digging holes, and we keep tossing the dirt onto that pile—which just happens to be directly under the skylight—" I stopped in mid-sentence. I was waiting for him to figure it out.

He reflected for a moment, and then a broad smile filled his face. "Then the pile will get higher and higher, and eventually we'll be able to climb up it and reach the skylight," he said. "Charlie, you're a genius."

I grinned. "And we'll get out of here a lot faster if we both dig."

"Oh yeah," Josh said. He ran over, pulled another shovel down from the wall, and joined me. He was now in a different frame of mind. He didn't seem angry with me anymore. He seemed hopeful.

For the next few hours, we dug and dug and dug. At one point it became difficult to get the dirt onto the top of the pile because it was getting so high. That's when Josh positioned himself about halfway up. Then we used the old assembly-line trick. I would dig up some dirt, pass it on to him, and he would scoot to the top of the pile and dump it. By the time the morning sun appeared, we were both dog-tired and our backs were killing us, but we continued on. It had to be about 7:00 A.M. when we were confident that the pile was high enough for us to reach the skylight.

"That should do it," I said.

"Now what?" Josh asked.

I ran over to the far wall and grabbed a pitchfork. "We should be able to break the window with this," I said.

"Let's do it," Josh said. He climbed about halfway up the pile, and I handed him the pitchfork. He crawled the rest of the way and then tried to stand on the top of the pile. It wasn't the best footing. He was a little unsteady.

"Can you reach the window?" I said.

"We're about to find out," he said. A second later, Josh closed his eyes, and as if he were a medieval knight thrusting his lance at an oncoming opponent, he attacked the skylight.

I immediately took refuge under my shovel as shards of glass came crashing down. We had done it. Sam's idea had worked. For the next several minutes, Josh knocked out pieces of glass from around the window frame.

"Okay, now, let's get out of here," Josh yelled. He exited through the opening and climbed out onto the roof. He poked his head back in. "Come on, Charlie, it's your turn."

As I scaled the pile, I thought back to a few of the second and third helpings of dessert that I had unfortunately chosen over the years. What I wouldn't have given at that very moment to be lean and mean. But it wasn't to be, and I just needed to make the best of it. It took me a few extra minutes, but when I neared the top of the pile, I could hear Josh's words of encouragement.

"Just a couple more feet. You can do it," he said.

At one point I was tempted to tell him to go on without me. I didn't want to slow him down. But I knew that he wouldn't leave me. I clawed my way the last couple of feet and gave out a long, loud sigh when I finally reached the top.

"Okay, take hold," Josh said as he extended his hand

in my direction. I grabbed on and with his help managed to climb out onto the roof.

From our vantage point, we were able to see the rest of the compound—Repentance Hall, Resurrection Hall, the auditorium—and most importantly, the front gate. That was precisely where we were headed. It was the only exit off the grounds. But first we had to get down from this roof, and jumping off didn't appear to be an option. Josh crawled to one of the corners.

"C'mon," he said. "We can shimmy down this gutter pipe."

One minute Josh was there, and the next he was gone. I crawled over to the edge of the roof. He was already on the ground and was motioning for me to join him. *Here we go again,* I thought. But, at least, this time, gravity was in my favor. I inched my way off the roof, feetfirst, and tried to wrap my legs around the gutter. I was hoping to descend in a very slow, gradual fashion. But no dice. I soon found myself sliding down the pipe completely out of control. The bad news—I had managed to scrape up my hands on the way down. The good news—I had landed on the part of my anatomy with a built-in cushion—my butt.

"Are you okay?" Josh asked.

"I'm fine. Let's go," I said. I pointed east, in the direction of the main gate. "We're headed *that* way." In pinball fashion, Josh and I zigzagged our way across the compound. We hid behind every tree, bush, or whatever object we could find that would provide cover. When we reached the main gate, we hid behind a large hedge. We immediately noticed a camp sentry sitting in a small guardhouse off to the side. I seemed to remember that the gate was motorized and that it opened inward. All we had to do was wait for a vehicle to enter or leave the camp, and we would be able to sprint to freedom.

We sat on the wet grass and waited for about twenty minutes, although it seemed like an eternity. Then in the distance, we heard the sound of an engine approaching.

"Someone's coming," I said. "Get ready." I peeked through the chain-link fence.

As the vehicle got closer, I couldn't help but notice that there was something strangely familiar about it. From a distance it looked like a big black station wagon. But as it got closer, I realized it wasn't a station wagon at all. It was a hearse. And not just any hearse. It was Eugene's hearse. The cavalry had arrived. This long nightmare was finally over.

CHAPTER 23

The Gull Next Door Caper

I elbowed Josh in the side. "We're saved," I said.

"What do you mean?"

I pointed to the hearse. "I know that guy. He's a friend of mine. He's here to take us home."

Josh smiled. "Really?"

My heart was racing, but in a good way. When the vehicle stopped at the gate, I could now see its contents even better. Not only had Eugene come to our rescue, but Gram was riding shotgun. This was awesome.

The camp sentry stepped out of the guardhouse and approached the driver's-side door.

Eugene rolled down his window.

"Do you have an appointment?" he asked.

"Sure do," Eugene said. "We're with the mayor's office. We're part of an oversight committee checking up on the how city funds are being spent."

"Let's see your credentials," the guard said.

Eugene handed him what looked like an ID card. A phony one, no doubt. I had a pretty good idea what Eugene was up to. He knew that he'd never be given permission to enter the grounds to search for me, so he concocted a plan about some city committee. It was brilliant.

"Well, I'm afraid you're not on my list. I'm going to have to ask you to turn around and go back to where you came from."

Oh no. What was happening? They couldn't leave.

"Call your boss," Eugene told the guard. "I'm sure he'll vouch for us."

The sentry pounded his finger on the clipboard. "If you're not on the list, you're not getting in. Period. End of discussion."

I couldn't let Eugene leave. He was our only hope. When he began backing up the hearse, I knew I had to take matters into my own hands. I ran out from behind the hedges and out into the open so he could see me.

"Eugene!" I yelled. "It's me, Charlie. We need your help."

"What are you doing there?" the sentry said. He started moving in my direction.

Eugene immediately stopped the car, jumped out, and ran up to the fence.

"Eugene, you were right about Colonel Culpepper . . . He's a phony . . . He's a fraud . . . He's behind all the burglaries in the area. We have to stop him."

"And we will," Eugene said. "But first we have to get you out of there. Just be patient and leave everything up to me."

Eugene was a rock. He was calm and confident. It didn't even seem to bother him when a half-dozen military vehicles suddenly pulled up and blocked him in. And he grinned when four armed guards surrounded Josh and me. I had heard about people smiling in the face of danger, but did Eugene have any idea what was in store for all of us? If the colonel had no qualms about making two kids disappear, he certainly would have no problem with adding two more people to the mix. When a guard ran up from behind Eugene and handcuffed him, he winked at me. It was almost as if this was all part of his master plan. I wished I could be more like Eugene, but I was confused and scared and uncertain of what the immediate future held for all of us.

The guards piled us into the backs of jeeps and transported us to—where else—Colonel Culpepper's office. I had a chance to give Gram a hug as we filed into the office and were instructed to sit, side by side, opposite the colonel's desk. Sergeant Stanley stood guard at the door—in the event we had any notions of slipping out.

"Nice to meet you, Josh," Gram said, extending her hand.

"Likewise," Eugene said.

I couldn't believe these two old-timers. They were

relaxed and smiling. It was as if they were at a social function.

"Hi," Josh replied nervously.

"Just shut up over there," the sergeant instructed.

"We'd just like to have a little conversation," Eugene said. "You can't even grant a condemned man his last wish?"

"I'll let you know when you can speak and when you can't. And right now you can't. Got it?"

Eugene turned his body so the sergeant could see the handcuffs still locking his arms together from behind.

"My hands are falling asleep," Eugene said. "Would you be so kind as to remove these restraints?"

"No, I wouldn't," the sergeant snapped.

"Well, I guess we'll just have to keep talking," Eugene said. "Maybe that'll wake them up."

The sergeant snarled and shook his head. "Anything to shut you up." He pulled out a key and removed the handcuffs from Eugene's wrists. "Not another word—and I mean it."

We sat in silence for the next twenty minutes. With each minute that passed, the more frightened I became. Whenever I managed to make eye contact with either Eugene or Gram, they would wink or smile. I just didn't get it. They were so cool under pressure. Maybe it was because both of them, over the years, had gotten themselves into so many scrapes like this one that they just knew they would somehow survive. I, on the other hand, with only limited experiences under my belt, was less than optimistic about our chances.

Another fifteen minutes passed before Colonel Culpepper appeared in the doorway.

"Sorry to keep you waiting," the colonel said. "I had to make a few phone calls. It's somewhat difficult to reach our elected officials on the weekend." He glanced at the four of us. "So, what do we have here?" He stared at Josh and me. "Why, it's the Houdini brothers. My associates have informed me how you escaped from the toolshed. Very ingenious. I commend you." He turned to Eugene and Gram. "And this must be the Dynamic Duo." He walked up holding the ID card that Eugene had given the sentry at the front gate. "I had a little talk with our friend the mayor. It seems there *is* no oversight committee checking into how city funds are spent . . . Mr. Johnson . . . or whoever you are."

"The mayor's a busy man," Eugene said. "He must have forgotten about us."

"He *is* forgetful," Gram added.

The colonel leaned in. He was nose to nose with Eugene. "I'm not here to play games, Grandpa. I want to know why you're here. And remember that your answer might just save some innocent lives."

"I already told you," Eugene said. "We're part of a committee that was—"

The colonel raised his hand as if he intended to strike Eugene, but stopped and sighed.

"You insist on testing my patience," he said. "Well, in that case, I have no other option but to charge you with high treason. And I think you know what the penalty is."

Eugene cleared his throat. "Listen, mister—"

"You will refer to him as the *colonel,*" Sergeant Stanley snapped.

"My sources tell me that your *colonel* hasn't served a single day in the US military," Eugene said.

"So he hasn't earned the title," Gram added.

"Why, you old—"

"There, there, Sergeant," the colonel said. "Don't allow this insolent pair to bother you. We won't have to deal with them much longer."

I kept waiting for something to happen. But nothing ever did. And what good did it do to argue with the colonel? He was just becoming more and more upset. I trusted Eugene and Gram, but I didn't know where this was going.

The colonel locked eyes with Eugene. "You do know what's in store for you, I hope?"

"Oh, I'm well aware of what you have planned for us," Eugene said. "But let me ask the same question—you do know what's in store for you, I hope?"

"A man in your position?" the colonel said. "There's nothing you can do to harm me."

Eugene turned to Gram. "Constance, exactly how long have we been here?"

Gram glanced at the clock on the wall. "I'd say about fifty-eight minutes," she said, "give or take a few seconds."

Eugene leaned back in his chair and locked his fingers behind his head as if to relax. "It won't be long now."

"Listen, old man," the colonel said. "I don't know what kind of game you're playing, but unless I get some answers, and fast, it's going to get ugly in here."

And right at that second, I could faintly make out the sound of a siren, then another, and another—and they kept getting closer.

Gram looked up at the clock. "They're a minute early."

"That's okay," Eugene said. "I don't mind." He stared at the colonel. "I'm afraid the ride's over, soldier. Time to get off."

Corporal Waters ran into the office. He was out of breath. "Colonel, the compound is under attack. There are cops everywhere. What are we gonna do?"

Colonel Culpepper glared at Eugene.

"SWAT teams to be exact," Eugene said. "You see, I told them that if we weren't out of here in one hour, then they should join the party."

Sergeant Stanley was perspiring. He turned to Eugene and pointed to his boss. "It was all *his* idea."

"We were just following orders," the corporal said.

"Shut up, you fools," the colonel shouted.

I could hear footsteps in the hallway. It sounded like a group of people running in our direction. I glanced at Colonel Culpepper. His expression had suddenly softened. He stared forward in a trance-like state. He was smiling. He seemed at peace.

"I did the right thing," he said. He didn't appear to be talking to any of us. "I saved those boys. I fed them. Clothed them. Put a roof over their heads. I was their shepherd. I rehabilitated them. If it hadn't been for me, they would have fallen prey to the system. Don't you see? I did them a great favor."

A half-dozen members of the local SWAT team charged into the room. One of the officers scanned the area. He seemed to be assessing the situation. He nodded to Eugene.

"Commander Patterson, are you and your party safe?"

"Quite safe, thanks," Eugene responded.

Another officer approached the colonel and pulled a paper from under his bulletproof vest. "We have a search warrant," he said.

I pointed to the portrait of General Patton. "You can start by looking behind that picture," I said.

A third officer began handcuffing Sergeant Stanley.

"I want to cut a deal," the sergeant said. "You be sure to tell the prosecutor that."

Eugene put his arms around Josh and me. "C'mon, boys, it's time to go."

As we exited the colonel's office, I glanced back at him. He was seated at his desk with his head buried in his hands. I don't know why, but I kind of felt a little sorry for him.

Gram patted me on the back as we walked down the hallway. "What did I tell you?" she said. "Didn't I say you oughta take on this case? Glad to see you took my advice."

"To be perfectly honest, Gram, it was kind of by accident."

"Whatever," she said. "You got the job done and I'm proud of you."

When we walked out the front door, there had to be at least a dozen police vehicles in the open field, all with their lights flashing. A few sirens were still blaring. It was quite a scene. As we approached one of the squad cars, the back door flew open and two familiar faces greeted me.

"Well, we did it again, huh, Charlie?" It was Henry.

"Wait a minute. You would never have known he was in trouble if it wasn't for me," Scarlett said as she slid out of the backseat.

"So apparently you got my text," I said.

Scarlett nodded.

"I couldn't believe it," Henry said. "When Scarlett

called me and told me you had texted her, I thought she was out of her mind." He shook my hand. "Charlie Collier . . . welcome to the twenty-first century."

Josh put his hand on my shoulder. "So, that's what happened."

I smiled. "Remember when we were in your room last night and I was admiring your new phone? I was texting Scarlett that we were in trouble and needed help. Of course, I almost wasn't able to send it. If you recall, you wrestled the phone away from me."

"Sorry about that," Josh said.

"And so Scarlett called me, and I called Eugene, and the rest is history," Henry said. "By the way, Charlie, I found your backpack in the bushes back by the police station—so I knew you were here. And I loved that note. Very creative."

"Thanks." I glanced back at the building we had just come from. Police officers were escorting Colonel Culpepper, Sergeant Stanley, and Corporal Waters to an awaiting vehicle. I assumed that other officers, at that very moment, were searching the colonel's office. Once they opened the safe and found the cash and furs and whatnot, this would be an open-and-shut case.

I felt a tap on my shoulder.

"So, another case closed, huh?" Scarlett said. "You're something else, Charlie."

I grinned. "Well . . . this was a real group effort."

Gram walked over and hugged me. "And don't you worry about your parents," she whispered. "I'll square everything with them."

Oh no, I had forgotten about them.

Gram placed her hands on my shoulders. "They won't be too happy to learn that you kind of stretched the truth about the camping trip with Sherman's family," she said. "But when they read about you in the paper again, I'm sure they'll be okay with it."

"I hope so," I said.

"You sweet-talk your mom, and I'll handle your dad," she said. "In our line of work, we sometimes have to fib to the civilians. It's for their own good, you know. We're just trying to spare them a little grief, that's all."

"Consider it one of the hazards of doing business," Eugene said.

A member of the SWAT team approached. "Commander, could we have a word with you?"

"Excuse me, won't you," Eugene said as he followed the officer. Gram joined them.

Henry slapped me on the back. "So, did you miss me, partner?"

"Henry, I've been gone less than twenty-four hours."

"You missed me. I can tell," he said confidently. Henry turned to Scarlett. "But you know what he really missed?"

Scarlett shrugged.

Henry grinned. "Peter's mother has three children. One is named April, one is named May. What is the third one named?"

"A brainteaser?" Scarlett said. "Now?"

"Why not?" Henry said.

Why not, I thought. "So Peter's mother has three children—one is April, one is May, and you want to know the name of the third one, huh?" I asked. He nodded. To tell you the truth, I would have thought that upon my return from a virtual death trap, Henry could have come up with something a bit more challenging. "If Peter's mom has three children, and one is April and one is May, then the third one has to be . . ." I smiled. "Peter."

"I was going to say that," Scarlett said. "Charlie beat me to it."

"Yeah, right," Henry said. "Like you had any idea what the answer was."

"I did too," she said.

"No way," Henry shot back.

"Did too."

As they continued to argue, I grinned and sighed. It was so good to be back.

The days that followed were pretty exciting, let me tell you. Not only was I interviewed by the local newspaper, but radio and television came calling as well. Henry,

Scarlett, and I were celebrities again for a couple of days there. And like before, Gram and Eugene chose to keep their contributions anonymous. The news was full of stories about how Colonel Culpepper had duped city leaders into thinking that he would solve their juvenile delinquency problems. The Oak Grove city community relations office immediately went into damage-control mode. But most residents weren't buying it. Radio talk shows were filled with callers who were demanding a recall election for the mayor and council. But when the dust finally settled, most citizens just planned to make their voices heard at the upcoming general election.

Most of the colonel's staff was taken into custody as well. Lesser charges were filed against them. As for the boys—the residents of Camp Phoenix—they were initially bused back to various police stations for processing. The more serious offenders were incarcerated. Others were sent to foster homes. But most were released to the custody of their parents, including Evan. I was glad to see that. All of the boys, however, were forced to attend a series of sessions with court-appointed counselors who really did want to try to rehabilitate them.

Scarlett, Henry, and I were on hand when Josh was reunited with Sherman and his mom. It followed a visit to the police station to determine if charges should be filed against Josh for his part in the colonel's burglary ring. Since Eugene, Gram, and I vouched for him, he was able to plead to lesser offenses without jail time. Instead, he was given one hundred hours of community service. And since much of that time was to be spent cleaning up the local forest preserve, Josh was perfectly fine with it. He was in his element.

And as promised, Gram ran interference for me with my parents. She had predicted that they would soften up once they saw the attention paid to me by the press. They were definitely proud of what I had done and even boasted about my accomplishments to their friends, but they weren't happy about the fact that I had lied to them. After hours of deliberation, we finally came to the understanding that as long as I was up front with them in the future, then I wouldn't be grounded for this offense. My dad was a tough sell, but Gram worked her magic, and as usual, he eventually caved.

When it came time to sit back and reflect on this whole experience, I wondered what it might be like to step into Sam Solomon's shoes—for real. More than once during this case, my life had dangled in the balance. And each time, I managed to wriggle free. I wondered how many more times I'd be able to avoid the inevitable. I was beginning to worry that I had taken on too dangerous a profession. If my life was flashing before my eyes at the age of twelve, then what possibly was waiting for me at twenty-two or thirty-two? As I pondered my future, I found myself creating a word picture of Episode #39—*The Gull Next Door Caper.*

In this particular story, Sam had been hired by an animal control officer in Clearwater Beach, Florida, who wanted to find out why seagulls were attacking tourists. While working on the case, Sam sought out the services of Caroline Roundtree, an ornithologist—a bird expert—to help him better understand the feathered attackers. Sam and Caroline spent long hours together. They soon fell in love and planned to marry. But when Caroline saw the dangers that Sam encountered each day, she gave him an ultimatum—he had to choose between her and the agency. Sam anguished over this decision. The more he thought about it, the more he realized that he would never be happy in any other profession. He thanked Caroline for her assistance and returned to his one true love—the private detective business.

Although I was concerned about my own personal safety, I realized that, like Sam, I wouldn't be happy doing anything else. And if that meant putting myself in the line of fire every so often—then so be it. I had clients who were depending on me, and I had no intentions of flaking out on them. They could continue to count on the one person who put their interests ahead of his own—namely Charlie Collier, Snoop for Hire.

So, there you have it. Case closed. Another successful mission. Did you figure out that Josh had actually been taken to Camp Phoenix? Did you guess that Colonel

Culpepper was behind all of the burglaries in town? Did you deduce that Josh was committing some of those crimes? Were you able to solve any of Henry's brain busters? If you answered yes to any of those questions, then you're one step closer to joining the agency.

But not so fast. You need to solve one more brainteaser. Here goes: An electric train is traveling at one hundred miles per hour headed directly east. A crosswind is blowing at fifty miles per hour out of the south. And so, based on that information, can you tell me which direction the smoke will blow? Now, take your time. Think real hard. Read it again if necessary. Maybe even a third time. Are you still stuck? If you answered west-northwest, I'm afraid you'd be wrong. You see, this is an electric train, and hence, there is no smoke. I know—it was kind of a trick question. Sorry about that. But if you hope to become a full-fledged member of the Charlie Collier, Snoop for Hire agency in the near future, then you have to learn to recognize the legitimate brain busters from the trick ones. Who knows—it just might save your life someday.

Stay on the case with

CHARLIE COLLIER

as he investigates

The Copycat Caper

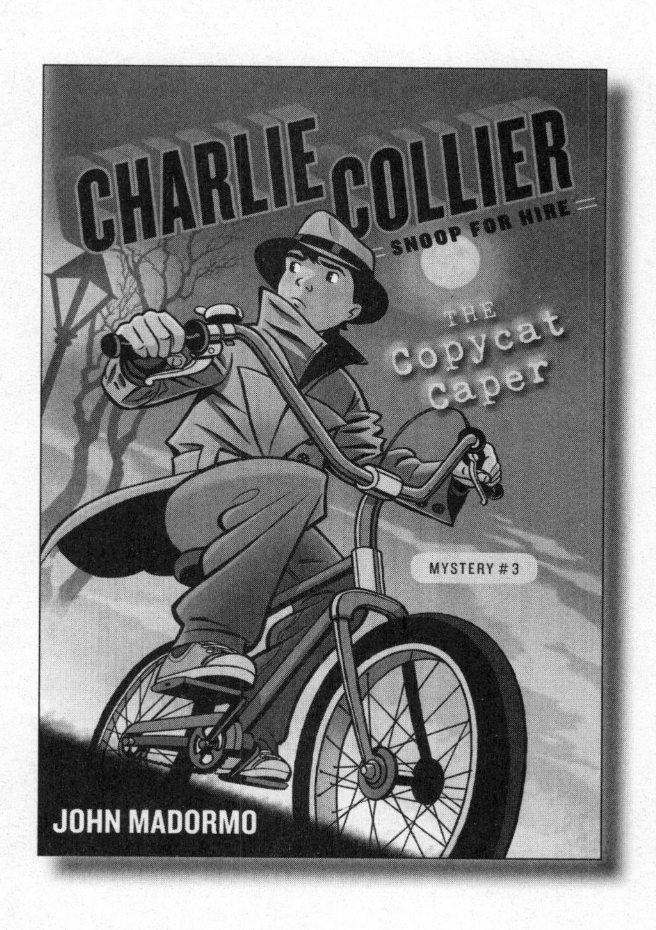

CHAPTER 1

The Well-Disposed-Of Caper

Scarlett appeared impatient. "I've got better things to do with my time than wait around here for clients who may never show up."

"I've told you before," Henry said. "We have to maintain certain office hours for walk-ins. It's the way we've always done things."

"Well, then I'd like to propose a new policy," she said. "From now on, we don't see anyone without an appointment. Then we won't have to sit around here and waste our time."

Henry made a face. "You can't make up a new policy just like that. We have to vote on it—and I vote *no*. Charlie, what do you say?"

You would think that after weeks of working together, Henry and Scarlett would have at least learned how to tolerate each other. It was almost as if they enjoyed confrontation. Most people go out of their way to avoid fighting, but not these two. They seemed to embrace it.

"So what's your vote?" Henry said. "Vote *no* if you want to continue to offer a necessary service to your fellow man . . . or *yes* if you're self-centered, self-absorbed, or self-indulgent." He smiled. He was proud of his command of the language. It didn't hurt that our list of vocab words at school today all began with the word *self.*

I folded my hands and set them down on the card table. "Why don't we just call it quits for today," I said. "We don't need to vote on any new policies. And besides, my mom's due back anytime now."

"Fine with me," Scarlett said.

I removed my fedora and flipped it across the room in the direction of the hook that I always seemed to miss. I wasn't even close this time. I unbuttoned my trusty trench coat and hung it up as Henry folded the card table and slid it behind a ladder on the wall.

"Bye, guys," Scarlett said. "See you tomorrow." She swung open the garage door and stopped in her tracks.

Standing in the doorway, completely out of breath, was Danny Reardon, one of the basketball jocks from school. He squeezed by Scarlett.

"I'm glad I found you, Charlie," he said. "You're still open for business, I hope."

"We were just closing up shop for the day," Scarlett said.

Danny was having a hard time catching his breath. "Listen, guys, this is an emergency. I need help . . . right now."

Henry reached for the cash jar on one of the shelves and shook it for Danny's benefit.

"There's an additional fee for a rush job," he said.

Danny threw up his hands. "Whatever, I'll pay it. We just gotta hurry."

"Okay," I said. "Let's get to work." While Henry and Scarlett opened up lawn chairs, I retrieved the card table and set it up. As I slid on my trench coat and fedora, I felt my heart racing. This is what I lived for—a chance to tackle a real caper—and one with urgency to boot. Danny had come to the right place. We wouldn't rest until the client was completely satisfied. It was the only way the Charlie Collier, Snoop for Hire Agency did business.

"Okay, Danny," I said, "what seems to be the problem?"

Danny stood and began pacing. "It's Rita. She's going crazy. I don't know what to do."

"Who's Rita?" Henry asked.

"She's my dog," Danny said. "We just got her from a shelter."

Scarlett folded her arms. "This is about some crazy dog? I'm afraid you've come to the wrong place. Shouldn't you be taking her to a vet?"

Danny shook his head. "No, you don't get it. A vet can't help with this problem." He sat down and tried to compose himself. "Rita loves this one tennis ball. And it fell down this hole in our yard . . . and we can't get it out. You just gotta figure out a way to get it for me."

I leaned forward. "How deep is the hole exactly?"

"Ten or fifteen feet."

"Why don't you just go buy her another tennis ball?" Scarlett said. "If you can afford to pay us, you can afford a new ball."

Danny plopped down into a lawn chair and squeezed the handles. "I've tried that already. It won't work. She only likes this one tennis ball."

"This doesn't sound like a real emergency," Henry said.

"Oh, no?" Danny said. He was getting upset. "Just how exactly would you define an emergency, then? Try this—Rita stayed outside all night. She refused to come in the house. She just stands over the hole and stares down into it. She hasn't eaten anything in twenty-four hours. Is that good enough for you?"

Before Henry could respond, I held up my hand. "Tell me, Danny, how wide is this hole exactly? And can you slide a ladder down into it?"

"No way. It's only about five inches in diameter," he said.

Henry got up and leaned against the wall. "What kind of hole is this anyway?"

"There was this old water pipe in there. Some workmen from the city came by yesterday and removed it."

"And they didn't fill it back up?" I said.

"They're gonna do that tomorrow," Danny said. "So we gotta get Rita's ball outa there before they come back."

I reached for a small pad of paper on a shelf behind me and began sketching images of the hole. I tried to think of what might be long enough to fit down there, as well as something that could grab the ball. The more I drew, the more frustrated I became.

"Have you tried using a long pole with some double-faced tape on the end?" Scarlett said.

"It won't work," Danny said. "The hole goes straight down for about six or seven feet, but then it turns to the right . . . maybe thirty degrees or so. There's no way to get something down there. I don't know what I'm gonna do."

"Why don't you just trade this dog in for a less crazy one?" Henry said with a grin.

Danny didn't seem to appreciate Henry's attempt at humor.

I sat back in my chair. There just had to be a way—an easy way—to get that ball. I tried to recall any Sam Solomon episodes that might help us find a solution, but I kept coming up dry. Then just when I was about to surrender, I had it. Of course, Episode #41—*The Well-Disposed-Of Caper.* In this particular story, Sam was hot on the trail of a country doctor who had improperly prescribed a drug that had left his patient clinging to life. To avoid getting caught, the doctor decided to discard the empty pill bottle at the bottom of a dried-up old well. The bottle might have remained there forever had not a torrential downpour occurred that raised not only suspicion, but the evidence as well.

I slid my chair up to the table. "Danny, you said this hole is in your backyard, right?"

He nodded.

"Do you by any chance have a hose long enough to reach it?"

"Yeah, I think so."

I rolled up the sleeves on my trench coat. "Here's what I want you to do. I want you to fill the hole with water—all the way to the top."

"What good would that do?" he said. "Then it'd be even harder to get the ball."

Scarlett grinned. She knew exactly what I had in mind.

"It's brilliant, Charlie," she said. "Don't you see, Danny? A tennis ball is hollow. If you fill the hole with water, it'll float to the top."

A smile began to form on Danny's face. "It might work. You *are* brilliant, Charlie."

"As long as Rita doesn't mind a ball that's soaking wet," Henry said.

Danny jumped out his chair, dug into his pocket for a pair of dollar bills, and stuffed them into the change jar.

"Trust me, that won't be a problem," he said. "It's always covered in her slobber anyway. She won't mind a bit." He waved as he exited. "Thanks, guys."

And so the trio of Henry Cunningham, Scarlett Alexander, and yours truly, Charlie Collier, had managed to crack yet another unsolvable case. You know, there was a time, not so long ago, when I had gotten tired of the ho-hum cases presented by fellow sixth-graders. I wanted nothing to do with them. Instead, I dreamed of tackling the types of capers found on the pages of a Sam Solomon novel. But after the Rupert Olsen and Colonel Culpepper capers, I've since learned that if you are patient enough, one of those lightweight cases could actually turn into the big score. The lost tennis ball was obviously not going to lead us to our next adventure, but I always made it a point to look at every client who walked into our garage as someone who might just present us with a challenge that could turn out to be life-altering.

Scarlett had only been with the agency for a few weeks now, but I was pleased with her progress. She wasn't as dedicated as Henry, and she didn't possess his rottweiler mentality for collecting cash, but she had an above-average intellect and frequently offered solutions to problems nearly as quickly as I did. It was also nice to have an extra set of eyes when surveillance missions presented themselves. And it was still hard to believe that I actually had the chance of spending time with her not only in class, but after school at the agency as well. Scarlett and I would never be an item. I had come to accept that. We traveled in different circles. But I figured that as long as I had a stage to demonstrate my amazing powers of deduction, then anything was possible.

We were deciding whether to close up for the day or prepare for another unexpected walk-in when the side door of the garage swung open. A cloud of smoke filled the doorway. In the haze I recognized a familiar face . . . in unfamiliar attire. My grandmother, Constance Collier, a free spirit who sported a new identity on an almost daily basis, unveiled her latest personality. She had a towel wrapped around her head like a turban, a short purple vest over a tight yellow T-shirt, red satin slippers with the tips pointing up, and sheer turquoise pants.

This was almost too much to bear on an empty stomach. All my fantasies about genies went right out the window at that moment. Gram placed her hands together with her fingertips pointed straight up and bowed repeatedly as she entered.

"Thought you might like to know that your mom is on her way," she said.

“Ooh, thanks, Gram,” I said. I turned to the others. “We’d better break this stuff down . . . and fast.”

“Thanks for the warning, Mrs. Collier,” Henry said.

Henry had seen my grandmother assume any number of identities over the years. It was nothing new for him, and he actually seemed to enjoy them. But this was all relatively new for Scarlett. I was hoping she wouldn’t hold it against me that I had a rather eccentric grandmother.

Gram continued bowing as she backed out of the garage. “Gotta run. Time to squeeze back into my lamp. See you later, kids.”

Henry was holding back laughter. He waited for the door to close. “I love her, man.”

“She is so cute,” Scarlett said.

Phew, was I glad to hear that. If Scarlett somehow found Grandma’s unusual behavior *cute* rather than *odd,* then I’d have nothing to worry about the next time she reappeared in one of her unpredictable ensembles.

As we flicked off the overhead light and slipped out, we could hear the grinding of the garage door opener. My mom was home and we had escaped in the nick of time. Had she found us conducting business again, there would have been serious consequences. I still was on probation following the Camp Phoenix Caper. They were proud that I helped expose Colonel Culpepper and successfully tracked down Sherman’s brother, Josh, but they were still upset about how I had deceived them into thinking I was on a camping trip. It wasn't that my parents weren't impressed with my amazing deductive reasoning skills, it's just that they would have preferred if I had exercised them at school rather than using them to solve problems for fellow classmates. My grandmother had lectured my parents at length about how they shouldn't suppress my talents and that they should embrace them. That would never be the case. My folks just wanted a normal kid who did normal kid things and didn't engage in life-and-death adventures every few weeks. My dad threatened to ground me if he caught me taking on clients again. And not just ground me—he went out of his way to use the term *house arrest.*

Henry and Scarlett were on their way home and I was safely in the house by the time my mom arrived. I had carefully positioned myself at the kitchen table and was downing a glass of chocolate milk when she came in. I sprinkled cracker crumbs on the table in front of me to suggest that I had been there for a while.

"The traffic was just horrendous downtown," she said as she plopped bags of groceries on the counter.

"I wonder why," I said.

"I'll tell you why," she said. "The police had Belmont Avenue blocked again. They were back at that carpeting store. They're still trying to figure out who stole all those Persian rugs. It's been a few days now."

"Really?" I said.

"Yeah, and they have no clues, no suspects, no nothing."

Gram appeared in the doorway—still in her genie outfit. "Sounds like a job for the Charlie Collier, Snoop for Hire Agency if you ask me."

"I would love that, Gram."

My mom made a face. "Please, that's the last thing we want." She pulled out a chair and sat down across from me. "Promise me, Charlie, that you won't interfere this time."

"But Mom, it sounds like the police could use my help. They're obviously stumped. I might be able to turn up something they've overlooked."

"Just let the professionals handle it," she said.

"Charlie's *almost* a professional," Gram said.

"Please, Mom," my mother said. "Don't encourage him."

"The boy's got a gift," Gram said. "It'd be a shame if his talents went to waste."

My mom got up and began putting away groceries. "If he wants to go into law enforcement when he grows up, I won't stand in his way. But for now, I just want him to be a normal kid. Is that asking too much?"

"But how will he ever know what he wants to be if you don't let him explore a little?"

My mom slammed the refrigerator door shut. "Do

you call nearly getting himself killed *exploring a little*? Mom, you have to let us raise our own son."

Gram sneered at my mom and motioned for me to follow her into the living room. Once we were out of harm's way, Gram put her arm around me.

"Ahh, don't worry about her," my grandmother said. "She and your dad'll come around one of these days."

"And if they don't?"

She smiled. "That's why I'm here," she said, pointing at her outfit. "You get one wish." Maybe she really was a genie.

I thought for a moment. "I got it. I'd like to be able to keep the agency open, without any interference from my parents, and to become a real private detective someday."

"You *are* a real private detective, Charlie. And as far as keeping the agency open . . . your wish is my command. Consider it done."

"But what about . . . ?" I nodded in the direction of the kitchen.

"You just keep doing what you're doing," Gram said. "And let me worry about Mr. and Mrs. Killjoy." She leaned in and kissed me on the cheek. "Now where the heck is that lamp of mine?" She winked. "Can't keep Aladdin waiting." She leaned over and whispered, "He's a nice kid, mind you, but very demanding. It's *all* about him."

Catch Charlie Collier's first case,

The Homemade Stuffing Caper